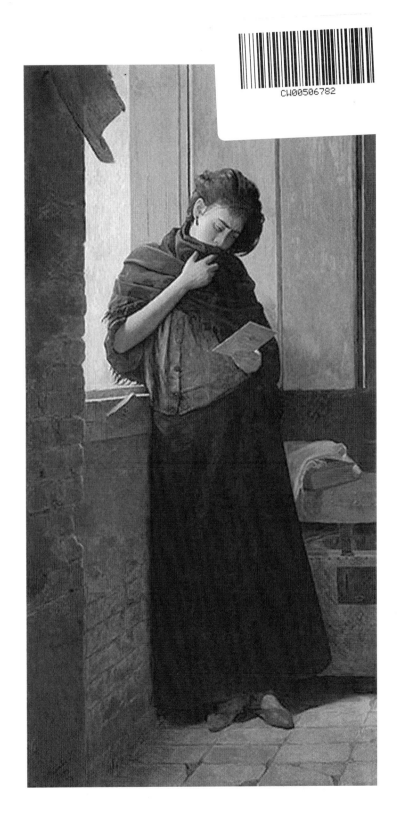

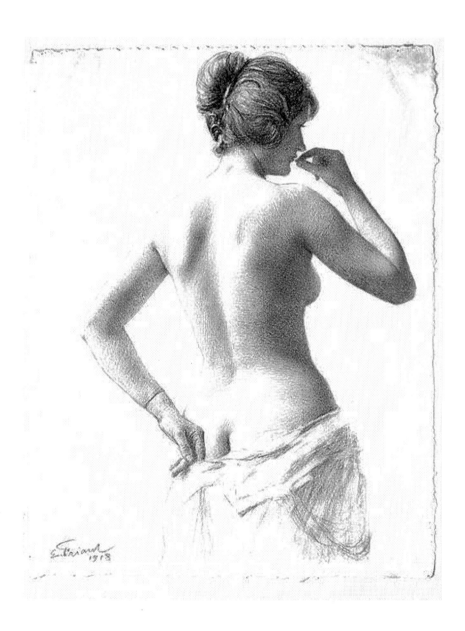

Sculpted love

Coming of age in the shadow
of the Beaux-Arts of Nancy

Marcus Bicknell

Les Éditions de la Fonderie

This edition first published 2020 on Amazon paperback,
e-Book and Kindle. All rights reserved.
Print edition ISBN: 979-8-6685952-6-6
Electronic edition ISBN: 978-0-9553751-3-2 ASIN: B08DKVPM1N
Audio edition: to follow

Sculpted Love is illustrated with pencil sketches by Robert Butcher (April
2020) and with late 19th century paintings in the Musée des Beaux-Arts,
Nancy, and elsewhere, including several by Émile Friant of Nancy (1863 -
1932). The frontispiece images are *Saudade* by José Ferraz de Almeida
Júnior and *Dessin Nu* (1918) by Émile Friant. Acknowledgements and
credits for the images are given at the end of the book.

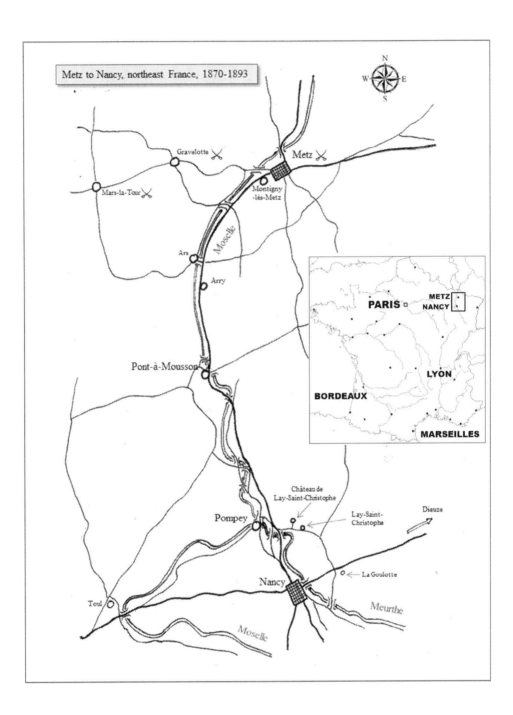

Metz to Nancy, northeast France, 1870-1893

Chapter 1 - Dust to dust

Blood, dust and stones. Duchien lay crumpled on his right side, pain coursing through his right arm. He could feel his legs and arms were grazed, his clothes torn. Blood obscured his sight. He could smell it. He could feel its sickly warmth. He put his left hand to his face and felt the dust and gravel stuck to his palm with more blood. He tentatively felt his forehead; blood flowed freely from a long gash.

He wiped the blood and dirt from his eyes enough to see he was on the edge of the dirt road. The low sun dazzled him. There was a large rock by his feet and another one near his head. That was all he could see; no, there were some people running towards him. He tried to roll onto his back to relieve the agony in his arm. The movement triggered a massive stab of pain. Duchien screamed. He had to get up. He had to help the others. He rolled away from the road again; less painful. The left arm worked well enough to push himself up to sitting and get his legs under him. He staggered to his feet, cradling his shattered arm in his left hand.

A few metres up the hill lay his upturned trap. The horse was still harnessed to the shafts and alive, its neck at an unnatural angle; one rear leg kicked spasmodically. Duchien spotted Émilie by a flash of her floral pattern blouse and staggered up the road. To his horror he found just her head and shoulders protruding from under the trap. Her open eyes stared into the blue sky. He touched her cheek in desperation, willing the eyes to blink. One arm stretched in the direction of their lifeless daughter. Pascale's head was crushed under a wheel, almost unrecognisable. Duchien screamed in disbelief and wept in denial, alternately. Blood. Carnage.

He kneeled between them to see what he could do to help. He shook his wife's shoulder with his good hand, and felt her torso under the wood and metal of the trap. He stopped when he felt the ribs cracking. He screamed again, his voice breaking and croaking. He turned to his daughter but it couldn't be her; she was such a mess he chose not to touch her. He tried to push the wheel off her head; the wheel only turned slightly, and the head came further apart making a horrific sound and releasing blood and grey matter onto the road. He retched and groaned but nothing came; just the tears flowed with the blood off his head.

As he knelt there, despite the physical and mental shock, the sequence of events came flooding back to him. In the bright light and warmth of springtime Saturday, after a happy and sunny afternoon at the little lake at La Goulotte, Duchien had been driving his wife and daughter homewards in the horse and trap. On this slight descent towards the bridge over the Meurthe, six men were working with a threshing machine in a harvested field alongside the road. A huge steam engine was driving the threshing machine with a long belt. As the men put wheat stalks into the machine it thrashed them with rotating rubber paddles, the grain fell through a grille and the stalks flew out the end. The men and the machines had been there in the morning and the horse had passed it without any problem. On the way back, as they drew alongside it, the pulley on the thresher broke. It made a loud crack; the belt flew off and flapped about in the air. The steam engine sped up, for lack of load, until the rev-limiter cut in, making a whistling noise.

Suddenly Duchien's horse was whinnying and at full canter downhill. He was unfamiliar with the borrowed trap and struggled to keep control. Stones had been placed to mark the edge where the road narrowed slightly. The right wheel hit a big one, sending the trap toppling over at speed. Duchien was thrown clear, headfirst into the line of rocks. Émilie and Pascale were kept in by the side-rails as the trap rolled.

'Monsieur. Monsieur.' The voices of the farmers were reaching him now.

'Oh Christ!' cried Duchien. 'What have I done?' His vision blurred. His head sank forward. He toppled sideways and collapsed unconscious.

The clouds, heavy with damp and cold, hardly moved; the bright spring weather had been overtaken by a sullen depression. Edmond Duchien stood a few paces from the open grave, shivering slightly in his waistcoat, his raincoat over his shoulders. The cast and a sling on the broken arm prevented him putting his coat on properly. His head was bandaged heavily and he leant on a rustic walking stick. His eyes moved slowly from one person to another. Who was grieving? Who pitied him? Who thought he was an irresponsible idiot for taking his family out in a borrowed trap? Who here loved him?

The pallbearers, Franz and Marcel from the café and two from the undertakers, had brought the two simple coffins, one adult and one small, up from the wagon. The two silver grey Percheron horses chumped audibly on their hay. The curé, Papin, opened his prayer book and started reading from it even though he had officiated at hundreds of funerals. After the first phrase he was aware of the drizzle curling the pages; he put it away under his black vestment and continued faultlessly from memory.

A big crow squabbled with two magpies. When they moved away the only sound was the distant clanking of a steam hammer at the marshalling yards south of Nancy's main railway station, partly visible through trees at the edge of the cemetery.

Duchien had been in hospital for three nights with concussion from the blow to his head. He was still dizzy and nauseous. He got out of the hospital only the day before the funeral so he had not had the time or means to tell many friends. Duchien recognised the few people there: Émilie's cousin Jocelyne who had taken the train from Metz; Antoinette, a friend who looked after the household of a rich industrialist; Bernard who ran the café-restaurant near Duchien's atelier; Franz and Marcel, two of Bernard's regular customers who knew Duchien; the undertaker, Guidon, who had no known first name; his teenage son; and a trainee priest. Behind the curé and the trainee was another person. He took a long time wondering about her, a lady on her own, until he realised, after a glance from her, that it was Evelyne Lefebvre, one of his muses from several years back, before his marriage. He had liked her. The sculpture had been very successful. Had she got married since? Why had she come to the funeral?

Duchien realised in his misery that he had no family at the burial. His parents were long gone. One sibling; his sister Marie-Angèle lived in the Massif Central and could not get to Nancy in time for the funeral. Anyway, they had negligible contact.

His wife and child died instantly as the trap rolled over them. The money owed to the owner of the trap, destroyed, and of the horse, who had to be put down, weighed heavily on him as well.

He had not only lost his wife but he had lost his muse, his model, his creative inspiration, the woman who had sat for countless poses and whose form elicited the most ardent and complimentary reactions from everyone who saw them, not least from men. Émilie's square jawline, cushiony lips on a juice-stained mouth, deep-set grey eyes, and thick black hair expressed as much intelligence as sexuality. Her unsmiling expression, seen in the paintings and sculptures he alone did of her, conveyed neither an inflated opinion of herself nor the coyness which makes many a young woman so captivating as a model; Duchien was proud that viewers of his portraits of his wife saw the suggestion of a complicated, closely guarded inner life. Only Duchien and Pascale had seen Émilie laugh, smile, wink, kiss and hold hands.

He had lost his only child, the warm and intelligent Pascale; at age nine she had already shown some talent in drawing and clay modelling in her father's studio. He had sketched and sculpted Émilie and Pascale together in life but now the image of the two of them, as death masks, haunted Duchien every moment of the day – and night. He was racked with guilt. He had been the driver. He had killed his wife and child.

Should the people gathered around the graves be consoling him? Or condemning him?

ৰ

Nathalie and I sat side-by-side on the bench in the school yard. We had similar looks – brunette, hair up a wide bun, pretty but not overtly beautiful, slim but not skinny, intelligent. This was a matter of amusement for our classmates; since we first started at senior school, they had called us The Twins even though Natalie was a year older than me.

'I hate maths, I always have,' I moaned. 'I just can't get my head round those interminable figures. My head spins.'

'Yes, but you find it easier than your brother does.'

'Indeed. He doesn't seem to be able to learn anything. But then he has never even spoken very much. I don't think he's going to get into the Lycée. He spends most of his time with Hubert.'

'Hubert? Who's that? The game-keeper?' asked Natalie facetiously. She had known for years that I lived in a château with servants but she had never asked about a game-keeper before.

'No. The dog, silly. One of the springer spaniels they take hunting. Hubert seems to be like Jean-Marc; happy with a quiet life, not too curious, not too demanding, not too bright, subject to tempers. They adore each other and go on walks together.'

'Twins like us. Don't worry about maths Cécile. Just relax and follow the rules. Everything always adds up in the end. Anyway, you've got your artistic side. Maybe you'll be an artist or something creative when you grow up.'

'When I grow up? When will that be? I feel like I'll never catch up with you.'

'Ha. You've been going on for years about me being a year older. I can remember as if it was yesterday, sitting on this same bench, you saying you were jealous of my breasts... and you were only twelve or something. Now that you're eighteen you look terrific, and, may I say, tastefully well-developed and attractive. I say 'tastefully' because apparently, small breasts on a more petite woman are all the rage nowadays – as far as fashion and men are concerned.'

It always impressed me how Natalie seemed to know the latest trends; and how to help me see thing in a positive way.

'And you're obviously clever because you've passed your bac

a year younger than me and secured your next move.' Implied in that remark was Natalie's acknowledgement that I would be starting at the École des Beaux-Arts, Nancy's best art school, in September.

'I think my specialisation in art, and whatever they spotted in me on the artistic side, that got me the place. If I had applied to study history or literature in the Faculté des Lettres at Nancy University, I do not think I would have been accepted.'

'Anyway, you're in and on your way. I hope that I can get the funding for my year's business course in Paris. If that happens then we will be apart for the first time since we were five or so. Strange.'

'I'm not looking forward to that, however much I am pleased for you.'

Neither of us spoke for a moment.

'Whatever happens, promise to be my big sister forever?' I blurted, to balance the anxiety of being parted.

The bell rang and the teacher set to shouting at us. Some movement on the road caught my eye, and I glimpsed the undertaker's black coach, devoid of coffin, drawn at a walk by two huge horses, its work for the morning done. The undertaker's boy looked back over his shoulder at us. As usual. At me?

We grabbed our satchels, lifted the hems of our long blue skirts and hurried back into class.

শ্র

Chapter 2 – Duchien: worries

Bernard's café, Nancy, a year later, August 1890

The evening service had finished at Bernard's café in the Place Thiers opposite the railway station. A few customers relaxed with their coffees. Bernard was at his usual place, drying glasses with a kitchen towel. The chef was getting ready to leave.

Mimi had taken off her black dress and white apron and was putting on her coat. It was a moment when she could share some intriguing intelligence with the regulars at the bar. The ears she chose to fill this evening were those of Franz, who worked in the town hall as porter and caretaker, and Marcel, who was good at arranging things like transport and work help without having a proper job. He had arranged the horse and trap for Duchien on that fateful day, a role which he did not like to dwell on.

'I don't mind saying, Duchien isn't playing boules in the square. He has hardly been in to eat. I hope he's alright.'

Marcel and Franz looked at each other to confirm they agreed, then back to the waitress. Marcel said 'It's true. I have not seen him much. Have you been watching out for him?'

'Yes. If it has been a few days I drop in on the way home and leave him some bread and cheese left over from lunch service. Or the dreg ends of a bottle of Merlot.' She motioned to the bag she carried.

'He has work; that I know. He's been making doors for a furniture company.'

Franz added 'He has to get some of his statues cleaned and mounted on stands because they're doing an exhibition of his work – the nudes I think. The Musée des Beaux-Arts people are working with the mayor. Maybe they think it'll help him and his career.'

Mimi was not convinced. 'That painter, Van Gogh, the one who cut his own ear off; he shot himself last week. Suicide. So they say.'

ॐ

Place Thiers, Nancy, 1890.
Postcard. Bernard's café is behind the statue

Chapter 3 – Sculpting & haunting

The atelier was huge by city standards, roughly eight metres wide and twice as long. It was beautifully lit because of the frosted glass overhead and the full-length windows of the back wall giving onto a yard.

Sculpture covered every bit of floor space. There was Duchien's big drawing table, a couple of smaller tables and two big chests of drawers for sketches and paper stock. But even these were covered with dozens of his sculptures. Some full-size women; some half or quarter size. There was only one man in the whole place, the mayor of a local village, Pompey, site of the two biggest ironworks in the Nancy area. He knew he had been obsessed by women for all 15 years of his sculpting life. Their form had driven his hands. The character and complicity of each of his models had driven his creative urges. The demand for the pieces drove his bank balance.

He enjoyed the initial sketching phase. He could let his imagination loose, doing a few alternative compositions before deciding which was best for sculpting.

Over the fifteen years since leaving the École des Beaux-Arts de Nancy he had worked in four media. He had started in plaster of Paris which is the cheapest raw material and the easiest to work. Duchien became adept at bending and soldering ten-millimetre-square aluminium rods into the skeleton for the sculpture, to give it structure. This meant that the person's arm could be away from the body, the fingers could be separate from each other and the legs could be apart. Plaster was forgiving because if he had made a mistake he could cut it away, put on a new piece and sculpt it again.

He dabbled in clay, literally, because it was so messy. But the sensation of doing it he found highly erotic. As he formed the curves of the female body with his hands he felt as if he was caressing the body of the model in front of him. In some cases his vivid fantasies were as good as reality. On other occasions, before he got married, reality overtook the fantasy and if the model were willing he would find himself touching her, exchanging smiles, letting the passion build until he was making love with her, wet hands, smeared clay on her breasts, shrieks of laughter.

The third medium he used was stone, chiselling the form from solid rock. He got some limestone from Euville and Senonville to the west, but with difficulty because most of their production

was chalk for roads and railways, too crumbly for sculpting. He was friendly with one foreman who put suitable pieces of hard limestone aside for him. Marcel could arrange transport at low cost, finding a charabanc which would otherwise be coming back from Bar-le-Duc or Reims with a part load. He had used the white sandstone from Lohr, Adamsweiler, Niderviller and Rothbach in the Vosges to the northeast but the Prussian occupation had made it difficult to get since 1870. None of his clients nowadays liked the pink colour of the most readily available output from the Vosges quarries so he did not bother with that variant.

Working in stone was no erotic moment. This was blister-making, bicep-building, brow-sweating hard work. But certain clients demanded it, especially full-size heroic pieces for public display. They paid well. The rapid expansion of the mining, iron and other industries in the second half of the 19th century had made a lot of rich men, and they were ready to spend their money to satisfy their vanity and impress their employees, clients or electorate. This explained why none of these full size stone sculptures, except one, rejected, remained in the studio. The others had been commissioned and were in the open air somewhere in the northeast of France, typically in a main square or outside the town Hall. Good money. Only two of the nude ladies in the atelier were in stone; he found it difficult to 'feel' the contours with the chisel and hammer alone. He did not get the sensation under his fingers. There was no joy in the creation. Just sweat.

The fourth medium was not strictly his own output. Certain pieces, especially the half- and quarter-sized nudes were highly sought-after, in Nancy, Paris and other cities round France, and they could be bronze castings of an original in plaster. Duchien's success with castings started with Jean-Christoffe de Platigny, the entrepreneurial manager of an expensive shop near the Place Stanislas in Nancy called *Art et Antiquités Montmorency-Laval* who saw one of Duchien's quarter-size stone sculptures in an exhibition in the Musée des Beaux-Arts and agreed to take on the cost of the lost-wax mould and the initial run of 12 bronze castings. The statue was typical of his nude women; all he had to do was attribute a facile and commercial name for the piece... *Dans la Baignoire, Nue, 1882*. Yes, she was standing, slightly stooped to gently wash her thigh with the flannel she had in her hand. De Platigny had the obligation to fund the manufacture, the rights to sell them and a satisfactory share of the income. He was the sole agent for the bronze and alabaster reproductions for several years, probably twenty different originals used, including four full-size ones, and an average of a dozen replicas from each one.

So the stone and bronze statues mostly sold. The plaster or clay originals were stored willy-nilly in the studio. Almost all were nude females, full-size and miniatures, done either as originals for casting, or just for the fun of it... a response to a creative need or to a lust-driven urge. In some cases the piece had been prepared for an exhibition and had come back afterwards. A few of the females were clothed, usually in diaphanous négligées or gowns which suited the style of the new art of the Nancy school. Some had a scarf or a towel, the minimum necessary to cover the midriff. In some cases such propriety was demanded by the exhibition curator, but in the quickly developing and heady atmosphere of Nancy, as in

Paris and Berlin, people were becoming more liberated, more sexually aware, more tolerant and even demanding of pieces showing the human form in all its beauty.

His agent, De Platigny, acting more as artistic adviser, encouraged him to depict the female in a more natural way, even rustic. He said there was less demand for the perfect woman in the style of *The Three Graces, Aphrodite* or the figures by the 18th century Frenchman Allegrain. Duchien turned to the girl next-door or the country girl, totally nude as if prancing in a meadow, her hair flowing, unkempt, the detail of her underarm and pubic hair without compromise and in full view. The market lapped them up.

Duchien did not feel for a moment that he was prostituting his art for the market. He loved doing it (and he loved the models who became his muses) and he earned and saved money.

The Romans and the Greeks were masters of sculpture of the male and female form without clothing. Yes, he felt he was the manifestation of a renaissance of what had gone 2000 years before. He wondered whether Roman sculptors had as much lust for their models as he felt. Was Michelangelo in love with *David*? Duchien reflected on these issues in the way they were debated in lectures at his art school, the École des Beaux-Arts de Nancy 15 years before. When Praxiteles of Athens sculpted *The Aphrodite of Knidos (Venus Pudica)* in the fourth century before Christ, of course he was aware of how the sexuality of the woman would play to those who viewed it; his female nude is reaching for a bath towel while covering her pubis, which, in turn leaves her breasts exposed. The sub-title *Venus Pudica* is suggesting that the woman had some modesty, but the statue, like the *Venus de' Medici* and the *Capitoline Venus,* communicate raw sexuality more than modesty.

But for Duchien, his appraisal of nude sculptures tended towards the intellectual, emotional or sexual link between artist and model. What was the relationship? How did the model look at the artist? Did the sublime curves of the body of these masterpieces come from the artist's adoration of not only the form but the person?

Venus after the Bath
Christophe-Gabriel Allegrain (1710-1795)

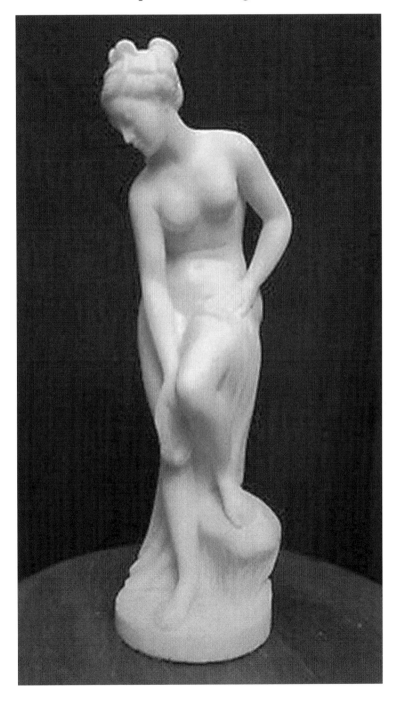

Those Botticelli women with fat tummies and bulging bottoms were not to Duchien's taste. He was much more into the modern woman, live, nubile and with petite features. Even on an older woman, in her forties say, he preferred the demure chest look – clothed or unclothed. The cast of characters in the atelier were testament to that. Most of them looked very similar to each other. This had been a self-perpetuating circle because Duchien would find himself befriending the slimmer girl to see if they would like to sit for him. Sometimes a woman turned up at the studio on the

recommendation of a friend, just for fun and to have a copy of any sketch he did of her, nude or head and shoulders only.

Bernard's café, where he used to have lunch quite often, and where he had a small sketchbook on the table, was a happy hunting ground; any solo lady arriving from Paris or elsewhere might walk across the square with their baggage and seek refuge in the café. Nancy was known for art and for artists; what would be more natural for a new arrival to be amenable to being immersed in art within minutes of arriving. Duchien was happy to engage in conversation those who were willing, mostly females.

Around town, in the shops, when he visited the museum or when walking, he found it easy to engage a stranger in conversation. He had a friendly face. He was never pushy. He would offer a cigarette even if there was no evidence the lady was a smoker. He could offer a café serré instead, a very strong coffee being a rather provocative notion.

He liked being polite and respectful of the girl he talked to, singular, one girl, and genuinely interested in her character and interests. He did not want to appear predatory but if she showed some interest in art, and in what he did, then she wouldn't mind if he asked her if she would like to see his atelier. Would she?

Many new prospective muses, when coming into his atelier for the first time and seeing what had gone before them, were initially shocked; but they quickly came to love the permissive, erotic and marginally immoral nature of stripping off for a perfect stranger and posing for him for hours a day over half a dozen days.

There was never money involved; maybe a meal together or another petit café. There was no paperwork, no discussion of rights to the images made and commercialised.

Some of them fell for those of his charms which were not purely artistic. His soft brown hair, strong-featured clean-shaven face, muscular arms, hairy chest and narrow waist... he remembered how in summer he stripped off his shirt and wore trousers cut off at the knee; disgraceful behaviour in retrospect.

How ostentatious he must have seemed to the women who did not fall for him. Each of those that did fall for him was special, however long the sittings or the affair lasted. Each had her own special characteristics and qualities.

He loved each of them intensely.

Le Turban (1929)
Émile Friant (1863-1932)

Sometimes he reflected on them to see if he could remember their names. Miriam Bensouma; Jacqueline Méli; Françoise Dupont; Madeleine Montbéliard; Alicia DeSousa; Martha Baltacha; Patricia Malkovich; Evelyne Lefebvre (who came to the funeral); these ladies he remembered well and he were still in contact with those that lived in Nancy.

He looked deeper in his memory. Aline Léon (a friend of his painter pal Émile Friant – he did a wonderful painting of her); Keiko Kagawa (a Japanese exchange student at Nancy University, the most boyish figure he had ever seen on a female); Agnès de Choiseul (classy girl, aristocratic family); Marie-France Callot (daughter of somebody famous, a Paris fashion designer?); Valérie (he never knew her family name); Angélique (the same); Giovanna Artegiani (luscious Italian looks, long black wavy hair).

Where did they all come from and where did they all go? Beyond a dozen he could not name them and could hardly even picture their face. Why did they all seem to be intelligent brunettes? Why did he not fall for the busty blondes or the short-haired androgynous ones?

Then came the woman he would marry. Émilie Corbin. She carried him away into a land which was her own, away from the throng of his models. She gave him life, character, occasional wild eroticism, laughter and happiness. He found that he needed no other. He was 24 when they married a year later. 1879. Their daughter was conceived just months after. So for years the only nudes he sculpted were her.

No, not quite; there were those with their daughter. He finished *Mother and Daughter* (1888) only a year before the fatal accident; Émilie standing, one hand over her head and the other curled to her own shoulder, looking down at Pascale, nine years old, who is stretching an arm upwards and looking up at her lovingly. Surely the best sculpture he had ever done and the one which now haunted him the most. He had played the pivotal role in their death. He was to blame. He must live with it.

Mother and Daughter
Robert Butcher (born 1961), as if by Duchien

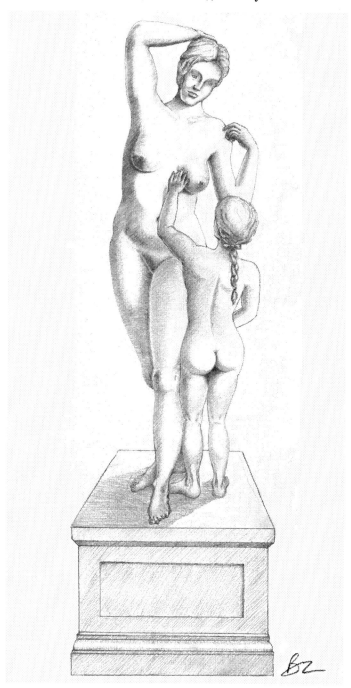

He knew that his depressions were serious and that they were having a physical toll. His bad shoulder and elbow, his aches and pains and general lethargy were the physical side. What worried him slightly more was the total absence of desire for a woman; a total absence of desire. He hardly glanced at the girls at Bernard's if he went for lunch. He never cupped his hand round a breast of one of the statues in the workshop. He had not done a single nude sculpture since the death of his family, nor had he felt the slightest frisson about a woman.

Some months after the accident some errant neuron of his imagination triggered the first and most dramatic of the nightmares that would thereafter haunt him nightly. He woke with a start, sweating slightly...

There was a noise downstairs, a crash, something falling. He heard indistinct voices, and some further movement. Christ, have some people broken in? He got out of bed, wobbled half-asleep to the bedroom door and listened, a sleepy man in his underclothes, to what was happening downstairs. Now he was certain there were two women talking. Now a younger girl's voice joined. Were they angry? There was a noise of the table leg jarring on the floor as somebody bumped into it. He started making his way down the stairs.

It was a difficult scene to comprehend. Several of the statues, the full-size ones, had moved and were dotted about the part of the workshop which had been cleared. It was a group of three of them together who were talking, quite loudly. They ignored Duchien. He turned his gaze to two others and noticed they were no longer statues but humans. He was not certain how that could have happened. His perplexity was short lived because they both walked towards him, smiling in a saintly way. Their hands on his body did not act in a saintly way. They both caressed him, put their lips where his bare flesh was, muttering sweet nothings. These were both girls who had been his lovers. But now he felt nothing for them. No inner forces driving him to touch them. No stirring in the loins. Nothing, except a faint disgust.

Why were they molesting him like this? Getting their own back? Reliving a great moment in their lives? For fun?

Now he was angry. He pushed them away and shouted at them. They both fell over. One toppled directly to the floor and broke into two pieces of stone. The other put out her hand and slipped across the table, knocking a three-quarter size nude onto the floor. They were both made of plaster and smashed irreparably. He went over to the three who were still talking and raised his hand to stroke them or to see if they were real. They crumbled into dust on the floor.

From that date on his women of plaster and clay visited him nightly without fail, to terrify him. He started getting the bad headaches but he could not establish whether the headaches came first or the nightmares. The terrible headaches made the days nightmarish as well. His work was bad. His income dropped off. He had frequent depressions. He withdrew into himself. On the rare occasions when he went out to eat he declined any invitation to conversation.

He looked in the mirror and saw a face wracked with pain; an unshaven and beleaguered face; a shadow of former self. He asked himself where on earth he could go for help. There was no-one else to lean on. He knew he needed professional help.

ৱ

I am floating in the air back into my workshop. The statue of the Mother and Daughter is there but so are all the other sculptures that were in storage at Bernard's friend Marcel. Only now they are all new nudes. They are dancing with each other and touching, all women. Some of them girls. They are gambling around like sheep. The gaiety is interrupted by my wife shouting at them, screaming abuse. Each of them in turn slumps down and melts into the floor.

Dessin nu - Fiche
Émile Friant (1863-1932)

Chapter 4 - Natalie arrives in Paris

Appartement 3A, 16 rue de l'Estrapade, Paris V^e

7 September 1891

Dear Cécile

Just to let you know, here I am. It was hard saying goodbye to you and everyone in Nancy but I feel excited about my step forward. The flat is absolutely tiny and I share it with a girl from Marseille called Marie-Pascale. But as all of this has been paid for by La Fonderie, I cannot complain. After we talked about whether your father, the boss, put in a word for me, did you ask him?

I have signed on and got some of the books second-hand to start reading. The business management lectures started yesterday. My college, which has the grand name École Supérieure de Commerce de Paris, has only just opened – I had not realised in advance – so the course structure is a bit chaotic. One of the lecturers and my tutor are really interesting and I think it will turn out well.

It was actually a good time to leave Nancy because I was getting really uptight about Manuel. Adequate as a Latin lover goes, but he just absolutely didn't do intellectual stimulus. Also, he was even more of a pauper than I, so, long-term, it would never have worked. Paupers for ever? Oh no, Cécile, not for you or me. I must get myself somebody delightfully rich, a brilliant conversationalist and totally in love with me. Does such a person exist?

We didn't have time in the last week to talk girl to girl, but I get the impression that you and Jean-François are at a similar stage. Tell me do.

Yours in haste and with love from Natalie.

ঽ

Nancy, 12 September 1891

Dearest Natalie

You know me so well. I did the right thing and I told Jean-François that it was over. He took it badly and almost cried, but I'm sure he'll find somebody else and do fine. In the meantime I can let my self-esteem recover and concentrate on my final year's studies, fine arts.

My god, this place is weird without you. Who do I talk to at lunchtime? You were always so present in my life that I probably paid less attention to the other people around me (except maybe one or two of the more attractive boys) but at age 20 it's difficult to have a casual relationship with a boy and just chat when their base instincts are always driving their urges. Why do boys want to progress to the kissing and petting stage when we have hardly been able to talk together and get to know each other? Anyway, Mama doesn't let me have anyone back to the Château so spare time can be quite dull. Oh, Jules Guidon, the undertaker's son, tracked me down and professed undying love. He's such a dolt though, and seems to have been influenced by the corpses he has to frequent.

Two girls, both of whom you know from the Lycée, are doing the same one year course at the École des Beaux-Arts. Julia has settled down and has been friendly, as has Françoise, and for some reason, maybe her reddish nose, she is called Framboise. Girls must try to be less spiteful.

In the two weeks since you left, I have taken a big step forward in my art. I am spending a couple of hours a day and my new tutor Professeur Méli, a friend of Daum, has said I am able to get an art diploma under his supervision. I think I will pursue that alongside the normal course elements.

No, I didn't mention it to Papa. Well done you. I presume you impressed them in the summer job.

Yours in haste...Cécile

Chapter 5 – Son of the Count

The Count Geoffroi Orlowski had a special place in his heart for his son. One Saturday in September father, son and I were at breakfast together. The Countess was still in bed. It was nice for the Count to be with us two, to coincide at the table at the start of a weekend. He was off travelling on business a lot and sometimes did not get back till later on Saturday. He sometime chose to go into the office at weekends. Not this time.

'We concluded the takeover of Equipements Nord-Est on Thursday. A great step forward for La Fonderie as we now have control and the extra profit margin from our products in the professional distribution sector. I can relax a little bit for the first time in months.' Jean-Marc was dunking a brioche with jam into his bowl of milky hot chocolate, his favourite. I gave him space to respond from between mouthfuls. He was less interested in the excellence of the business deal than in his father's intention to be at home for a change.

'Papa, that's good. I'm glad you'll be here this weekend'

'Thank you Jean-Marc, my dear boy. Would you like to do something with me today?'

'Yes Papa. I'd like to. What were you thinking we could do?'

'Woodwork. We will use the walnut to make something useful. There is a choice for you. I have made plans for an outdoor table, a bench or a hay manger. Which would you like to make?'

'The table. Yes, the table. Picnics, Papa. Yes. Let us make something again.'

'Shall we go after breakfast?'

Jean-Marc looked at me to confirm our understanding of the arrangements. 'Papa, I'm taking Cécile on her errands round town this morning as usual. Could we go after lunch please?'

'Certainly. See you then.'

☙

The Count spent some time writing letters, ones he wanted to do personally. He walked round the house and stable block checking on maintenance. He informed his driver-come-handyman Binder that Jean-Marc would join them on some woodwork in the afternoon. He took coffee in the mid-morning and the Countess was still not up. The savour of his cup of coffee transported him to Reims, then Brussels, then Paris, places where he sometimes had a moment to relax. He associated the taste and smell of coffee with some particular bistros or hotels. He reflected on the people he had met on his travels and on the occasional woman. He felt he had been faithful to Leonora for twenty years or more if one allowed that the one or two flings he had conducted were not long-term and did nothing to disturb family life. He knew he was not without sin. But he also considered how difficult life with her had become; how their relationship had been without love since Jean-Marc had been a toddler; how he missed the touch of a woman, the emotional and physical love which he was largely denied; how she was focussed solely on climbing some imaginary social ladder, ingratiating herself to people with a title, abhorring any activity which had a creative or useful purpose; how her mood swung from self-isolation in her spacious apartment upstairs, separate to his, to manic furies and outbursts. The staff lived in terror of her; his own life with her was unpleasant.

Thought of her social circle made him reflect on her private life. She was madly beautiful when he first knew her and she threw herself at men in a flirty way. It was just her lifestyle. She might have thought it was normal. She might have thought it helped the Count with client relations when La Fonderie guests were concerned. She might have thought that generous hospitality and her personal attentions increased the kudos of the Orlowski household. But had she taken any lovers? If so, she had been uncharacteristically discreet. The Count could think of one or two men who might have been attracted to her and might have found the opportunity to conduct themselves improperly with her. Yes, he had often travelled midweek. Yes, she had opportunity. Maybe she would be more relaxed and less subject to tantrums if she did take a lover.

This brought him back to his own state of mind and lack of

love in his life. He yearned for a woman that would love him but he knew it was not Leonora. Should he have sown his seed more during their twenty-one years together? Had he wasted a large part of his youth and middle age in denying himself a lover – or lovers? He drained his coffee cup with a sigh. There were no evident answers.

The Count and his son spent the afternoon together. Jean-Marc only felt at ease with people one-on-one; a reason he did so badly at school. He got fits of rage, sometimes involving symptoms of *delirium tremens* like beating his hands on his head or rolling on the floor. His temper-prone mother probably saw some of her own genes in the boy, which forced a wedge between them. He needed attention and appreciated it; from the Count's point of view he enjoyed giving whatever extra love was available because Jean-Marc got none from his mother. He had a 19-year-old body but the behaviour of a pre-teen; difficult. He loved the time his father gave him.

They had cut down a walnut tree a couple of years before when extending the stable block. The trunks had been sawn by a woodsman with a full size mill into planks. Jean-Marc had helped with stacking the planks, putting slats between each of them so that air circulated between them as they dried out. So, now, quality hardwood from their own domain, dry and ready for use. Today they had the help of Binder, the German who had been with the Count for so many years as his coach-driver, groom, retainer, stable-hand, hunt and shooting-party organiser, and maintenance man. He lived with his wife in the stable block in an apartment next to Jean-Marc's and they had grown to like each other. Hubert, the springer spaniel, sat quietly on the flagstone step to Jean-Marc's rooms.

The three were company not a crowd as they lifted the three metre planks off the stack in the end of one of the barns where they had been stored. Each plank was nearly 3 centimetres thick and 30 to 40 cms wide so each needed two or three people to carry. They got half a dozen of the planks down to small table-mounted circular saw driven via belts by a small steam engine which the stable man had stoked an hour before. Once a plank was on the saw table he could push it through the blade, the purpose now being to trim off the edge of the plank, the curvy and knobbly bark surface, to leave a straight edge. Jean-Marc was keen to help and walked each plank through after the blade, a position of relative safety.

On a work bench in the barn the Count had a paper plan of the outdoor table they were going to make, constructed just of these 3cm planks. The legs were two planks in X shape at each end of the table. Under his guidance Jean-Marc used a set square and tape to mark and hand saw to cut each plank to length. By four o'clock all the pieces were cut. Where joints could be secured by wooden dowels, the holes had been drilled with a hand brace drill with a wooden pommel to apply pressure from the chest. All three worked each structural piece with chisel and hammer to get them to fit.

Jean-Marc had the honour of final assembly; pinning the X legs together, fixing their horizontals then pinning the boards of the top surface. A garden table in near-white walnut, 2.2 metres long and 1.2 metres wide. By five they were finished.

As Jean-Marc got a big bear hug from his Papa he said 'Thank you for being my Papa. I'm with Papa. Don't make me do things with Mama, please. Just Papa, Cécile and Hubert. Please'.

'Of course. Thank you for being such a good son. I understand. I am here for you.'

৯

I am walking down the stairs to see what is going on in the workshop. I'm going too fast. I lose control and trip over a stone. I lie in a daze and put my hand to my head to find where the blood is coming from. Blood is pumping out of the gash in my head in time with both my heartbeat and the chant of the women. I try to get to my feet to ask them to stop but I slip on my own blood. 'It was him'. They are braying for me to be punished. 'Guilty. Guilty.' They carry two bodies off, one adult, one child.

Chapter 6 – Natalie writes

Appartement 3A, 16 rue de l'Estrapade, Paris V^e

17 September 1891

Dear Cécile

Yes, getting the art diploma would be very good. Now, dearest friend, the important things. Hurry up and find somebody to take your boyfriend's place otherwise you will start being mopey. I know you.

Here, life is so busy I have hardly been able to think about men friends except that the nice lecturer I told you about is making eyes at me and is warmly chatty, not all about business studies if you know what I mean. He compliments me on my dress sense and says I have intelligent eyes. Have you had this? Men must think we are blind to the fact that their anodyne chat-up lines are anything other than a seduction technique which can remain blameless if the girl does not respond in the way he wants.

The course is quite easy at the moment because many of the financial and management topics are ones covered last year.

How is your good-looking father? I wonder if they will replace me in the finance department and whether they will take me back next summer when I finish here. I already have a debt of gratitude to him and the company so I do not have a right to go back. We will see...

Natalie

༄

Appartement 3A, 16 rue de l'Estrapade, Paris V^e

Sunday, 28 September 1891

Dear Cécile

I promised you I'd tell you everything: I bedded that nice lecturer last night, the one I mentioned! Nothing serious. He was not bad, but I think I can do better. I think he agrees, so that will save some embarrassment at college. By the way, you must be wondering, Marie-Pascale and I have an arrangement, as we share a pretty small apartment. Alternate Saturdays I have the apartment to myself up to one in the morning. She stays out on the town or at her boyfriend's before coming back, then vice-versa the week after. Nice and clear even if a bit sordid in its practicality. But then love will have its way.

Went with Marie-Pascale, and a man she has 'in tow' (see above for the meaning of 'in tow'), and another guy from the college who I do not have my sights on, to the tower built by an engineer called Eiffel for the Exposition Universelle in 1889. It's 324 metres tall and has 1665 steps! Did you know the iron came from Fould-Dupont, at Pompey, near Nancy? They must be the big competitors to your father's firm. We went up to the top. The view is amazing but it's a bit scary. There are lifts most of the way up then we walked all the way down.

There are motor cars. Have you seen one? They make a huge noise so you can hear them coming just as easily as carriages and cabs, and they keep on breaking down. I like Levassor and Panhard cars, the French manufacturers.

Stop a moment. Sorry. I just re-read this letter. Did I really say that about the lecturer? I am mortified! Are you destroying these letters? I sincerely hope so. If your mother or a servant or your brother got hold of this one they would make sure our relationship got destroyed. They keep you locked away in the Château too much anyway.

Miss you. Natalie

২

Chapter 7 - Duchien misses the opening

> *I am chiselling a relief on a door, one of five to do today. Émilie and Pascale are watching. They ask if I know what it feels like to be thrown off a speeding trap and to have the head crushed by a wheel. I fall off my stool in turn; my head falls under a giant stone wheel of a nightmarish pre-historic chariot driven by semi-clad maidens and Boadicea warriors with tattooed bodies and blue faces. The pain in my head is pounding in time to the rotation of the stone wheel.*

The depressions came every few days, in waves, at any time of day or night, unpredictably. The feelings of guilt, of shame and of worthlessness assailed Duchien unceasingly. At the nadir of each phase of depression came the pain. It started as a tingle in the brain or a buzzing like when a loud noise has been replaced by silence and the eardrums are singing; then a subliminal rumble of thunder announcing the spasms of pain in the head. Sometime they started in one side of the head like a migraine, sometime above the eyes, sometimes all over. The headaches would exacerbate his other physical pains like the scars over his forehead and elbow. Within seconds he was forced to stop what he was doing, to drop his tools and to give himself up to the agony. Many times he could do nothing but collapse to the floor where, if the gods were smiling, he would lose consciousness. After a few hours he might be able to get up and stagger aimlessly around, maybe even get some water. But it could be days that the pains last, at the end of which he would be an unshaven, hollow-eyed, dishevelled and stale-smelling wreck.

And so it was that on the day of the opening, Duchien the renowned sculptor was in the third day of a massive headache attack. He was aware of the date and the obligation to be at the Musée des Beaux-Arts, just a few blocks away. He was expected at the opening of the new exhibition 'L'École de Nancy 1892 – Cinq

Étoiles' including new paintings (some of them nudes) by Émile Friant and eight stone statues by him, the room sign-posted as 'Duchien and the Ladies of Stone'. No-one used his first name, even if they knew it, and his family name had become something of a trademark in its own right like Gallé and Daum, the eminent glass and ceramics maker. He wanted to be there, of course; to meet clients, to revel in the acclaim, to get a boost to his fragile morale. But he was wracked by pain, in the worst state imaginable, and had not got up all day. The nagging voice telling him he should be there added to the misery.

Now, among the voices of his daytime nightmare, there were real voices. He could distantly hear people in the atelier downstairs, calling his name. He usually left the front door unlocked. When they came up he could identify them. He knew Franz Saarschneider, the museum's caretaker. He was friendly with the second person, Émile Friant, painter, acolyte and the rising star in the École de Nancy firmament.

Duchien lay in bed, the curtains closed. They implored him to come but all he could do was groan and shake his head on the pillow. They knew it was the headaches. They also knew that the anticipation of being in a big event with a crowd of people giving him more attention than he wanted would probably have been the trigger for the attack.

'Duchien, come. Get up and get dressed. It is already after five o'clock and a crowd is waiting.' Franz shook him through the blanket. He smelt Duchien's body odour and was appalled at his wasted and unkempt face.

'Franz.' Duchien's eyes were open but appeared glazed, unseeing. His dry mouth moved with difficulty. Émile saw a glass of water and passed it to Franz who lifted up Duchien's head to put some to his lips. 'Franz. Five o'clock. Is it today? Is it Saturday?'

'Yes, come. They're waiting; the Mayor, Gallé, the Daum brothers, Méli, Dupont, Orlowski. Everyone. '

'Aagh...' It was clear Duchien was in the middle of a headache attack. Franz had seen it happen once before in the middle of a meal. He had to help him home, semi-conscious. 'I can't come. My head. It is unsupportable. I have not moved since Thursday. I wish I could be dead.'

Émile was distressed, clenching his hands in a nervous rhythm. He had not seen his friend like this. He had mood swings himself and it flashed through his mind whether this was the condition of all artistic people and what might lie ahead in his own case. He watched on.

'Are you sure Duchien? I am so sorry that you suffer like this. Shall we tell them to go ahead without you?'

'Yes. Tell them I am sorry. I will better one day, or I will be no longer with you. Do what you have to do.'

'Is there anything we can do for you? I can come back later.'

'No Franz. Thank you. Put my suffering out of your mind. Nobody can cure me but myself.'

The two men left him and rushed back to the museum. If Duchien had been alert enough they might have recounted to him what he was missing.

ॐ

In the main atrium of the Musée des Beaux-Arts, a large throng of the great and the good of Nancy waited impatiently for the speeches which would mark the opening of the special exhibition. The director of the museum, Monsieur Aristide Majorelle, was talking intently with the Mayor of Nancy, Nicolas-Émile Adam, an excellent man to have at such an event; born and bred in Nancy, he had been a cavalry officer when young, then a career politician, Mayor since 1888 and President of the Société Lorraine des Amis des Arts. He greeted in turn Professeur François Méli of the École des Beaux-Arts de Nancy.

Three of the other great artists, sculptors and designers whose work was in the exhibition were being fussed over by the curator of the exhibition, Méli's daughter Jacqueline, a good friend of Duchien; Louis Majorelle, the director's cousin, had a group of chairs and a table in the exhibition and his wife Jika and 6-year-old son Jacques close at hand; Émile Gallé with his wife Henriette; both the Daum brothers, Auguste & Antonin, with assorted family and colleagues.

Dessin Nu (1918)
Émile Friant (1863-1932)

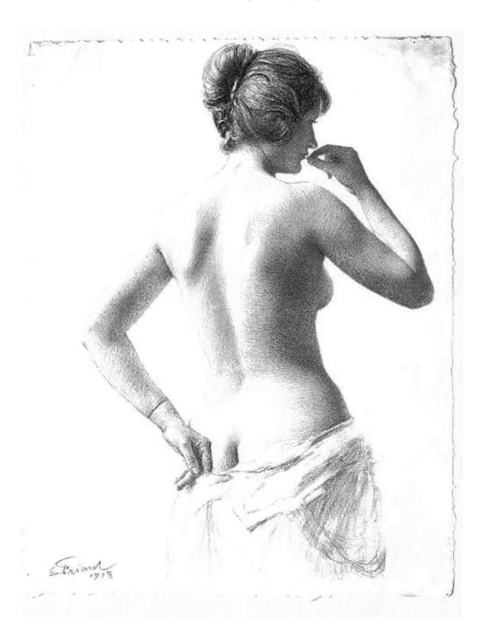

The fourth exhibitor, Émile Friant a specialist in society portraits, realist romantic scenes and eroticised nudes from life, was one of the artists featured in the exhibition, but he was absent for twenty minutes while he went to try to get Duchien, the fifth.

Art dealer Jean-Christoffe de Platigny hovered round this conversation, ingratiating him when he got an opportunity; Fanny Reinemer, Gallé's former business partner, was too infirm to attend but the two of her family who ran the Reinemer crystal and porcelain shop represented the family. The director of the Orchestre Symphonique et Lyrique de Nancy was invited but the mayor did not know him by sight and therefore did not know if he had come; he did recognise Albert Dufourmantelle, organist and choir-master of the Cathédrale Notre-Dame-de-l'Annonciation et Saint-Sigisbert of Nancy.

The station-master was there, Hypolytte Lyautey, less often known by his official title Directeur-Général-Adjoint des Chemins de Fer Français Region Est. The ever-present Léon Goulette, the owner, editor and managing director of the recently launched newspaper L'Est Républicain was there with two of his reporters and a photographer with his hardwood tripod, a large collodion wet plate camera and one of the new flash powder lamps.

France's north-eastern industrial powerhouse was represented by the competitors with the biggest iron works, Auguste Dupont of Fould-Dupont (they had provided the iron for the Eiffel 's giant tower in Paris three years before) and Le Comte Geoffroi Orlowski of La Fonderie (with his wife Leonora and daughter Cécile).

The Count Geoffroi Orlowski was a fine upstanding man, a benefactor of the museum, son of a banker in Metz and of a cultured mother. He was of average build, not particularly tall but well proportioned. His face was all but invisible behind a magnificent facial hair. He never cut them back severely, but he trimmed the moustache and beard away from the lips and he waxed their extremities to have them sharply silhouetted. His eyes shone through; dark brown, sparkling and intelligent. When he spoke it was with a deep voice and well-chosen words although he had the habit of extemporising by adding exclamations to the beginning of a sentence. He seldom abbreviated or used slang.

Catalina Pietri de Boulton (1920)
Émile Friant (1863-1932)

He was respectful of the title and sensitivities of the person he might be talking to which made him a good leader of the people in his factory. He behaved more maturely than his 45 years; this radiated both self-confidence and the stature which made people around him confident in him. His body language could give the impression of posturing but he did not take himself too seriously and he had a dry sense of humour. He always dressed impeccably, as today, usually in his work suit with a waistcoat, watch chain and full-length jacket. The collar open today, he sported a foulard in a quiet dark blue and discreet pattern; nothing to show off about. When he went out in the winter, even for the commute from the Château with his own driver, just a few kilometres to the works, he made an impression with his short top hat, a black cape over his shoulders and an ebony stick engraved with the family crest. It certainly looked like a family crest, but because its origins and its connection with the Orlowski family were not known, those who noticed it could not be certain of its authenticity. He took to wealth well; he invested wisely, he looked after his staff and he gave to certain charities. As for his private life, those who knew him well could see that he had an eye for the fair sex but in the presence of his wife it was she who dominated the relationship; they never appeared to be a loving couple but she had forced him over the years to behave as if they were close.

This wife, the Countess Leonora Orlowski, was a larger-than-life character, a caricature of herself. She had a face which might have once been beautiful, with strong eyes, strong eyebrows, large lips and a long if slightly sturdy neck. Her cheeks were now a bit flabby and her eyes sunken into grey pits, whatever the make-up she applied. Her double chin exaggerated the old-age look even though she was probably in her early 40s. The rounded face and large nose gave her the look of a Romany gypsy, as did her dress sense; she wore voluminous full length dresses, all day every day, such as a favourite in bright pink organza with a bow at the waist and voluminous sleeves. Another was off-white cotton striped with green and red silk in the style of a gentleman's boating blazer. She wore her red-brown hair up in a high bun, secured with loud jewellery brooches; but she always managed to make it look unkempt. She threw her weight around, with her family, her staff and her friends. It was apparent to all that this extrovert behaviour was to compensate for an essentially nervous and insecure psyche. Therefore the most telling part of her physique was the twist of her mouth; the listener (and she could talk endlessly without any pause to let her interlocutor speak) could not help feeling that it was a mouth that knew how to spill evil. Indeed her temper episodes were astonishingly violent and protracted over hours and days.

Duchien did not meet the Count and Countess that day. He missed all of this. The event went ahead without him. Friant said some words on his behalf.

Listening and watching from the back were Antoinette, Marcel and Mimi from the café, plus Bernard himself, who had been admitted through the employees' entrance by their drinking companion Franz. Antoinette had to avoid being seen by the Orlowski, head of La Fonderie, because she was his housekeeper.

Chapter 8 – Cécile in Nancy society

Nancy, 2nd October 1891 (Sunday)

Dearest Natalie

You are a brazen hussy. You fix your sole access rights to the apartment for the purpose of luring your lecturer, for heaven's sake, back there to seduce him and, as you so appropriately say, bed him. You didn't make love then? You didn't have a quiet moment of intimacy? You were not able to conjure up any ladylike words? I am so shocked. But I still love you. And I love reading about your life in Paris.

I don't know about Fould-Dupont. Papa has not said much about work recently. Home life is ruined by my dreadful mother picking a fight with him every time there's an opportunity. I do not know what's wrong with her. Two days ago all the staff heard them in the orangerie having a fit of rage. Antoinette told me she threw a Sèvres porcelain vase at him and it smashed as it went through the window. Not good. I can never even tell what the subject of the problem is. It's mostly jealousy about how well he is doing in business but it comes out in other ways like criticising the people that come to dinner, many of them his friends. Did I ever tell you Monsieur and Madame Gallé came for dinner recently. He's the famous ceramics designer. They are perfectly charming but Mama behaved in such an offish way, almost spiteful, that it embarrassed me. I sometimes think Papa will have to review the situation or read the riot act.

The École des Beaux-Arts is fine and my courses have settled into a pattern; some history with literature but mostly history of art and art. I couldn't be happier especially as the practical art is going well and I get to do quite a lot of input under Méli's supervision. Boyfriends less well. Jules is an idiot. I can do better.

Went to the Musée des Beaux-Arts for an exhibition opening yesterday, in the early evening. Professor Méli, my parents and all the big-wigs were there. His daughter is nice, Jacqueline. She had curated the exhibition. Got champagne. I met Monsieur Daum – they make the most beautiful decorated glassware.

After that I went to a ball at the Poniatowskis. I hate the idea of being a debutante. It's really a cattle market where we luscious ladies line up for the dilection of the spotty would-be-aristocrat boys. I knew one from school, Thierry, but no others. The areas round the ballroom and the terrace were patrolled by various middle-aged female chaperones, including Antoinette who had been roped in by mama for the evening. Even if there had been any cheek-to-cheek and the desire to 'talk' quietly as a couple that would not have been permitted. Depressing.

Yours in haste, Cécile

ঽ

Chapter 9 – Duchien: survival

Nancy town centre, 15th October 1891

Duchien sat at his big drawing desk with his head in his hands. Two years had passed since the funeral. He could not keep the tears from flowing. Several times a day his distress would attack him like a beast, without mercy. Above all he felt a sense of guilt for the death of his wife and daughter. How could he have been so thoughtless to borrow a trap that he didn't know, drawn by a horse he didn't know? Could he have known that the gentle ride to the country and a picnic would be fatal to the two most dear people in his life? Could he have done anything better to prevent the horse running away downhill? Why had God not taken him the same time as the women? He prayed at the end of his bed. He went to church a few times to see if God could help. He couldn't. All he got was lugubrious and repetitive condolences and *Ave Marias* from the curé Papin who had taken it upon himself to give him extra attention.

The trauma of the accident, the death of his loved ones and their funeral weighed heavily. There might be friends and contacts in the art world who might have been thinking that he had been careless or downright stupid. His loneliness weighed heavily. Several times a day a huge weight came down on him from above, squashing him into his self, squeezing his brain. The weight squeezed the tears out of his eyes. It made his fingers tremble and his shoulders sag. It made him unable to do anything constructive. His work suffered and both his glassmaker clients, Gallé and Daum, started to question whether he could deliver good work on time as in the past. And even when the weight lifted slightly, he would still be in a depression that sucked his spirits, made him want to hide from people and made him half a man.

Those were the psychological effects. But he still had physical sequels to the accident. His right arm had healed as far as the bone was concerned, but his right elbow still hurt and felt disjointed. Maybe a cartilage was cracked or a ligament permanently damaged. Sculpting was almost impossible. He could write and draw with the right hand but after an hour the pain was too much and he had to stop.

Even worse were the headaches. He had a small scar above his right temple mostly under the hairline, but the impact, the concussion and the day of coma must have done further damage. The headaches came suddenly, like a mortar bomb going off. There was no warning. The pain was excruciating. None of doctors and their remedies made any difference. He just had to lie down for an hour or two before the headache eased at all, and even then the rest of the day's work would be lost.

He felt lonely. He had lost his family and now all these ailments made it impossible to see people. He imagined he would be unattractive for people to want to be with. From time to time he would pluck up the courage to walk over to Bernard's but he could not even bear the smell of pastis, let alone drink it. Coffee was too strong and he attributed the onset of each headache to it. So having a squeezed lemon juice – a citron pressé – or an ice cream were the only pleasures available to him there. If cash permitted he would eat a plat du jour, a blanquette de veau, a pot au feu or a steak minutes frites. If someone said 'Good morning Monsieur Duchien' he found himself glaring at them as if they were intruding. After a while they gave up trying. He began to wonder about the purpose of this lonely painful existence; although he was never suicidal he consciously thought that an early death from natural causes would be preferable to the life he was forced to lead.

His atelier was uncharacteristically untidy, the upstairs apartment even worse. His spare statues were shuffled to the side, some of them under dust sheets, to make space for drawing and water-colouring - designs for ceramics - on a tilting drawing desk and woodwork on a big workbench. He had kept the one half-size bronze of mother and daughter holding hands uncovered but he found he had to avoid looking at it because he started crying. After a few weeks he covered it with a dust sheet too.

He had taken on a contract with furniture maker Louis Majorelle for sculpting the front panels of cupboards and this contributed to the mess. The best-selling item was a full height cupboard, drawers up one side alongside a hanging cupboard for clothes with a mirror inset into its door. The door surround for the mirror was sculpted freehand with a light hammer and chisel by Duchien with designs of a composition of leaves and tendrils in the new style which had grabbed Nancy and discerning consumers further afield in Metz, Strasbourg and around France. The British were already calling the style by the French name art nouveau and it gave him some satisfaction to be part of a movement. The chiselling was laborious and it made his elbow worse not just painful. He walked on wood shavings all day and spent hours sharpening his chisels.

Duchien had also been commissioned to create designs for Gallé and Daum, the two eminent manufacturers in Nancy of decorative glass and crystal vases, jugs and lampshades. He had not lost his touch in making designs for them for the glassware, but other artists charged lower rates and there is only so much creativity that one man can put into how to decorate a vase. They also put pressure on him to work at their workshops not from his own atelier; being with others made his headaches worse and he was not able to hide the weakness of his elbow and take sufficient rests.

Sculpture? He had not touched clay for two years. As for stone, it was much too painful to wield a cold chisel and hammer. He could not bring himself to think about sculpting.

২

I hear noises downstairs again. There are no stairs down to the workshop, just a long winding road with stones. A gentle slope. I lose control going down and I'm tumbling head over heels. I smash into my wife and daughter. I sent them flying to the corner of the room and they turn to stone.

Chapter 10 – Cécile: reflections on Natalie

CHÂTEAU DE LAY-SAINT-CHRISTOPHE,
LES BORDS DE NANCY, MEURTHE & MOSELLE

Nancy, 5th of November 1891

Dearest Natalie,

What's your news you moody friend who goes to Paris and forgets me? Three weeks without a letter. I know your love life must be full to brimming and of course you will tell me because you feel morally obliged. Or is that amorally obliged? Who is the latest lecturer / professor / co-student / man / woman (wouldn't put it past you) / someone you met you fancy a quiet moment with etc.?

So it turns out that my art teacher François Méli knows Monsieur Daum (Antonin... there are two brothers) and fixed a meeting for me. The company, Daum ceramics, now want me every Saturday morning, starting now, in the workshop near the Place Stanislav which is good. I'll be doing the filing, listing stock and unsold works and visits into town to pick up work completed by contractors. Thank God for Jean-Marc. My funny brother's greatest joy in life is driving the trap into town on a Saturday, waiting outside with the dog while I'm in their glass workshop and then transporting me round Nancy while I do the pick-ups. He is lovely, and in his own way adorable. I am the best friend he has except for Hubert. A dog can be a very good friend.

Mama seems to despise Jean-Marc. She treats him as a wine stain on the pure-white double-damask tablecloths of her oh-so-perfect life. Papa is much nicer to him and they do things together like woodwork and fishing. He is allowed to come on a shoot if he stays 50 metres behind the line and he is good at looking after the dogs. My spare time is full of painting. I am obsessed with the tendrils of plants at the moment, the way they intertwine. I see this a lot in the new art which is dominating the designers in Nancy. With a big hug, not in haste, just to let you know you owe me a letter.

Cécile

ॐ

Appartement 3A, 16 rue de l'Estrapade, Paris V^e

10th November 1891

Dear Cécile

Mea culpa. I apologise and it won't happen again or else I will ask a man to spank me.

Yes, since you asked, there are men here and in my life. Don't worry about me. I am perfectly capable of getting what I need. In fact, there is so much detail that, firstly, it would not fit in a letter, and secondly, being in such poor taste, I should not put it all in writing in case you left my letter lying around in your boudoir in your posh château with nosey domestic staff and a curious brother roaming round, to say nothing of your horrid mother.

Suffice it to say that my mind is highly stimulated by the business course, the people are brilliant, and my body is battered and bruised from night-time cruising, carousing and courting. Some of the damage is from dancing, but, honestly, not a lot. Marie-Pascal, similarly, is something of a soul-mate because we can compare notes and give sisterly guidance. On a serious note, being absent from you I realise how much you have always been the sister I never had and I thank you for that.

I send you the biggest hug that can be contained in an envelope and sent via the post.

Your sister Natalie

ॐ

Saudade (*Longing*) (1899)
José Ferraz de Almeida Júnior (1850-1899)

The postman came when I was at the stable block talking to Jean-Marc and Hubert. I liked it here; an earthy environment other than the ornate furnishings of the main house. I opened the letter from Natalie immediately and read it where I was. No need to risk being intercepted by either of my parents with a letter in my hand; it's Saturday and they are both at home.

I was worried about Natalie's lasciviousness. I read this latest letter. 'The people are brilliant, and my body is battered and bruised from night-time cruising, carousing and courting. Some of the damage is from dancing, but, honestly, not a lot.' My goodness, Natalie, what are you doing? This sounded like a girl who was sleeping her way round Paris. I wondered how many partners she had taken? 'Battered and bruised' sounded like the effects of sex at least once a night. I wondered if she was exaggerating, and why? Was she trying to impress me?

I compared this excessive behaviour to my relatively quiet existence. I had not had a boyfriend since September (Jean-François) and even then our intimate acts had hardly registered on the scale of passion. I had no desire to make an effort to go out and find another. I was very motivated by my work and soaking up the praise of Méli and other tutors at the École des Beaux-Arts. Was Natalie becoming a different person? Was it just a phase? Were we diverging too much for our friendship to endure?

When I looked in the mirror I saw an attractive girl. I knew men found me attractive... by their looks and their casual words. Was I jealous of Natalie? Did I want more lovers, more nocturnal escapades? Living with my parents in this formal environment and outside the city I knew that was quite difficult. I looked forward to the time when my love could be directed to one strong man; someone who would sweep me off my feet; someone who could be the love of my life. I didn't think I wanted lots of lovers.

There was also the practical me. I feared for Natalie in her promiscuity in Paris in a time when girls got pregnant, all the time. The phrase 'to put a bun in the oven' made the act of getting a girl pregnant as commonplace as baking bread. Natalie seemed to be expert when talking about birth control but I wondered what she did in practice. I would talk more to her about that when I next saw her, when she came back for Christmas. I wanted to be certain about her wellbeing; and I wouldn't mind being more expert myself.

I chose not to write any of these nagging doubts. I went back into the house and up to my room. I sat down and wrote the jolly letter she would want to read. But I had doubts about my reasons for doing so.

২

Nancy, 14th November 1891

Dearest Natalie, dear sister

I read your letter in the corridor to Jean-Marc's room; to be alone. I almost cried. Thank you for those words. You are definitely the sister I never had and, if I may go further in the tributes, you are also the Mama I never had. Leonora, my mother, has got even worse. She is so abusive to Papa, the staff, to Jean-Marc and to me. The temper outbursts are every few days. I just hope that I have inherited none of this temper that she and Jean-Marc have. Anyway, there is not a shred of love between her and any of us, maybe occasionally some forced civility. I have no direct evidence but I can't help thinking from Papa's reactions that she has threatened to walk out. He would be perfectly willing to let that happen. Not much fun for me and Jean-Marc, or for Hubert, who always looks doleful.

The Daum job is quite good fun. I get to meet people. Some are really offish and treat me like a post boy or worse; Gustaf St.Pierre, an artist who does designs for Daum is really horrid to me. Ignores me at best. My favourite is Duchien, a sculptor, who always has a kind word and a smile. He lost his wife and daughter a couple of years ago and I think it's acceptable that I try to cheer him up. He doesn't seem to have a first name. I was there this morning, just a few minutes, rushing on.

Christmas is just round the corner. I suppose you will be back. And I do hope so. Mistletoe is so romantic. But then maybe you need your mistletoe in Paris right now. Probably not.

Please tell me your year-end plans.

Yours with more kisses than could ever fit into an envelope via the post,

Cécile.

Appartement 3A, 16 rue de l'Estrapade, Paris V^e

7 December 1891

Dear Cécile

Well, I am exhausted (mentally and physically). I need a break. I will take the train back on the Friday 18th of December arriving late. See you on the Saturday. Meet at the Hôtel de la Poste at ten; or somewhere else?

What did people do before the railway? It would have taken two days in the charabanc. Rutted roads. Highwaymen. Changes of horses. Would a young lady feel safe spending the night in Vitry or Bar-le-Duc or somewhere ghastly like that. When I get back please let me have a break and some rest. No men, promise? Just girl talk. Although, have you honestly been keeping me up-to-date with your love life? You know you have to tell me all.

Sorry I haven't written for ages.

With love from your sister Natalie

ঌ

Nancy, 11th December 1891

Dearest Natalie

We are the only people in the world who say anything to each other, on any subject. I have come to the conclusion that marriage is a vow of silence between two people, not a promise to be open.

I have been keeping you sort of up-to-date with my love life as much as you have been keeping me up-to-date with yours. Ha ha. See what I did there? I might just be able to keep my latest news to one page of a letter, but as you suggested yourself, you would get more details when we chat face-to-face around some log fire at Christmas, or a Marc de Bourgogne and a petit café at Bernard's or at the Hôtel de la Poste.

Jean-Marc will pick you up from your mother's at ten on Saturday 19th December and bring you up to the Château. Mama is usually out on Saturday mornings - important society coffee dates. She thinks she is so aristocratic but her behaviour is so bourgeois. I sometimes wonder whether her titled ancestry is in fact all made up.

It's cold here. Hurry back.

Your Cécile.

ঽ

Jeune Nancéienne dans un paysage de neige (1887)
(Young girl from Nancy in a snowy landscape)
Émile Friant (1863-1932)

Chapter 11 - Cécile and Natalie: tête à tête

Pompey, north of Nancy, Saturday 19th December 1891

I looked forward to seeing Natalie. This had been the first time she had been away since we knew each other; fifteen years, more? Since we were in primary school together. Maybe because she was a year older I had struck up a special bond with her. I always looked up to her. She was the leader of our pack of two. As girls growing up this had been easy; she enjoyed mothering me a little bit. We both knew my mother was difficult to get on with and did not show much love to Jean-Marc and me; Natalie didn't mind me putting my head on her shoulder, talking through the latest bad feelings at home, asking advice, getting a dose of confidence-building. As a result she increased in self-belief and took seriously her role in showing me the way.

I looked through the letters from Paris and compared her delightfully open attitude to her life and the people round her with my relatively staid existence back in Nancy. I had hidden from her that I had not had a boyfriend since she had been away; I found myself growing up into someone less flirtatious, more keen on wondering what it would be like in a long-term relationship, maybe even with a man with experience. I wondered whether she and I were diverging as characters, whether she was being too frivolous about her relationships.

Jean-Marc brought me and his dog down to Natalie at her mother's home in Pompey after breakfast; I couldn't wait to be with her so I went too. We came straight back up to my home with Natalie riding as royalty with us. We went walking and talking in the woods for a couple of hours, Jean-Marc and Hubert zig-zagging round us. We got some lunch in the kitchen with Antoinette. The Countess, not Natalie's favourite person, was due back mid-afternoon so we judiciously left the Château to get back to Pompey at about two, making it less complicated for Natalie. The bruising presence of the Countess on two occasions in the past had made her feel unwelcome. My Papa and Mama really did not know my best friend.

Pompey was the village of our childhood. I felt at home here with Natalie. Pompey's village school was the one where Natalie and I spent seven years together, Natalie always a year ahead but inextricably linked to me. We would gravitate towards each other if there was no other priority. The school was only a kilometre and a half to walk for me, unless my father's driver picked Jean-Marc and me up in the trap, so I had some freedom in how I used my time after school. I could often go back to Natalie's.

Natalie's mother was Angela Duhamel but I knew that she and Natalie had changed their name from Büdenbaum when she was a baby. Madame Duhamel liked me and had made the effort to get to know me; or maybe she enjoyed chatting to me. She was most days at the school gate at the end of lessons to walk Natalie fifty metres home. When Jean-Marc was not with me then I felt tempted to go with Natalie for a while. It was she who gave us girls lemon drink and biscuits. She fussed over us and made me feel welcome. She encouraged to relax and talk as much as to do our homework or do some drawing. I even mucked in with domestic chores or did some sewing.

On this occasion, when we got back from the Château, Madame Duhamel chatted away intently with us, mostly about Natalie's latest news from Paris, that is, the bits which she could recount in front of her mother.

Natalie was fascinating, committed and informed; not at all the flibberty-gibbet of her letters. She had a pack of postcards about the Exposition Universelle of 1889 because she had visited what was left of some of the pavilions. She was fascinated by the construction of the Panama Canal. The project led by the French engineer de Lesseps went bankrupt in 1889; an estimated 22,000 men died from disease and accidents, and the savings of 800,000 investors were lost. The scandal rumbled on; some of those deemed responsible were prosecuted, including Gustave Eiffel. She showed Eiffel's magnificent Tower in various stages of construction; the engineering, the speed of build and that fact that it was still standing after two years enthralled her. She showed postcards of Sacré-Cœur at the summit of the Butte Montmartre; construction had started in 1875 but it was nowhere near finished. You could see the scaffolding and the first tower from all over Paris. Engineering could well be her career; her good start with La Fonderie, the summer job and the bursary for the Paris studies, pleased her. It pleased me to see her so excited.

It interested me more when Natalie started talking about art, fashion and how ordinary people were; although few people in her circle of interests are 'ordinary'. She showed with more post cards that Paris fashion was moving away from the stiff, moralistic, style of the Second Empire and the depression which had started in 1873. New technologies, such as the introduction of electricity into clothing manufacturing, produced a boom in the ready-to-wear clothing market, so even middle-class ladies wore new fashions. Women enjoyed new levels of independence, intellectual expression, the right to ride a cycle and play sports. The protruding bustle, the voluminous derriere look, was disappearing in favour of skirts fitting smoothly over the hips, a nipped waist, smooth bodices and loose gigot sleeves. She saw women (and read about them enviously) who could start the day, or go to work, in classic high necklines and long sleeves, then move to a dress open at the neck and shortened sleeves in the afternoon, and finish with a daring décolleté and bare arms in the evening. Even if she could not afford the clothes Natalie was transported by so many aspects of the changes in society and the role of the new woman. She clearly thought of herself as one, a new woman, and was mapping out the life which that state-of-mind would give her. I knew I could be a new woman too and that Natalie would support me in getting there. I did not know what path this would take other than having the feeling that my Papa would let me buy some of these clothes. I wondered when I could ask him and what I could wear them for.

Natalie's mother served tea at four o'clock which was not a normal habit for her but which she thought might be suitable for the daughter of a count. I didn't say that I had never had a 'cup of tea', as a formal event, in my life. I did not say why I thought that might be, but I did wonder sometimes if my parents actually behaved like aristocrats... or if they were indeed aristocrats. I knew there were plenty of false counts in France and always had been, even before 1789, but I did not know how I could check.

In the mists of time, Madame Duhamel had had a serendipitous link with my parents. Her mother left Metz as the German and Prussian invaders arrived, in the summer of 1870. With the infant Natalie wrapped around her chest, and a single case dragged behind, Angela Büdenbaum, as she was then, made the trip to Nancy, on foot, 60 kilometres over three days. She had heard it say that the Count and Countess had also escaped from Metz at that time; she wondered if they were on the road at the same time. I knew nothing of this from my parents. 70,000 people left Metz for Nancy after the invasion and before the date by which the Germans forced them to decide which nationality to take, October 1872, so it seemed unlikely. The Büdenbaum home had been destroyed by a stray shell during the German bombardment; luckily she and Natalie were out. But Natalie's father Alexander had volunteered for the French army and had been killed a couple of weeks previously; Natalie had never known him. By a miracle, Madame Büdenbaum's employer, a manufacturer of electricity generators, had to move without delay to Nancy and offered her a continuation of her job in the new location. As a good Catholic, she had plenty of good fortune to thank the Lord for every Sunday at the Église Saint Jean-Baptiste. With the name Duhamel, changed by deed poll, she was a competent person in production and sales administration, respected by her colleagues and clients and secure... 20 years later.

At about six Natalie and I put on every bit of warm clothing we could find and ventured out into the cold evening. Just across the road was the village school; we sat on the bench where I would wait with Natalie when her mother was late. We reminisced for a minute until the cold forced us to continue on down to the main Metz-Nancy road, cross over and enter the Hôtel de la Poste. The half-timbered façade, sharply angled roof and small windows made the inn look more like an elf's forest cabin. The restaurant felt homely with a crackling log fire and a place where two young women, 20 and 21 years old, on their own, could feel comfortable.

Over a long meal we talked like old friends but without the frivolity of the letters we had been writing. I was conscious of the attractive sensation of growing up and she encouraged this. We were intrigued by each other's personalities; two people becoming quite different from each other and yet remaining so close. I commented that this must be how non-identical twins must feel.

Natalie thought I was more beautiful – 'more serene' were words she used – more mature than six months ago. We stood up, perched on the footrests of the bar stools and looked in the mirror behind the bar. I had to agree with her, I looked terrific, even if I feel I have a slightly shy look. She is certainly more out-going. Physically, we looked identical from a distance; quite tall without being willowy; slim-waisted; feminine without being busty; brunette with our hair in a flat bun. Natalie's hair was now slightly darker than mine. Her facial features were slightly darker and more acute too, a sharper nose, firmer lips, pointier chin, deeper eyes... quite womanly and very attractive. She said I had retained the doe-eyed look of the girl you would want your son to marry; charming, intelligent, permanently young-looking and fresh-faced.

On interrogation of our private lives, Natalie had to admit that she was the more extrovert and active. She could hardly deny it because she had put quite a lot in writing! She had no complexes with men. She enjoyed seeking one out, especially the older man. She was adventurous in the sense of wanting to learn, wanting to lap it all up. I was comfortable with the modesty and reticence expected of the daughter of an aristocratic family, if that is what I was. I wondered if my coyness increased my attractiveness, especially to men. I was aware of two co-workers at Daum who had chosen to work on Saturdays just for the dubious pleasure of some possible interaction with me when I came in for my weekend job. The attention was flattering but I did not take easily to chirpy greetings like 'Salut Cécile chérie'; quite right for lovers and just about acceptable for working class people. But really? Natalie pushed me for more. One of the contractors I had to visit on my Saturday rounds, a sculptor called Duchien, was a person of brooding and manly silence so when a compliment passed his lips it was quite pleasant. I was keen to prevent any work relationship from getting serious; but these contacts made it obvious to me that I had not only eloquence and charm but some sexiness as well. I had no real love in my life since Natalie left in the autumn; Natalie and I wondered whether I was missing out; whether I was being left behind. I suggested I might be keeping my powder dry for the battles ahead and she chided me for using such a masculine metaphor for a young woman's behaviour. We talked about different types of men, those we had met, those we would like to meet and a lot about more experienced men. She clearly knew much more about all that than me; I hung on to her every word.

This was the moment to ask her how she avoided getting pregnant. She didn't blush but she did incline her head while she told me to make sure we were not overheard. What she said did not fill me with confidence. More often than not she would just get the man to pull out at the last moment; if necessary by bouncing him out by a well-judged thrust and twist of the hips, or by rolling him over and getting off. Would that work? It might work better than politely asking. I giggled. She added to my embarrassment by adding some mucky detail about how to give the man some alternative satisfaction. Then she went through her understanding of the rhythm method to be able to predict ovulation dates and choose the times of the months to have sex. I had read that you have to log your cycles every day, every month, on a calendar to be certain of the danger dates. Natalie was worryingly dismissive of the need to keep such accurate records; she said she just knew what time of the month it was.

I impressed on her my hope that she was right and that no mishap would ever befall her.

We left the table long past ten at night, happy, impressed with our own sincerity and looking forward to more time together. We embraced warmly on the pavement outside the Hôtel de la Poste. Natalie walked a few hundred metres to home. I got a lift up the hill by a friend of Natalie's mother who had a pony and trap for hire.

I am floating high above the river Meurthe and the road where my family died. My arms are outstretched. I flew down the road from my bedroom to the workshop. I pick up a casting of the statue of the two of them, my wife and my daughter. I know I must get rid of it to stop my torment. I pick it up but the bronze turns immediately to fine dust and it flows like water into the cracks between the floorboards. I can't reach it to get it out.

Chapter 12 – Duchien and the hypnotist

'Yes, there has been much written about these extreme headaches, worse than migraines and neuralgia. A doctor called Professor Charcot at the Salpêtrière Hospital in Paris - well, you may know about it, a home for the clinically insane, a lunatic asylum - I was at medical school with one of his assistants, Georges Gilles de la Tourette - has shown that these headaches are a distinct type of affliction, caused by a physical incident like a concussion or head injury but exacerbated by a mental condition such as depressions. Or they are the cause of the depression; this last piece of the jigsaw is what is so fascinating about such studies today. The pain is described by some patients as a pain worse than dying. I do hope that is not your case Monsieur Duchien.'

Dr Tenneberg put down his pencil and looked his patient in the eye. 'You are lucky to be alive of course. But at the same time you are <u>un</u>lucky to have survived the crash. Despite this brilliant research work in Paris and the diagnosis of these physio-psychotic illnesses – they call them psychosomatic illnesses - they have not proposed any cures. It may be that you have what they have named a neurasthenic condition, nervous exhaustion with insomnia, phobias and so on. I'm not boring you am I?'

Duchien shook his head slowly, his eyes averted.

'It is more likely' continued Tenneberg hardly taking breath 'to be what Professor Charcot calls a neurological condition caused by a lesion, a cut or swelling, in the brain or spinal cord which causes problems of the nerves from that point. Despite these vast strides being made in these disciplines, I am afraid there is no pharmaceutical product I can prescribe to you to relieve the pain or to help you make some progress in re-establishing a normal life. From this point of view, you are most <u>un</u>fortunate.'

He paused to look intently at Duchien. Seeing no reaction, he finished up with 'I wish you a good recovery by whatever means it comes. If you can immerse yourself in your work and give yourself something to live for, then of course your chances of recovery are much higher. But I know that it's not always easy. '

Duchien fiddled with his cap and looked at the floor. His

Christmas and New Year had been a continuous nightmare. He felt suicidal at times, his depression still exacerbated by the headaches and pains in the chest and in his right elbow. He had to seek help. Dr Tenneberg seemed very young for such a reputed expert, in his early thirties maybe. Really there was nothing to say.

Tennenberg had another idea. 'You might consider consulting a specialist recently settled here from Paris. If there is no remedy for you in standard medical practice, then I'm sure Dr Bernheim would be interested in your case, and he might well be able to find some therapy to help you.'

'I can't afford a specialist, you know that'.

Tennenberg continued 'I have just been reading his new book *On Suggestion and its Applications to Therapy*. It is not to the taste of everyone because this science of hypnotism and neurology is on the outer frontiers of science. He is also in direct opposition to the theories of Professor Charcot of the Salpêtrière in Paris, so the waters are murky. But Bernheim has moved here to Nancy and the nature of your trauma (especially as manifested in your dreams) is such that he might take you on at little or no cost for the purpose of continuing his research, which I think you can assume would not risk harm to you. Here, let me write down his address'

❧

I am sitting at a round table on the street. Bernard comes over with a bottle of pastis and two glasses. One glass is large and it's my wife. One glass is small and it's my daughter. I tried to stop my sneeze but the energy of it makes Bernard lose the balance of the tray. The bottle and the two glasses full to the floor and smash to smithereens. I see I have destroyed the ones I love.

Duchien did eventually, after five weeks, take Tennenberg's advice and took an initial consultancy appointment with the famous protagonist of new-fangled ideas, the mad-doctor (as some people called psychiatrists), Professor Hippolyte Bernheim, recently arrived from Paris.

His practice, a few blocks towards the river from Duchien's atelier, was in a large upper room with three desks and a large patient's couch. The two desks other than Bernheim's were occupied by intense young men, one of whom turned out to be named Jacques. Bernheim, resplendent in a high white collar and formal frock coat, white moustache, knowing eyes and receding hairline, took some details from Duchien and confirmed that the initial session would be free of charge. Duchien protested about the costs in the longer term but Bernheim continued with initial questions about Duchien's symptoms and mental condition. He wanted to know everything about his late wife and daughter, the accident, the people around him thereafter, their roles in his life, his sleep patterns, his mental breakdowns, the chronic headaches and the calendar of each of the stages of his illness. He silently observed the sunken eyes, the drooping head, the tar-stained index finger and the awkward position of his right arm.

'What you have told me is of great interest to me. The symptoms are those of a condition which might respond well to the techniques we have been developing in this practice and I would like to delve deeper into the issues today, if it were to please you and if you have the time.'

Duchien did not object.

'Many episodes of psychosis like this, where a patient might give the impression of taking leave from reality, are caused by an event in the past which may be unknown to the patient. In your case, Monsieur Duchien, the trauma is of course the death of your wife and child and your involvement in the accident. You had an injury to the head, which should normally be giving you no further symptoms. That is clear. But in the sequel there may be other influences, in your life or in your psyche, which exacerbate the effects of the trauma and which, frankly, from what you have told me, make your life unbearable.

'In many cases, gaps in certain memories are distorted by false information from friends or from other unrelated events, especially when the signals are received by the patient over and over. This phenomenon is known as suggestibility. The patient receives some input and accepts it readily even if it is not an essential cause of the trauma. If the patient experiences intense emotions then he or she can be more open to ideas and these can make the psychological condition worse. It is often impossible by classic methods to find out what these triggers or underlying reasons are.

'But now we have various means to enter into the psyche of the patient, with his or her cooperation, in order that we can hear directly what might be the root causes of the problem. Abuse as a child is a frequent cause. A loss of someone or something which does not seem important might be another. Furthermore, when the patient is sleeping, or under hypnotism, the psyche releases information which is of great interest to the consultant neurologist, that is, today, to me. My colleague Professor Charcot at the Salpêtrière considers that only mental patients with hystero-epilepsy, hysteria, can be hypnotised, i.e. people who would otherwise be in a lunatic asylum. But we, that is Professor Liebeault Ambroise, also here in Nancy, and I have found that this is not the case. Hypnotism now has an important part to play in analysing and curing mental depression even when the health and intellectual capacity of the patient is otherwise perfect.

'I am confident from the way in which you have described your situation, Monsieur Duchien, that your health is excellent and your intellectual capacity too. I therefore think that we would find out an enormous amount and be able to take the first steps towards analysis and cure in your case, if you were to agree to hypnotism: to being hypnotised.'

The two young students leant forward across their desks, bright-eyed and lapping it all up. Duchien was shocked.

'Do you mean, do you want to put me to sleep now, to hypnotise me and then I, by talking, inform you of things of which I am not aware? What planet do you live on Dr Bernheim. How do you do it anyway? Is there any risk of pain?'

Professor Bernheim, Faculté de Médecine de Nancy (1895)

'No no no. There are no risks. Furthermore if the patient is becoming upset or we see some other incipient danger, we can immediately take the patient out of the hypnotic state by a click of the fingers.' There was silence in the room.

The three medics waited expectantly for the patient's response. 'Well. What have I got to lose? I am desperate. And what about the headaches, doctor; each time I have an attack it feels as if I am dying... or dead already. In this weakened state I don't think my body and my mind can survive much longer.'

'I understand my dear sir. But there is a strong likelihood that if we are able to cure the underlying psychosis and a neurological condition, then the physical symptoms disappear. On this I can tell you that Charcot and I agree entirely; there are many case histories where a patient with mental problems of the sort we have been talking about makes a complete recovery and throws off the physical afflictions.'

Duchien left another silence. Then he got out of his chair and looked around the room. He looked at each of the students, back at Bernheim and then at the couch. He unbuttoned his tunic, took it off and put it round the back of his chair. He took three paces to the couch, with its headrest raised at 30°, took off his shoes, lay down on it, felt his shaved chin with the flat of his hand and relaxed his head on the pillow.

'Well, very good Monsieur. Let us proceed.' Bernheim gathered up his pad of notes and a pencil, moved a chair to the couch and sat down where Duchien could see him. The elder of the two medics went to the window, opened it, closed the shutters from outside and closed the window firmly. The other turned on the table lamp on Bernheim's desk and turned off the ceiling chandelier.

'Hypnotism. Psychological analysis. This is how it happens' thought Duchien. Aloud, he said, 'You really think you're going to put me to sleep here and now?'

Bernheim let a silence descend on the room. Being on the third floor there was little or no noise from the street. The medic brought out a little bell on a cord ten centimetres long. Nothing in the initial hypnotism was out of the ordinary. Then he asked Duchien to look at the bell and to follow it with his eyes as

Bernheim wafted it slowly from side to side.

'Yes, that's right. Continue looking into the bell. Look all the way through it. Empty your mind. Feel your breath in the movement of your chest. Feel the distant beat of your heart. Now... now you are feeling sleepy. You have had a tiring day. You will be going to sleep shortly. When you hear the bell and a click of my fingers, then you will wake up. You are feeling sleepy. Now... you are feeling very sleepy. You have closed your eyes. Good. Now... you are asleep.'

The man lying on the couch had totally changed demeanour. The nervous and fidgety sculptor was now totally relaxed, looking blissful and serene. The professor glanced at the two medics and the three of them exchanged nods.

Bernheim left another moment of silence, then... 'Now you are fast asleep, Monsieur Duchien. You are at peace with yourself and with us. There are people around you who respect you very much and who care for you. You will now be telling us more about what is in your mind and what events or emotions are at the origin of the trauma.' Bernheim put the bell down silently and picked up his pad and his pencil. The two students were already prepared to take notes.

'What is your name, Monsieur?'
'Duchien.' He sounded completely normal.
'Where are you right now?'
'At home, above the atelier. I'm lying in bed.' The two medics glanced at each other.
'Do you remember the accident in the horse and trap, when your wife and daughter were killed?'
'The horse was killed too.'
'Who is left? Who lives with you now?'
'No one. I live alone here.'
'Do you think about the accident in the daytime? '
'I try not to. I start crying, at any time of day.'
'Do you dream about the accident at night?'

'No, not about the accident. Well, yes, the accident is always there in the background but it's the statues that are always in my dreams. And women.'

'Tell me one of your dreams where the accident is involved.'

Duchien's voice changed in pitch; upwards. He recounted with a more nasal tone and an uncertainty in his delivery.

'There is a crash in the middle of the night. I sit bolt upright, straining for the source of the sound. I hear an angry voice downstairs and get out of bed to hear what's happening. The stairs are not there anymore so I jump and crash to the floor of the atelier. My wife is shouting at my daughter. 'It was his fault. It was all his fault. Stupid man. Why did he think he could drive a horse and trap'. But she was beating up my daughter not me.'

Bernheim left a silence to be certain Duchien had finished and then said 'Thank you Monsieur Duchien. Now tell me another one, maybe when the statues are involved, as you said.'

The two students wrote as fast as possible to catch up.

'My wife and daughter are a statue, holding hands. They let go of each other and walk towards me but their legs are not moving normally. They each stretch out a hand to me and beckon me to walk with them. Secure between their hands I float with them, the three of us, out of the atelier and into the street. I am looking downwards, arms stretched out holding them, watching the streets move past. We float upwards, now out of control. It's windy. I look down and I see Bernard at one of the outdoor tables, looking up at us. Then Pascale screams. We drop like stones, our legs windmilling helplessly. We smash against the pavement.'

'Pascale is your daughter?'

'Yes. Was'

'Can you remember another of your dreams?'

Duchien's voice is normal for an instant; 'Yes, I remember all my dreams.' There was hardly a hesitation before his nightmare voice continued.

'There is a commotion downstairs. I cannot get there so I look down where the staircase normally is, down the long road with stones. All the statues have come alive but they are still bronze or stone. The statue of my wife and child holding hands is in the middle, pleading with them not to knock them over. They bustle round, ignoring her. They knock my daughter over and my wife bends to help her up. She falls under the weight of the other statues pushing in on her. I can hear her cries but I am impotent to stop what's happening. The shouting of the statues comes to a crescendo and then there is silence. My family has gone'.

'Do you remember all your dreams?'

'I remember all my dreams. They are nightmares. They haunt me. I am thinking of ... I cannot sleep without being tortured by these memories. I cannot, I cannot... I did not...'

Duchien got more and more agitated, hitting his fists on the couch, his head thrashing left and right. Bernheim picked up the bell, rang it once and clicked his fingers.

Silence. Duchien composed himself into the relaxed state as when he was first put to sleep. Slowly, he looked around him, wondering where he was. He did not seem worried about it. He looked at the Professor.

'My name is Professor Bernheim. Your name is Monsieur Duchien. You have been asleep and you have been recounting images and stories from your subconscious. This has been one of the most revealing hypnotic sources I can remember in my many years of practice. I congratulate you and I thank you. I'm telling you that you are a patient who makes it easy for us to find the reasons for your condition and the cure for it.'

'How long have I been asleep? I feel quite well. Can we do some more now?'

'No. At the end of your trance you became agitated and I thought it better to end it at that moment. But I confirm that what you have told us is spectacular in its interest for us and in what you have revealed about yourself. May I suggest that we bring this consultation to an end and set a rendezvous for another?'

Duchien gestured with his arms apart and the palms up to ask how he could possibly afford it. 'No, if you do not mind us keeping a record of these conversations and the treatment protocol for a case history, I think we would be pleased to continue the consultations without charge. Shall we say, Tuesday again, in two weeks and at the same time?'

Duchien muttered some thank-yous, took his coat over his arm, shook all three men tentatively by the hand and left

২

'How do you feel today?' asked Bernheim when Duchien was comfortable on the couch. The young medics had their pens poised.

'Alright. No, well, the same. My nights are a torment. The headaches unbearable'

'Yes, I understand. I would not have thought there would be any improvement yet. With your permission Monsieur Duchien, we will now seek out any other factors, including those arising out of suggestibility, which have muddied the waters of your subconscious and your reaction to the tragedy of the loss of you wife and daughter. We consider that in the first séance we did not learn anything unexpected about your trauma; guilt about your role in the accident, a feeling of impotence at having been unable to prevent it. I propose now to delve a bit deeper into your psyche... in aspects which initially might seem unconnected to your awareness of your case. But permit me to elaborate on my thinking after one or two more sessions.'

Duchien blinked, pursed his lips and inclined his head, firmly on the pillow, in agreement. Bernheim commenced the process of putting Duchien to sleep; his talent for hypnotising even recalcitrant patients was well known in Paris and abroad. By the time he put down the bell and took up his pencil and notebook, Duchien was miles away; serene, asleep.

'What is your name, Monsieur?'

'Duchien.'

'Where are you right now?'

'I'm lying in bed.'

Who lives with you now?'

'No one. I live alone here.'

'Are you lonely?'

'Yes.'

'Why? Why do you not have friends?'

'They do not want to be with me. I am a spent force, a nothing man'

'Can you consider a life in the future when you might find a life partner and adopt a conjugal life again?'

'No. A woman would consider me impotent. I am a spent force. I have no libido. I have no lust. The naked female form leaves me cold'.

'Do you dream about this impotence, about the lack of libido?'

Duchien hesitated. 'Yes. I think so. I am not certain about those dreams.'

'Tell me one, please, if you like'.

Duchien did not speak for a moment. His eyes quivered. The two students had caught up with their notes and watched him with rapture. Duchien then launched, firmly and with little further hesitation, but with his more high-pitched and strained voice, into a new dream, most revealing.

'A girl comes to the atelier. Her summer dress shows her bare shoulders, the shape of her firm breasts and legs bare to above the knees. She is the most beautiful creation in the whole world. I can smell her young flesh and a slightest hint of an eau de cologne. She stands a few metres from me and says she loves me. She wants me. As she speaks to me in this way, slowly, she undresses. I see her nipples erect. I see the flush in her cheeks. I see the waves of her downy pubic hair. She lets me look at it all, in her own time, in my own time. She looks up and down my body and then nods to indicate to me that I should take my clothes off too. I do so but with terrible pain. I have a headache. When I am naked in front of her, I am ashamed. My penis is soft and shrivelled. I put my hand there, out of modesty, and I find I have no testicles. They have withdrawn inside the body. She comes to me and starts holding me and kissing me. I want to participate, to reciprocate, but my body is frozen. My mind is frozen. She strokes my penis but I feel only revulsion. She becomes annoyed and asks what is wrong with me. A moment later she gets dressed, jerks her head disdainfully and leaves.'

Bernheim glanced at the medics and they exchanged excited glances.

'Thank you Monsieur. You are showing great certainty about the detail of such a dream. It is very positive for your restitution to normal life, for conquering your psychosomatic ailments, that you open up and expose your inner feelings like this. Would you like to remember another?'

'I am floating high above the main square of Nancy. All the people are statues, static. I see one of them is my daughter. She has no legs because she's a statue. She floats across the ground and across the street to my atelier. She has now come to life I am inside the atelier at my normal place. She comes in and takes her clothes off. She comes into my arms naked and I am embarrassed, but then aroused. She is kissing me passionately but now it's not my daughter. It is the mistress of a rich man, someone famous? I don't know her. She starts to undress me but my wife comes down from my bedroom, screaming abuse at me.'

Bernheim chose not to speak. The medics and he caught up with their notes and Jacques whispered 'Freud!' to his colleague. Bernheim made an angry face to demand silence. Duchien continued without prompting; another nightmare.

'The girl comes from the factory. From Daum. Ceramics. She asks me if the work is ready. I look at my feet in shame but my feet are not there. I have not done the work. She walks up to me and slaps me in the face. She rips open her shirt and shouts at me 'I come here to pick up the work not to be your prostitute'. When I look up she has turned to stone'.

The patient now tossed and turned his head, apparently with the force of his shame and his impotence. His face and neck were red. His eyes remained closed, lids quivering. There were beads of sweat on his forehead. But presently he calmed himself and reached further into his subliminal memory.

'I fly away from the centre of town, high in the air, looking down, my arms spread. I have been invited to a factory for the unveiling of a statue; a statue I've made out of stone. A man, in formal clothes. It is ugly. In front of the mayor, his wife, my wife and my daughter and all the senior executives, I am naked. It is cold and my penis is shrivelled to the size of two peanuts in their

shell. My wife and daughter are there and they burst into tears. I look down at my feet with shame, but I have no feet. I am falling. I wake up with my head beating and my body quaking.'

'These characters in your dreams, Monsieur; I infer from what you told us about your artistic activities that they are real people. Who is the girl from the factory; from Daum ceramics? Is it the same factory where your statue of a man is unveiled?' Duchien does not appear to be listening. He commences recounting another dream.

The rich industrialist has a daughter. I have never met them but she is with me in the atelier. She is beautiful, brunette, slender, and young. I cannot tell if she is bronze or real. She undresses herself and gives herself to me. She takes me upstairs and I find I have lust for her, for her touching me, for my touching her body, everywhere. She tells me I am erect and she kisses me there. She takes me in her mouth. I hold her head and marvel with amazement at myself. But my wife and my daughter come into the atelier and float upstairs to my bedroom even though the stairs have gone. The girl and I lie naked on the bed having made love. Her face and neck are flushed. My manhood is flaccid now but I'm not embarrassed. My wife looks at me with hatred then her expression turns into a Mona Lisa smile. Disdain. She takes the hand of my daughter and their bronze effigy melts into a pool of pastis on the ground.'

Duchien is sweating profusely, his face drawn with lines of stress and misery. After thirty seconds it is clear that he is not going to speak again. His head moves slowly from side to side. His right hand is twitching. Bernheim reaches for the bell, rings it and clicks his fingers. 'Now you are perfectly awake. You have had a relaxing sleep and you are now ready to renew the activities of the day. But may I suggest, dear Monsieur, that you stay lying down on the couch for some moments more while we talk.'

The patient is surprised to find his brow is sweaty; Bernheim passes him a hand towel, for which he is grateful, and retires to his own chair at his desk.

'You have been in a hypnotic state for nearly half an hour and you have revealed some dreams which are extremely useful in our analysis of your case. May I congratulate you again on your positive attitude and your openness with me.'

'I have not consciously intended to show a positive attitude and certainly not openness. That is not my nature.'

'I understand. Nonetheless, when you hear the details of your dreams, as much as we will be able at some future moment to recount to you, you will be impressed, and most interested, both at the detail and at your openness. Now, if I may ask, because some patients are in state of great lethargy and fatigue after such a séance, how do you feel and would you like to continue with the consultation this morning?'

'I feel fine. I have no headache. Whether I would like to continue with the consultation depends on what you have to say Professor.' There was the tiniest hint of cynicism in Duchien's voice which Bernheim ignored. The medics take up their pads and pencils. Bernheim speaks authoritatively and freely, without referring to his notes.

'I asked you at the beginning of the hypnotic séance about loneliness and whether you would find a life partner. With little further prompting you recounted five separate dreams, each of which have given detailed accounts of sexual encounters. Each showed some evolution from the previous, especially in the degree of inadequacy you felt, in your awareness of your own lack of libido. We will start there, and then come later to your expression of libido refound.

'You might be aware of the ground-breaking work of Sigmund Freud who visited us here last year. Among his patients 'psychical impotence' was a highly prevalent complaint, 'psychical' meaning that the problem emanates from the mind rather than a malfunction of the body. He argues that this dysfunction is caused by an unresolved neurotic fixation leading to an inhibition and an arrest of the libido. The neurotic fixation can be a conflict between tender and sensual sexuality on one hand and an oedipal-based castration anxiety and hatred of women on the other. This is the so-called 'Madonna-whore complex'. The degree of this divide determines the extent of the sexual dysfunction so caused. The erotic life of the vast majority of civilized people tends to be affected by this condition, this innate conflict.

'It is clear from what you told us under hypnotism that you have no hatred of women, in fact, Monsieur , much of what lies in your subliminal is sexually aware, positive about women and their sexuality, is of a strong innate libido and which, to be honest, cries out for sexual release and a warm personal relationship. How can we tell you have a strong innate libido? Freud maintains that dreams of floating serenely high above the ground are a direct indication of sexual potency. I and the bulk of the world's psycho-medical body agree. You, Monsieur, mentioned flying several times in your dreams. In a dream last week and in more than one today, you said, most eloquently '*I am flying high in the air, looking down, my arms spread*' or words to that effect. There is no doubt in my mind that you have no fundamental problem with your sexual potency, only a temporary inhibition caused by a malaise of the psyche.

'The notion that your condition is temporary is confirmed by your frequent reference to 'having no legs' or 'no feet'. This is universally understood to mean that you feel inadequate – this notion is so engrained in human nature over the generations that we use the phrase 'no leg to stand on' to refer to a lack of self-confidence, a void argument, lack of authority – but also that the inadequacy is temporary. The act of 'putting your feet back on the ground', when the conditions make it possible for you to do so, is not difficult.

'I would like to direct your thoughts to another positive signal from your dreams. I can quite understand that you have never been able to interpret your thoughts because of the blockage caused by the lingering memory of such an awful trauma. But in more than one dream today you expressed strong attraction for a young woman. You call her a girl; this gives the impression that you think of her as young, lustful, a new path for you, someone you could love. The ways in which you speak of this attraction, and the intense relations you entertain with the girl, show that your subliminal thoughts are already strongly in favour of converting this dream into reality. I recall that, in various incidences with the girl or girls, you refer to her differently or give her a different identity. Do I remember correctly? One is the girl from the ceramics manufacturer Daum; one is your daughter; another is the daughter of an industrialist.' He paused.

Duchien looked at him and looked at his feet again. He gave a shudder of self-loathing at the thought of his daughter in the context of 'intense relations'.

'It cannot be my daughter. The girl from Daum comes on Saturday but not every week. She passes by the atelier. I have never had feelings for her, but she is attractive. I don't know the daughter of an industrialist.'

Bernheim permitted himself a self-congratulatory rubbing of the hands. 'Excellent. This is excellent progress. Permit me to tell you a final positive signal from what you told us today. In your last dream, prior to unilaterally giving clear signals to me, even in your hypnotic trance, that you had arrived at the apogee of your discourse, you describe an interlude with the girl which indicated that your libido had returned. I must say, without wanting to embarrass you, that you recounted your love-making with the girl with affirmation and pleasure. The physical description of certain aspects showed us that we, you, have nothing to worry about in the context of you libido, your virility, your manhood or your ability to please, and be pleased by, a woman. Furthermore, even when your late wife encounters you in a post-coital state with the girl, you are not embarrassed. Remarkable.'

Before Duchien could protest at the depth of the details of his sexuality which is claimed he revealed, Bernheim continued.

'You may wonder what brings the malaise to an end. What is that liberates you again? In some extreme cases, sex therapy, behavioural therapy or group therapy may be helpful to those suffering distress from sexual dysfunction. More serious sexual perversions may be treated with drugs, electric shock treatment or natural remedies to help restore hormonal and neurochemical balances. But your case is not in the bit extreme, that is, despite your headaches and other effects of your trauma being extremely painful for you today, the underlying psychical problems are easy to understand and probably easy to cure. I am most optimistic on that point.'

The onlooking medics looked at each other with

amazement at their guru's apparent skill. Duchien showed relief on his face, then puzzlement.

'Indeed', said Bernheim, picking up on Duchien's signals, 'you may ask what the cure is. I can tell you that it is quite possible that you are already cured. While some patients take many months and many sessions to make progress, you have unburdened yourself so completely that nature, and a full return of your libido, will take its course. Some incident, an exchange of words or an encounter with a girl, might lead directly to a new awakening in your psyche and immediately thereafter, in your body. There is no need for drugs. There is no need for physical therapy, although corporal massage can be therapeutic. It is difficult to think, given the enormity and, frankly, splendour of what you have revealed today, that further sessions here would reveal more to me about your psyche. The only request I permit myself to make is to ask you to come back a few times to keep us informed of your situation so that we can assess the value of our interventions and write them up for the psycho-medical fraternity with adequate notes on the results.' Then he took a breath and leaned back in his chair.

'Is it appropriate for me to see what I told you? In writing maybe?'

'Yes. Given my positive assessment of your psychology as of right now, I can see no reason why not. In fact, your knowing the detail of both your problem and how you can deal with it, could be a further beneficial therapy. We will write them up and get them to you at your address.'

'Thank you. And if I understand you rightly, I might now find, without any further effort, that an encounter with a potential mate could lead to ... well... could lead to where I would like it to go, and that neither my thoughts nor my body would stand in the way... that the memories and nightmares of the accident and the loss of my family would recede.'

'That is correct'.

'Thank you.' Duchien got up, put on his tunic and left.

রা

Chapter 13 – Ice in the ink bottle

Appartement 3A, 16 rue de l'Estrapade, Paris V^e

Th. 3rd March 1892

Dear Cécile

It has been so cold here, including in the apartment. I should have written more often but it is difficult to hold a feather quill when one's hands are in gloves. The quill is not strong enough to break the ice in the ink bottle. Yes, there is only one thing for it; that is to find a mate to get warm with in bed.

I promise I have not been changing partners too often. The current one is an Englishman, Sebastian, from Sevenoaks in Kent. He speaks beautiful French and I am busy teaching him the words he did not learn in his French primer at school. There are some parts of the body he struggled with, the French translations that is. He has now got a better grip on them and I on his.

Does your father remember me? I did not get to see him much when I did that internship but he seems really nice. I sometimes wonder whether it was he who persuaded the charity board of the company to fund my studies or whether he actually doesn't care. By the way, do you sometimes thank your lucky stars that you have your father's genes... terribly good-looking, a bit suave, humourful and a little bit sexy even for a man of his age. Jesus; if you had turned out like your mother... maybe we would not even be friends. Just think. Life can be so serendipitous

I'm going to come back at Easter just for a few days. It's April 17th and I will try to get away on the Wednesday 13th.

Your devoted representative in the real world

Natalie

ॐ

Nancy, 10th March 1891

Dearest Natalie

I open your letters with joy in my heart. Everything you say is worth reading two or three times, with a big smile on my face. I am in the real world too you know, Madame Paris person.

I asked Papa about you and I think he really likes you. He said he thinks of you (or was it people like you) as the future of business. But, a woman! He was aware of your bursary and, yes, he did influence the charity board to fund the year in Paris. Maybe they will take you on when you're back.

I've never had a love letter from a boy because I've never been away. What would you think if I came to Paris for Easter?

With love from Cécile

Chapter 14 – The Countess's tirades

Place Thiers, Nancy town centre, 16th March 1891

Antoinette had her day off. Mondays. She downed her double espresso, leaned closer to Marcel and lowered her voice. 'You know my old friend; I hate what I'm seeing at the Château. The countess's treatment of her son is appalling.' Franz, on the other side of Marcel, inclined himself discreetly towards them, ear cocked. 'Why, what's happening now?'

'She is always telling him that he is an imbecile and that she is ashamed of him being her son. Yes, he finds school difficult, even the village school in Pompey; not like his sister who went on to the Lycée here. Jean-Marc is a bit slow, but he is a kind soul and has a good heart. Today the dog, which I think of as his dog, came in from a walk and got into the hall. Muddy footprints on the carpet. She launched a tirade at Jean-Marc and hit him over the top of the head. He sobbed and screamed. I really don't think it's acceptable and it will end unhappily, probably as much for her rather than him. And all the time the Count seems to be helpless. He keeps out of her way as much as possible but he does spend time with Jean-Marc in productive activity in the grounds, making things.'

Marcel was an observant man and aware of what went on around him. His place at Bernard's bar, on the Main Square facing Nancy railway station, gave him the perfect viewpoint to see the goings-on. 'I used to see Jean-Marc quite often when he was driving Cécile around in the trap, doing her errands for the ceramics company, almost every Saturday. Not recently though. They often parked right here when she jumped off to go into Duchien's atelier down the street. The best part is how much the dog seems to like Jean-Marc, always sitting next to him faithfully. And in that situation Jean-Marc seems happy and on top of things.'

'Yes he and the dog are beautiful to behold and I think he would fall apart at home without him. But then Cécile adores Jean-Marc as well. She is a lovely sister to him, a life-saver considering how awful the mother is'.

'Can she do anything about the Countess?'

'No she's is as helpless as the father. And I am just a humble employee. The Countess trusts me, for the moment, and I do not want to risk losing my post. I can't do anything about it. It's worse for some of the others. The Countess picked a fight with Ursula in the kitchen over a change in menu and she waved a candle-stick over her head at her, white knuckles, stamping feet, red-faced, screaming at the top of her voice. She's a danger to all of us, I can feel it.'

ঽ

I am woken in the night. There are voices downstairs so I walk down the stairs in my nightshirt to see what is going on. The mad-doctor Bernheim is giving a lecture, but the contents are incomprehensible. He has a long baton which he is waving about randomly, pointing at nothing in particular. His audience is made up of ladies; now I recognise some of them. Each is based on one of my statues or on one of my muses. They are fully clothed in garish satins and silks as if they are going out dancing. Indeed, presently they start glancing at each other and nodding as if a pre-determined time has arrived. The lecturer takes no notice and continues delivering his nonsensical monologue. I am not surprised when the ladies, one by one, rise from their chairs and leave the room without a word. I feel some pity for Bernheim, but, unusually, none for myself. When the room is empty of his audience, I feel a massive release of tension. I smile at Bernheim and he looks at me with a fixed expression, not understanding what has come over me.

Chapter 15 – Body to body

Appartement 3A, 16 rue de l'Estrapade, Paris V^e

17 March 1892

Dear Cécile

That would be a good idea, you coming to Paris for Easter, but 1) there is little or no room in the apartment so you'd have to sleep with me and 2) I have to get back. My mother misses me a lot as her life is difficult as you know and there is no-one else except her neighbour Agnès. So I must come home for Easter. We will have time together anyway.

As it happens, I don't think I have ever had a love-letter from a boyfriend either. I'm sure they are not as good as they are cracked up to be. Why would you want to read his words on paper when the lure of body to body and face to face, contact is so delicious?

Of which more anon when I see you.

N

ঽ

Chapter 16 – The Count commissions his statue

'My dearest Countess, how nice to be together with you at breakfast this fine Saturday morning. What plans do you have?'

'Indeed Monsieur le Comte, how perceptive of you. I have Madame Valentina coming in only half an hour to do my hair and my nails. I must not be late for coffee with Madame de Montesquieu at half past ten in town.'

'That's wonderful. I'm sure you'll have an entertaining and productive time.' The Count hesitated before opening up the subject for which he had made such an amicable conversational prelude. The housekeeper Antoinette, on duty in the absence of the serving maid at the weekend, served them both another coffee, wondering how on earth they had managed for twenty years to keep up this pretence of liking each other. 'My dearest Countess, I have wondered if I may ask of your ineffable knowledge of the people and the culture of Nancy to help me with a problem with which I have been wrestling. My colleagues at La Fonderie think I should commission a statue of myself, the director-general. We would put it on podium in the big entrance lobby. The problem is, we have not been able to find the sculptor for such a work, especially as it is proposed that the statue be life-size.'

She puffed herself up and replied 'Well, Monsieur the director general, surely you have people to tackle such problems, among all your so talented staff.'

'Well, no, we...'

The housekeeper interrupted him with two discreet but meaningful coughs.

'Yes, Antoinette. Were you thinking of speaking?' asked the Countess over her shoulder.

'Begging your pardon Madame La Comtesse, Monsieur Le Comte, and with apologies for overhearing totally inadvertently your conversation, it may be that I can suggest a suitable sculptor.'

'Yes?' asked the Count.

'Indeed Monsieur. I have the fortune on my days off to occasionally pass some time in the city centre of Nancy where I can rub shoulders with people from various disciplines and those that know them. It's so happens that one of those friends is Monsieur Duchien who is particularly well known for life-size sculptures. He works mostly in stone but I know that he has had one or two cast in bronze. His reputation is primarily in females, that is, ahem,' Antoinette coughed again, 'ladies, which are very popular with certain people nowadays, but I know now that he has done classic and formal renderings of important people, fully clothed.' Antoinette blushed and fidgeted.

The Count tried not to laugh. 'Well this is excellent information and I do thank you. Would it be possible to introduce me to the sculptor? I could even go down to see him and discuss the matter *tête-à-tête*.'

'Indeed Monsieur, it would be an honour to render you service in this way. It also so happens that your son Jean-Marc will drive me down in the trap this morning to run some errands. The Count would honour us by joining us for the trip and we could see if Duchien is at home.'

'Very well. Thank you. Shall we leave in half an hour, say?'

'Yes sir, of course sir'. The Countess lifted her eyes to the ceiling and down again, in a dismissive but futile gesture.

&

Antoinette and the Count left Jean-Marc with the dog and the trap outside Bernard's café, walked round the corner and knocked on the door of Duchien's atelier.

'His health is poorly from time to time, but let's hope he is well this morning' said Antoinette. There was no answer so, showing some fore-knowledge of the habits here, she opened the door, stepped in and call out 'Duchien. You have a visitor.' They heard a voice from the back 'Come on through.'

'His workshop studio is at the back. Follow me.' The Count took in the shambolic front office with a desk stacked with drawings but was more impressed when he stepped into the atelier, bright with light from the full height windows on the back wall merging into opaque glass roof lights overhead. There were a dozen statues of people, some of them full size.

'Duchien, good morning, I have a client for you, Le Comte Orlowski'.

Duchien brushed some shavings off the door he was carving, took his cigarette out from his lips and put down his hammer and chisel. He had been feeling a bit better since the second session with Bernheim and the physical pains had been easing. He shook hands warily with the Count but managed the rights words. 'I welcome you to my atelier; it's an honour'.

The Count deflected his eyes form the nude females and addressed Duchien directly. 'Thank you kind sir. I understand you are a very high quality sculptor, Monsieur. I would like to talk to you about the means by which we could commission you to do a full-size statue which I have in mind. I see some of the items here, including that full-size gentleman in robes, a piece which seems to me to be similar in size and style to what I have in mind. Excellent. Would this be a commission of interest to you?'

'No, sir, I'm so sorry but I'm not taking commissions at this moment in time. My creativity is presently as flat as the water on a millpond and I am constrained by financial rigours to work on this sculpting of doors for furniture and designs for ceramics.'

'I cannot help you with your creativity except to address your financial requirements, an act which might in turn stimulate the creative juices. I think you would find my commission to be the solution rather than a problem. What would be your typical fee for a life-size sculpture in stone?'

'Well sir, if I were accepting commissions, and depending on the material and scope, sometimes the price would be as much as 600 to 800 francs. A sculpture takes such a long time you know, and the base product, the stone, it's expensive. Then there is the issue of transport and...'

The Count interrupted by making an offer Duchien could not refuse. 'Let me interject by proposing a fee of double the higher figure, so, 1600 francs, and we take delivery here when it's finished, hopefully in six weeks? The 18th of May is the 10th anniversary of the incorporation of my company, La Fonderie Société Anonyme. I am prepared to pay half in advance.'

Duchien was flabbergasted and showed it with an open mouth. 'Well, I see. In such a case it might be inappropriate for me to turn you down. Yes, I think I might be able to squeeze you in. What will the subject be?'

'The subject shall be me, dear sir. I shall be the subject. Le Comte Orlowski, President-Director-General and 75% owner of the steel works at La Fonderie will be the subject. I would like a sculpture of me in my working clothes, more or less as you see me today, in a noble pose with dignity but not arrogance. I hope that these are characteristics you can convey. '

'Indeed sir, I think I can. Stone.' He counted on his fingers. '8 weeks. You are a hard task-master but... given the generosity and clarity of purpose of this commission I find I am unable to refuse you. There remains only the fixing of a rendezvous to start sketches.'

'Will this time next Saturday be suiting to your calendar?'

'Yes indeed. My regular work load will be somewhat less by then.'

'Permit me to ask you your first name Monsieur Duchien, as a matter of completeness. That is my nature.'

'Indeed, sir. My nature is not to use it. Pray tell me the first name of Michelangelo, Donatello or Bernini and I will be happy to tell you mine. We sculptors, you know...'

'Very good, I understand. Most impressive. Excellent. Until then, I wish you a good day and a propitious week.'

২

I am having a pastis at Bernard's. The Count is striding down the rue Gambetta towards my atelier, the statue of my wife and child under his arm. The street is water and he is floating across it. Now they are separated, one under each arm. The Mother and Daughter under his arms are real. They are screaming. He is knocking their heads together. 'It was your fault to go with him'.

Chapter 17 – Maelstrom of liberation

Nancy, 23rd March 1891

Dearest Natalie

Is it not extra-ordinary and very pleasing that we can talk like this when we write? I imagine when we are talking face-to-face there is all the other psychological accoutrement getting in the way, not least, people overhearing us. And I think of you in your little starched white collar and your formal work dress, dark blue, all the way down to the ankle and all buttoned up.

And what are you wearing in Paris, dare I ask? I see photos of the most outrageous costumes. There are low necklines. There are skirts and dresses which end at the knee. I bet you are wearing something like that at your lectures and when you go out.

Tell me all.

We have been learning about the origins of man as part of the history of literature course. Abbé Pierre, the lecturer, a good catholic, got into a terrible tizz because the way in which people all over the world have reacted to the new sciences around the evolution of man, well, of animals in general. It's over 50 years since Darwin and Wallace, the Englishmen, published their theories and more like a hundred since Jean-Baptiste Lamarck (I think he's much more important than the English) started the movement.

It has taken people an age to realise this means that it is not 100% certain that God created the heaven and the Earth. Heresy. It's called natural selection i.e. the pressures of nature and the law of the jungle make each generation more fit for purpose than the previous. So you and I are what we are by a natural process of science not by a miraculous birth at the hand of an omnipotent creator. Oh dear, poor Abbé Pierre. He hasn't a leg to stand on.

That leads me to wonder whether you and I are at the epicentre of a new wave of evolution.

There we were, prim and proper in our homes and at school in Nancy, and now we as humans seem to be liberated from the constraints of religion. Am I going too far? And women in particular find new ways to express themselves. I feel it myself. I feel I can be a person on an equal footing with a man and in some respects superior... because of my scintillating intuition (and my good looks). Therefore if you or I choose to be more extrovert and more open with people around us then that is our privilege, our right. If that means we can enjoy a relationship with someone to whom we are not married, then so be it.

I see lots of people doing this even here not just in Paris. Social intercourse can lead to sexual intercourse unless there is some very strong prerogative preventing you from doing so. This liberation of the mind and the body I find astonishing and revolutionary. I wonder if history will look back on us and think of us as the first of a new race of women. Might we be criticised for skirts showing the knee, make-up in public and décolleté tops. Might men in this new world be criticised for wandering eyes, preying hands and lustful thoughts? Or will men's defence be that women are provoking them by their self-affirmation and openness?

Will the human race turn to even deeper licentiousness, and depravity? Is this the beginning of the end of the human race?

My god, that sounds rather philosophical. Apologies.

Where are you and I in this maelstrom of liberation?

Your thoughtful Cécile

ৱ

Appartement 3A, 16 rue de l'Estrapade, Paris V^e

2nd April 1892

Dear Cécile

Where are we indeed, in that maelstrom of liberation? I know where I am! Plumb centre.

There is a night spot in Montmartre called the Moulin Rouge which opened three years ago. Girls dance the can-can without a lot of clothes on. I need to find someone to take me there. Did I tell you this city and its people are unchained, liberated and uninhibited. I sometimes think I must be dreaming. Your little Natalie from a village near Nancy, here in Paris when all this change is happening?

Paris is the centre of the new world in so many ways. Did you hear about the telephone link between Paris and London opened last April? Some connection of Marie-Pascale's father in Marseille and this guy in the Administration des Postes et Télégraphes head office invited us to come to a celebration of the first anniversary, yesterday. We were introduced to the Minister in charge, Monsieur Coulon, heard voices in London coming over the telephone and got loads of champagne.

No boyfriend at the moment, you'll be sad to hear. What about you? I am actually working quite hard because I have two sets of exams, early May and mid-June, then I'm done. Looking forward to seeing you.

Devoted

Natalie

ॐ

Chapter 18 – Paris, Nancy

Nancy, 18th of April 1892

Hello sister N

I have seen Patrick Lambert a couple of time. He was in my class last year. Do you remember? He's doing natural science at the Lycée Imperial so I don't see him every day. Some action but a bit tepid. We normally have nowhere to go because I can't take a boyfriend to the Château except for tea in the orangerie, but last weekend we went to his home because his parents were away. Not a great experience.

Do guys seem superficial to you? No experience of life, no real conversation, little masculinity? Maybe I am being too demanding. There has to be something better (someone better). Isn't the earth meant to move? When you're back you'll have to help me find my prince charming.

Paris is the centre of the new world? Yes to a certain extent but you forget your home town although you like me do not really know where we originated. I in Nancy? I think so. Your parents in Metz, or heaven knows where? Anyway, since the Prussians occupied Metz in 1870 a huge number of successful business people and artists left Metz to come to Nancy.

Papa waxed lyrical after dinner on Friday so I learnt more about him being one of them, with Mama. Nancy's population tripled in the last 20 years because of people leaving Metz. Not just people involved in industry like Papa, but artists, designers, architects, doctors and thinkers. Like his competitor here who you mentioned, the Fould-Dupont ironworks only a few kilometres north of Papa's works. I met Monsieur Dupont, their founder, recently at a reception. He was very charming and asked to be addressed as Auguste. Papa said they had both been forced to leave Metz. Fould-Dupont indeed won the contract to supply iron for the tower built by Eiffel in Paris which you went up, but Papa said Dupont made next to nothing on the deal so he's not unhappy.

Do you remember me telling you about Émile Gallé when he came to dinner, with his wife Henriette? He actually fought in the Franco-Prussian War in 1870! Now he is universally famous for his glassware with floral designs in this new style everyone is talking about. They have a shop in Paris. Please go and have a look, 12 rue Richter in Paris. Do you like the designs? Do you think there is a market for the pieces? But Gallé is absolutely a Nancy concern, which I am quite proud about. I might quite like to work for him. p.s. Gallé is drop dead gorgeous, moustache and well-trimmed beard, kind face, permanent smile, bright piercing eyes; like Duchien, except for the facial hair.

Actually, Duchien is even nicer. We don't speak for long but he seems to be on the same wavelength and seems to like me.

I am still working Saturdays for Daum, who are more or less a competitor to Gallé, but they are both at the forefront of this new art in Nancy, celebrated often by mentions in the press and by exhibitions in the Musée des Beaux-Arts. The old man died a few years ago and the sons Auguste (what's with the name Auguste?) and Antonin run the business, which is at the Porte Sainte-Catherine down by the river. Their blown glass vases and objects like that, decorated (some of their techniques are patented!) with designs by famous artists from all over Europe including Duchien, are selling very well.

Exciting times. I wonder how it will strike you when you are back here in June. Bye for now.

Cécile

ᘒ

Appartement 3A, 16 rue de l'Estrapade, Paris V^e

3rd May 1892

Dear Cécile

Patrick Lambert! Awful. A wimp. You can do much better than that. You need a MAN.

No, my parents were both from Saarbrucken originally. We'll ask my Mama when we're next with her. Yes, I was born in Metz and Mama walked all the way to Nancy, carrying a little me about a week old, as the Germans attacked the city. My father was killed in the war just before.

Went to see Gallé's shop in the rue Richter. Impressive. Lovely stuff. Eye-watering prices. All the customers had fur collars and a car with driver (peaked cap) waiting outside. Do you know about René Lalique? He is another pioneer of what they call here *Art Nouveau* style, set up his workshop in Paris six years ago and is doing well. Lalique's shop is impressive as it is the head office, unlike the Gallé shop here. You would love his glass pieces. I prefer it to the jewellery.

Yours in haste.

Natalie

క

Chapter 19 – The Count's statue unveiled

Time passed quickly for Duchien. He was busy with his jobbing work on some Majorelle furniture and some designing for Daum. He was busy enough that he did not notice that the headaches were becoming less frequent. His right elbow hurt less.

When the invitation card and note from the Count came he sat at his desk in the front office, got out the diary, and put Wednesday 18th May in his diary.

Le Comte Geoffroi Orlowski, President-Director-General of La Fonderie, la Comtesse Leonora Orlowski and
the Board of Directors of La Fonderie
request the pleasure of your company at the unveiling of the statue
of Le Comte by the eminent sculptor M. Duchien
at 5:30 p.m. on Wednesday 18th May 1892
in the presence of
M. Nicolas-Émile Adam, Mayor of Nancy and President of the Société Lorraine des Amis des Arts,
M. Aristide Majorelle, Director of the Musée des Beaux-Arts and Professeur François Méli, Director of the Ecole des Beaux-Arts de Nancy.

Champagne reception. RSVP.
La Fonderie, rue Pré à Varois, Pompey/Nancy, Meurthe-et-Moselle

---

The statue was finished, except for the 20 millimetre steel bolts to fix the statue to the plinth when installed in the entrance lobby of La Fonderie's office block. The contractors were going to come in a few days to transport the two elements to the site and erect them.

Duchien felt curiously serene, and pleased, of course, that

he completed the commission without stress despite being so ill only three months ago.

When the day came round he was pleased to have been offered a lift by Monsieur Majorelle, director of the Musée des Beaux-Arts despite letting him down at the exhibition opening last year. It was reassuring to arrive in the company of someone else who would draw some attention rather than on his own. Majorelle had been supportive for several years; before the death of Duchien's wife and child he had made the arrangements for the purchase by an anonymous benefactor from Duchien of his life-size *Mother and Daughter*, some four years ago now, and it seemed to be on permanent exhibition. The piece had a special place in his heart so he was glad it had recognition and a place in such an excellent gallery as the Musée des Beaux-Arts.

There were some 80 guests, carriage hands outside, cloakroom attendants inside and uniformed waitresses with champagne in wide gold-rimmed crystal glasses. Duchien managed to smile throughout the speeches, four of them. He smiled when the editor of the Est Républicain shook his hand with congratulations and asked if he would spend a few moments with his reporter. He knew the reporter, an admirer of his work and of that of his friend, the painter Émile Friant; a suitable article and photograph appeared in La Culture section of the paper on the Saturday after.

As for the sculpture, it really was not too bad. What had the Count asked for? Authoritative but not arrogant? He looked terrific. He was looking into the distance like one of Napoleon's generals surveying the scene of another victory. Duchien loved his local stone, not yellow and not off-white; between the two.

He slept well.

ॐ

The steel works at Pompey (1895)

Chapter 20 – Flattery from the Countess

Château de Lay-Saint-Christophe, three days later

The Count and the Countess were having breakfast on Saturday as was their weekly habit. The maid was on duty. She served oeufs en cocotte with wholemeal toast and coffee.

'My dear Count out, what a wonderful evening on Wednesday at La Fonderie. The company's 10th anniversary. You must feel so proud.'

'Yes, thank you my dear. I was most pleased with the reaction of my colleagues, the guests from around Nancy and indeed even the gentleman from the newspaper.'

'And the sculpture, my dear, is excellent, such a success. It reflects your position in society, your success in business and your role as a leader of men, in a most complete and artistic way.'

The Count hesitated, a spoonful of eggs halfway between the plate and his open mouth. The flowery compliments were as so unexpected that he fleetingly wondered whether there was a hidden agenda. This woman, for want of using the word lady, was effectively an estranged wife living under the same roof, and he could not remember a complimentary word for years.

'Yes my dear,' she continued, 'I thought your personality came through so excellently in the statue, and it is suitable to have that imagery of you to honour your position in the extraordinary industry that you have created. It has been occurring to me that a similar image, some other work, might grace the front hall of this humble dwelling in the stairwell.'

Now the Count could not believe his ears but he did not expect what was coming. The Countess continued in full flow. 'So, as I am the mistress of the house and the person with whom nothing in your life outside business happens, it would be such a good idea if we commissioned a statue of me to be displayed there. I think my guests would be absolutely delighted, I mean, our guests, my dear.'

The Count hesitated and wiped his mouth with his double-damask table napkin. He spluttered slightly as he responded. He could not, for the life of him, think in the split second of any grounds for turning her down. 'Yes of course my dear Countess. Let us do that. A capital idea. May I leave it to you to make the arrangements with the sculptor, maybe the same one?'

'Yes certainly my dear husband and provider. You are a creative genius. Consider it done.'

&

Chapter 21 – The cooing of pigeons

Duchien felt in quite a good mood this Saturday in spring. The sun shone. He had been to Bernard's for a proper lunch, the plat du jour and a glass of wine. Franz persuaded him to come out to try to reinstate the regular game of boules. The barren area in the middle of the Place Thiers was most suitable for the game and regularly used by the railway men - the station being on the west side of the square – and all manner of locals. Little wooden stakes marked the edges of the pitches with so that several games could be played in parallel. He cherished the moments when he could forget his misery and when the headaches were not assailing him.

After their half-hour match, by way of a break, he turned some of his dream-like attention to an old lady playing the accordion. She, her white stick and a mess tin to collect coins perched on a bench opposite the station. She was a pleasant contrast in sound to the occasional train stopping at Nancy's main railway station then ten minutes later starting off, direction Metz or Paris, with the conductor's whistle, the slamming of the doors, the wheezing and puffing of the steam engine and the lazily accelerating clickety-clack of the wheels. Here was a lyrical and musical sound at the hands of the frail lady in a hand-knitted shawl. She played a classical tune which might even be Chopin; some dance-hall polkas; a romantic ballad; a country folk song, plaintive.

She contributed more to life on the square, in Duchien's humble opinion, than the massive statue erected in 1879 in the centre of the Place Thiers of a man from Nancy who no-one remembered but who had been President and Prime Minister of France, Adolphe Thiers. He could not be so negative about the execution of the statue because many of his own money-earners were in this same realist style. He succeeded in ignoring the statue, and this conundrum, by sitting with his back to it.

❧

I had finished my rounds and had eaten a late sandwich alongside Jean-Marc outside Bernard's. The clink of the boules, the strutting cooing of the pigeons and the tricoteuse with her accordion made a pleasant backdrop for a moment of relaxation. I only noticed Duchien, sitting on a bench, after a while. I was drawn to him. I patted Jean-Marc on the knee and the dog on the head; I wandered into the centre of the square and quietly sat down beside him. I had not for a moment formulated an objective or had assessed the consequences. I was drawn by a force with its own objectives or by the random influence of tumbling dice.

A moment later, I felt Duchien jogged out of his reverie by the awareness that there was somebody sitting next to him. He turned his head to see it was me, the girl from Daum, the girl who came from time to time to pick up work for the factory, his designs, or to bring a letter from Antonin Daum. He recognised me. I looked at him in a friendly but non-intrusive way. I saw Duchien studying my features for a moment, a moment long enough to inform him, to take me in, but not so long as to be rude. I could see he found me beautiful. He looked at me with an appreciation that I had never seen when visiting him in the atelier. There was nothing about my features that he would describe later in categorical terms; he saw darkish hair, neat, in a wide bun held by a navy blue ribbon matching my navy blue cotton full-length dress, modest in taste but good in quality. He saw my dark intelligent eyes and a petite mouth. I wondered if he saw his late daughter in me. I hoped he would think I was as pretty. No, she would have been much younger.

'Good afternoon, Monsieur'. I didn't need to smile. I hoped my calm face communicated friendliness just as readily as a smile. And he must have thought that I had sat down next to him intentionally; even with intent, or as a gesture of friendliness

'Yes, well, of course. Good afternoon Mademoiselle. The efficient young lady from Daum.'

'Yes sir. Thank you for the kind words. I hope I am exactly that. And my name is Cécile.'

'Yes of course. Cécile. It's a pleasure, I'm sure. Thank you for joining me on this humble bench in our favourite square between the station and Chez Bernard.'

'You flatter yourself Monsieur. I am not here solely for you, although I must confess this is a pleasure. I am running some errands.' I made a movement of the head towards Jean-Marc and his dog sitting patiently on the driver's seat of our single-horse trap a few metres from Bernard's café.

'That's my little brother. Two years younger than me.' I continued with a little sigh and said 'Nothing for you from Daum this week. Do you have work due to them next week?'

'Yes, I believe I do. I think I am making satisfactory progress on some new designs I am creating for them; dinner plates; a dinner service; more of the idea of plants and flowers, tendrils intertwined... the new style.'

'I find the new art movement so interesting. Daum and Gallé are at the forefront. I am finishing my art diploma at École des Beaux-Arts de Nancy with Professeur Méli. He says the British, the Belgians and Prussians, people all over the world, are using the French term art nouveau for this style and that Nancy is considered the creative hub of the movement. That could even mean you, Monsieur.'

'That is flattering Cécile. From where I sit, it feels as if the commercial balance is not swinging in the direction of those that create this art nouveau. My paltry bank balance is testimony.'

'Don't be disappointed. At any stage of your career the income from sculpture, wood carving or designs for ceramics and glass can suddenly become significant. I am sure of it.'

'In my case?'

'I am sure of it... from where I sit.' I glanced down at the bench, suddenly self-conscious. I had not intended the double-entendre. Duchien took the opportunity to look, under the line of my long dark blue dress, at my chest, torso, bottom and legs. I saw his eyes searching, briefly.

'The way you sit Cécile, I am sure you are right.' I deserved that retort. I glanced at him, blushed and smiled. He saw me holding my lower lip between my teeth. The unexpected humour pleased both of us. Just then, Antoinette came round the corner with two wicker baskets full of provisions. I took a last glance at Duchien, noting that his salt-and-pepper hair, the white strands probably resulting from his depression which I knew about, actually made him attractive. He was clean-shaven so, with his soft and expressive lips, he looked a bit cherubic. His eyes were kind. I did not want to draw Duchien's attention to Antoinette; he knew enough about her to know she worked for the Count. He would have put two and two together if he had watched me driving off with Jean-Marc and Antoinette together. I wanted to withhold from Duchien the fact that I was the Count's daughter, so I just said 'I must go Monsieur. Excuse me. I wish you a good afternoon and good health until I next come by.'

'I look forward to that. Thank you for your presence in my life.' I thought that was nice but I left it there. So I smiled at him, broadly. I turned and walked off to join Antoinette with Jean-Marc and Hubert on the trap for the 10km trip to home up the river near Lay-Saint-Christophe. I turned to see him watch us drive off. We were surely too far for him to identify the woman in the trap with us.

☙

As the horse's hooves turned silent, Duchien found the sound of two other boules matches was relaxing, as were the sparrows twittering. He reflected on how the second consultation with Bernheim had ended. What had been said? That someone would appear and that would be it? That his heart was open to someone after everything that had happened? Could somebody as obvious as Cécile be an answer? The answer? Was she too young? Did they have enough in common? The questions themselves were soothing to Duchien, maybe even attractive. He did not need answers. Yet.

Before returning home for a siesta after which he would get back to work, Duchien walked away from Bernard's across the Place Thiers to the railway station to buy the Est Républicain. He bought it on Saturdays because their section on La Culture kept abreast of arts and artists in Nancy and the region. Two weeks ago he had been mentioned in an article about the market for bronze figures and the commercial success of Jean-Christoffe de Platigny. He was passing the accordion-player and about to cross the road when a voice from behind him said 'Excuse me Monsieur. Bonjour Monsieur. Monsieur Duchien I think.' Duchien could not place the willowy young man in a travel coat and hat, hauling a very large suitcase, a trunk almost. The traveller struggled up to him and shook his hand. 'Rebière. Jacques Rebière' he announced, smiling broadly. 'Ah' said Duchien, 'Jacques. Jacques from the psychiatrist's practice. I do not think I knew your family name.'

'Indeed Monsieur. And may I ask after your health and welfare?'

'You may, and I will answer. I am well thank you. I was thinking of Professor Bernheim and our sessions only a few moments ago. I was in the company of a young lady whose company I found most pleasant.' Rebière listened all the more intently as Duchien inclined his head and lowered his voice. 'And I have to confess to you that for the first time in two and a half years I have unexpectedly found myself thinking of a female in terms of, how shall I say this, with the feelings which had deserted me. Whether or not my libido is reborn, as Bernheim predicted, I do not yet know for sure.'

'A revelation indeed, but not unexpected for me'.

'Yes, I understand, but this girl is one I could... maybe... get to like a lot. Excuse me, this all happened in the last few moments so I am not expressing things well. Do I remember correctly that the Professor said that I might just bump into someone and I would find my heart is open?'

'He did. And you have proved to me by the manner in which you are talking that he was correct, that you have responded remarkably to these extraordinary treatments of which he is an acknowledged master. I will write to him of our meeting in case it's of use for his case notes, unless of courses you will be in touch with him yourself?'

'Write? Will you not be seeing him at all?' Rebière looked at his trunk and back at Duchien. 'No. I am leaving. I travel to Paris today to re-join my wife and her brother, another member of our august profession, curing those with mental health problems. Then on Tuesday we leave for Graz in Austria to set up a new sanatorium in the mountains to continue our research in a clinical institution with real-life patients.'

'Real-life patients. Like me I suppose'.

'No, these will be long-term patients, for whom the cure

might last a life time. So the sanatorium will have hotel and catering facilities; we will charge accordingly. We would think of you as someone with the effects of a trauma which can be cured by therapy, with or without hypnotism.'

'But will you find such fascinating patients as me, so easily disposed to being hypnotised and cured?'

'Indeed not. That would be impossible.'

'Or patients able to pay for such residency and care?'

'We believe so, yes. Now I must leave you because I have eight minutes in which to buy my tickets and get on the train. I would say au revoir, Monsieur, but I think it is more to be good luck and adieu.'

'Thank you. Thank you for everything. I wish you luck. Oh, good sir, one more thing. I never got a transcript of my dreams which the Professor promised'.

'Indeed. We wrote them up. We read them through. All three of us felt that the sexually explicit detail of your dreams would not be a positive influence on your conscious psyche... yet. Certainly, as the second séance evolved, it was clear that you would not have the slightest problem of libido. Ask the Professor for a copy sometime, when your heart has led you to a destination.' There was a gap in the traffic and they crossed the road to the station together.

'Adieu, Monsieur Duchien.'

As Duchien retraced his steps with his newspaper in his hand, the accordionist said his name. He stopped in his tracks. 'How did you know it's me?'

'I am partially sighted. I can see outlines. And I smelt the cigarettes on your clothes. Forgive me for stopping you, but I was moved by your conversation with the medical man. My ears are as good as my nose. Permit me to say that I find your attitude towards difficulties is enviable; I wish you success in your life and in love.'

'You heard everything we said?'

'Yes sir, enough to judge the truth in your heart.' Duchien was stunned but not displeased. He put five centimes in her bowl.

'Thank you Madame. I wish you a good day'.

ৱ

Chapter 22 – The girl from Daum

Nancy, Sunday 29th of May 1892

Dear Natalie

Big event at my father's works on Wednesday of last week. Jean-Marc and I were not invited; just business people (and press of course). I saw the statue on the Saturday a week before; Duchien has made an impressive job of the statue of the Count. Life-size and quite imposing without making him look arrogant which he isn't really (unlike my mother).

For some reason, I am hesitant about telling Duchien that I am the Count's daughter. Am I wrong? Tell me sister what your advice would be. In a way I was glad not to be invited to the unveiling of Papa's statue because Duchien would have seen me there. I want to be thought of as just an ordinary girl. For him I am the girl from Daum... and he said so! Yes, this is the reason for writing. I spoke with him yesterday. He was in the Place Thiers on a bench and really relaxed watching a game of boules. I just sat down beside him, just like that! We talked about art and things like that, just for a moment, five minutes maybe. We joked a bit, about my bottom I think, or was it the way I sit? And I could have sworn he looked me up and down.

Anyway he seems so nice and I think he likes me. He is a bit dreamy. Too old for me?

My mother has commissioned him to do a sculpture of her now; I didn't mention it. How would I know if I am just the girl from Daum?

With love from the birds and bees in Nancy and your friend

Cécile.

જ

Appartement 3A, 16 rue de l'Estrapade, Paris V[e]

2nd June 1892

Dear Cécile

Go girl, that's what I say. I have not even met him and I like him. Too old? Have you not been listening to yourself? Nota Bene: the longer you wait, the older he gets.

Back Wed 15th June. Do you finish college on the Friday? If you are still in lectures or whatever and are not free in the week, can you pick me up on Saturday morning like the last time? Otherwise please leave me a letter at my mother's.

La Fonderie has sent a letter to offer me a job, full time. I start straight after the Bastille Day holiday, Monday 18th July. I can't believe it's happening.

Bye for now

N

অ

Natalie and I met up on Natalie's first Saturday back, for the first time since the Réveillon of New Year's Eve. We walked in the forest with Jean-Marc and Hubert, as we had in the past, in the early summer sun.

Natalie was very excited about the job at La Fonderie, and grateful to my father for the opportunity; a dream coming true; an immediate occupation to put to use her year's business studies in Paris; secure employment; an income stream. She expressed her excitement of course, but at the same time she was mature and focussed. Coming to the end of education and starting real life she had taken on the character of an adult. I should have been jealous but I wasn't. I loved Natalie and was proud of her. At the same time, I was on the verge of my 21st birthday; I was leaving college, embarking on a real life. Working Saturdays for Daum gave me enough self-confidence to know I could compete with her.

We continued through the day talking in my big bedroom with the windows open across the lawns towards the forest. I made sure to tell Natalie that I had achieved a special merit in art on my final exams. We spent some time spreading drawings from my portfolio over my bed to look through them. We walked down to Pompey and ate at the Hôtel de la Poste.

ঽ

July 1892

My father had organised a dinner for my 21st birthday and it would be on my actual birth-date, Wednesday 20th July. It turned out to be as much a celebration of my graduation as of my coming of age. I was thrilled; I never really knew with my parents, how much I featured, what was the nature of their love for me, what events in my life were of interest to them – but this one he made an effort for. He had booked a private room for dinner at La Gentilhommière, one of Nancy's best and most fashionable restaurants, in the centre of town. I asked Duchien about it; he told me it had by far the best cuisine in the region. Even Mama seemed quite pre-disposed in favour of the event and was looking forward, especially as another lady she quite liked would be there; Professeur François Méli of the École des Beaux-Arts de Nancy (who ran the art part of the course which I had just completed) would be bringing his wife Sophie. She was particularly favoured by my mother because she was born Sophie Gendebien De Liederkerke, of a very good family from Belgium. Their daughter Jacqueline Méli, the exhibitioner organiser, was coming; I had met her a few times, once at the event at the Musée des Beaux Arts, and liked her. Antonin Daum was invited; eligible bachelor, junior partner with his brother Auguste in the Cristallerie Daum glass manufacturers and the man who looked after my Saturday employment there. If Papa had intended this to be a smart move, as with each of the guests probably, he turned out to be right.

I was excited by Papa's openness and desire to please. He had asked if I would like to bring a close friend. Of course I said yes please. So Natalie was on the guest list; he knew she had got a holiday job at his company last summer, had got the bursary for her year in Paris and an offer for permanent job. Did she get all of this independently of his influence? I wondered. But he hardly knew her socially, as my friend, because she chose to avoid the Château when the Countess was there.

So some of the Saturday before my birthday dinner had been spent by us two young ladies going through my modest assortment of dresses to pick the right one; I knew I had enough, including two evening dresses I had never worn, that I had not needed to buy a new one. We chose my new off-white taffeta silk with narrow straps over the shoulders; bare arms; rounded neck line; a chest-full of flowers embroidered in chestnut and tangerine silk; and a simple pleated waist.

On Sunday, Papa's driver took me down to Natalie's home to finalise her evening wear for my birthday. She had one evening dress from Paris which pleased her; off the shoulder; neckline plunging in a curve but nothing shocking; slender waist with no belt; no bustle; full length; cream in colour with deep green floral motifs. This was an occasion for which we both felt we wanted to dress our best.

ॐ

The guests were invited at six; I had taken the initiative of going into town early, picking up Natalie on the way, with Jean-Marc driving. Hubert had to stay at home. A coachman at the restaurant looked after the carriage. Jean-Marc was not really looking forward as he was uncomfortable in company and never spoke much. I had butterflies in my stomach with anticipation. Natalie was a calming influence but was warmly looking forward to my big event. My parents played at being the Count and Countess by being an annoying - but fashionable - half hour late. This gave 28-year-old bachelor Antonin Daum, a punctual arrival, the opportunity to usher me, with our champagne glasses, onto the landing of the first floor private room, to talk privately. I saw that Natalie watched me, smiling and nodding, through the open doorway.

So I was prepared for Daum's contribution during dinner. After the main course when Méli had already proposed a toast of thanks to the hosts for the dinner, Daum got to his feet, lifted his gold-plated fork and rang a sonorous sound on his crystal wine glass.

'My Lord, dear Lady, Orlowski.' He exaggerated their titles for effect and the Count batted the fluff away with his hand, smiling. Natalie winked at me. 'Cécile and honoured guests. In proposing the toast to Cécile, 21 years old today, I have an announcement to make which she will, I think, further to a brief conversation here just before dinner, consider to be a suitable and welcome birthday present. You are aware that Cécile, a talented artist and draughtsman in her own right, has graduated with highest marks from her fine arts course at the École des Beaux-Arts de Nancy under the guidance of our eminent friend here Professor François Méli, whom I salute and thank. You may also be aware that Cécile has worked every Saturday with us for the last year. I am delighted to announce that I have today offered Cécile a permanent post with Cristallerie Daum starting as soon our closure for the grandes vacances ends on Thursday 1st September, and she has accepted. She will start as assistant designer in the new products department and as personal assistant to me and my

Cécile Orlowski, diplôme Beaux-Arts
Professor Méli, Nancy, mai 1892

Cécile Orlowski, diplôme Beaux-Arts
Professor Méli, Nancy, mai 1892

Cécile Orlowski, diplôme Beaux-Arts
Professor Méli, Nancy, mai 1892

Cécile Orlowski, diplôme Beaux-Arts
Professor Mél, Nancy, mai 1892

brother Auguste as time permits so that we can give her as much input as necessary for her to become a vital part of our growing enterprise. Permit me to invite you stand and drink the health and future of Cécile Orlowski'

My mother took an intake of breath; it might even have signalled pride not just shock. She made a big effort not to spoil Cécile's evening but one of her pre-occupations was certainly that she did not think young ladies should have careers or go into business, even in the fine arts. The party stood, drank noisily, complimenting me and Antonin together. I stood too and thanked Monsieur Daum. Everyone, including I, clapped when they had put their glasses down, then we sat down. The Count stayed standing, overjoyed. 'My dear Antonin, this is remarkable. You fill me with joy and I'm sure my daughter too. She has my full support in venturing out into the great world of business and of the arts. I wish a thousand times good luck and happiness. I propose a toast to the friends who have been so faithful to my dear daughter.' Applause. Appreciative laughter. More toasting.

Natalie rushed round the table to embrace me. Jean-Marc stood, applauded and then gave me a brotherly and embarrassed hug too. The Méli family showed surprise and pleasure; all three knew I had some talent but had not anticipated the speed with which I would get snapped up by an employer. Nor had I. All of a sudden, I had a foothold in Nancy's rapidly developing sector; the arts, architecture, design and the manufacture of ceramics, glass and furniture.

Those who glanced at the Duchess would have seen a face trying hard to be delighted when assailed by the insult of an important announcement of which she had had no fore-knowledge and by the thought of me being a working girl – with talent of my own – rather than among the most sought-after of Nancy's debutantes. It would have been difficult to see in her darkening eyes that she had realised how much she must accelerate her scheming and her search for a suitable husband for her only daughter.

On the way home I thought I would be going to sleep with tears of joy and hope. But, in my night-dress, looking out of the open window onto the forest illuminated by a half moon, I felt curiously rational. I hoped Mama was happy. I thought of the support Natalie had always given me. I thought of Papa's generosity, tonight and over the years. I thought of Duchien sitting on the bench looking at the pigeons, the boulistes and the accordion lady; I wondered if he would be proud of me when I told him.

ৱ

Chapter 23 – Natalie: down to business

La Fonderie, Pompey, north of Nancy, Wednesday 3rd August 1892

'Good morning Monsieur Le Directeur. May I come in for a moment?'

'Certainly, Mademoiselle...?' he said, racking his brain for her family name and wondering how she had bypassed his secretariat.

'Duhamel. Natalie Duhamel.'

'Yes of course. I do apologise, I was miles away with the problems with the new Bessemer converter. Ah, you came to my daughter's birthday. Of course. I apologise. And we sent you to Paris for your studies. What can I do for you?'

'Yes sir. I graduated and I have been working here for nearly six weeks. I have the Profit & Loss Account by department for March, and I thought you might like to see them. Monsieur Schmidt the finance director was ill on Thursday and Friday and again today he is not in.'

'Very well. Pass them here.' The Count Geoffroi Orlowski, President-Director-General and 87.5% owner of the steel works 'La Fonderie', started reading them at his desk. Presently he asked the young lady to take a seat. With two hands she lifted her dress at the knee by two inches to sit down while ensuring it did not ride too high. She could not tell his reaction to her work.

'Very well. Very well. If Schmidt is absent who was it who put these figures together...' he glanced at the calendar '...on only the fifth day of the month?'

'It was I sir. I have been doing them since July 18th when I came back from Paris and the year's business school course which the company so kindly facilitated for me and started here fulltime.'

'I see. Very well. These figures look very good. I have noticed that the presentation changed in the last few weeks and I find it easier to see the trends. Thank you. Good day Mademoiselle.'

ॐ

The day after, despite the curt dismissal, The Count spotted Natalie in the corridor and asked her to step into his office and take a seat. She flushed with embarrassment and the thought she might be in trouble for overstepping her position vis-à-vis the Finance Director.

'Mademoiselle; those figures from yesterday. Let me ask you, after your year at college in Paris, what do you learn from these figures? Apply your educated business brain to my company as if it were a business school case study.'

Natalie hesitated for a second while the warmth of the compliment chased away her nervousness. She clasped her hands on her lap, sat up even more alertly, and started.

'Well this depends how deep you would like to go into the detail, Monsieur le Directeur. But I could start with, on the downside, the bottleneck in Smelting and Converting, as you mentioned yesterday, has been a severe handicap on our total production output since September. I understand the present limitations on production are temporary. The figures show, on the contrary, that the Casting shop is underworked, and it would be suitable to study the potential impact of an increase in the marketing budget, or some attention-getting promotion, to inform your clients of our skills and production capacity in that area.'

His eyes were glued to her. The moment she hesitated, he made a little upward motion of the head to beckon her to continue.

'On the upside, the company is in rude health. Turnover has increased as normal this month by a couple of percentage points. Your business is defined by the turnover being affectively proportional to the raw materials available and the products made, so your gross profit margin as a percentage remains stable. But this month you notice that the net profit is higher, in actual money terms, because of control of costs and the rationalisation of the workforce, especially sharing transport across various departments. I think my business school professors would be quite impressed, as I am, if you would permit me the remark, Monsieur Le Directeur.'

There was an expectant silence.

As he looked at her she could not help noticing that his lower jaw dropped a tiny amount. He lowered his eyes to the paperwork again, and went through each of the six sheets for a second read. She waited, pleased with herself, quietly confident and enjoying the moment. She also had the pleasure of studying the man, his strong features and the warm eyes.

He looked up, interrupting her gaze, and said 'Very well. Well, well, well. This is good work and I am pleased and, frankly, impressed that at such a young age, whether by intuition or by your good training, you have been able to put such an informative report together, both the figures and the accompanying commentary. This is what a finance department should be doing, see? Helping management see the trends, and early enough to take corrective action if needed.'

The tone of his voice seemed to be critical of the existing finance staff, or at least their reporting. He paused, then 'I imagine you've had some help.'

'Certainly, sir. The department heads and their finance people work with us in the finance department and provide their raw figures. All I have to do is check with them certain aspects of their work to ensure that the figures are all prepared on the same basis, 'apples and oranges' you understand sir, and then compile them in my daybook. After that I can write a commentary from my own appraisal of the figures I see, and submit them to Monsieur le Director des Finances.'

'Yes, and then you write out the figures and your text in long-hand.'

'Yes, sir, that is somewhat laborious and of course not all the management team can see the report immediately otherwise days would be spent on writing copies. For this reason I have asked Monsieur Schmidt whether it might be appropriate for us to have a type-writer to improve upon the handwritten report that you have in your hand. They have become available in the last few years; I would be able to make a stencil from which to reproduce copies within half an hour for all the management staff, which would be another step to good communication and performance targets.'

'Yes, I can understand that. But already in this form it shows that you have a good grasp of the company's finances and I thank you warmly for your contribution.'

He looked at her in a relaxed way which Natalie inferred

was not all about the figures. 'I hope we have the occasions to continue to work together Na... I mean Mademoiselle Duhamel. I thank you and I wish you a good day'

ও

At five past five on a Friday evening a few weeks later, Natalie took her coat and bag and made for the stairs. Monsieur Schmidt was back at work so she had no excuse to go to see the Count. But he happened to be there, looking intently at an engraving of an 18th century map of Alsace-Lorraine from Metz to Nancy and east to Saarbrucken and Strasbourg. He looked up, feigning surprise, and addressed her haltingly and with a wry but warm smile.

'Ah, good evening Mademoiselle Duhamel. Just leaving I see. I was wondering. I hope you don't mind, and that you do not have a pressing engagement, although it is of course Friday evening and you must have a busy social calendar... err... would you be willing to spend a moment talking further about... yes, about the figures, and your interpretation of them?'

'Certainly sir, it would be my pleasure and, if I may say, an honour. You know that my respect for you and for the industry you have created is without measure. You flatter me in thinking I have a busy social calendar. I intended to warm the soup at home and share it with my mother, then collapse into bed at the end of an exhausting week.'

He ushered her back into his office and offered her the usual seat in front of his desk. After serving her, and himself, a glass of yellow Chartreuse, he sat on a nearby couch, against the wall.

'Let's drink to your health, Mademoiselle' and he raised his glass.

'I drink to our health' responded Natalie smiling, 'and I

drink to your generous and unorthodox gesture of inviting me for a drink in the office, if that is what it is.'

'No, no, not all, I mean, yes, I would not be asking you in for a drink if members of the management staff were still milling around, but I find you presence in the company re-assuring, I find you interesting to hear from, and for heaven's sake I am the boss. I deserve some moments of relaxation, even at work. But what was on my mind is this. I was interested in your remark about the Metal Casting department needing some way of stimulating growth or even new clients. As we have nobody skilled in the fine black magic of marketing, I wondered if you had anything in mind.'

'I was thinking about that, out of work hours of course, and have the germs of an idea. Would you permit me to think about this over the weekend and come back to you with something coherent?'

'Yes, of course, how professional of you not to blurt out some half-baked idea. You see, no-one in the company has any idea about how to stimulate demand. We are all operational people. We know how to make things out of iron and steel. If I cannot find a solution to this issue of demand then it will stagnate the company's growth.'

Natalie took a second sip of the Chartreuse. The yellow version was a bit sweeter than the green and easier to drink; she nonetheless felt warmth come to her cheeks. The director did the same, quite a large sip.

'Next month on the 10th I have another important event. Duchien's statue of the Countess will be unveiled at the Château and she is organising a gala, whatever that is.'

'Monsieur le Comte must be delighted that she likes yours here so much that she desires another. Of herself.' She couldn't stop herself.

'Ha, Mademoiselle. Something like that. We drink to... the fine arts. Santé.' They both took a third sip. The warmth was welcome.

'I am sorry you cannot be included on the guest list Mademoiselle. There would be some jabbering tongues, especially that of my wife.'

'What on earth would she and they be jabbering about, Monsieur? Except that I am a junior employee'

'That's correct. Which is a reason why you would not be able to come. Anyway, you know how people are; even if nothing has passed between us, people would take two and two to make five. Jabbering is a plague.'

Natalie could tell by the mist in his eyes as he looked at her that he was thinking about what could be; what could pass between them. She thought about that too and felt she wouldn't mind giving the mauvaises langues something good and proper to jabber about. The Count took off his glasses, leant back in his seat and looked at the young lady again. In a moment he heaved his chest and let out a long sigh.

'Is Monsieur Le Directeur not happy about every aspect of his life?' Natalie surprised herself with the forwardness of her question. The Count probably knew how close Natalie was to his daughter – she had chosen her to come to her 21st birthday dinner – and wondered how openly Cécile spoke with her.

The Count continued to look at her, hesitated, and pursed his lips. 'You would think that I should be a man filled with immense satisfaction, running a successful industrial concern which I created from scratch despite being bundled out of Metz by the Prussians in 1870. It was as if I had to start my career again, but now we have created the enterprise you see around you and whose financial status you have understood so well. I should indeed be very pleased. But I find that my life is not rounded and I get little satisfaction except when I am here at this desk or looking through those windows onto the shop-floor with the glow of the molten iron and the noise of the converter and the hammers. You understand the figures, Mademoiselle Duhamel. Do you maybe understand something about me too?'

'But Monsieur has such a wonderful home in the country with a wife and children who by all accounts are the most loving you could imagine. Cécile is adorable, my best friend, someone I have known since we first went to the village school.'

'Oh, you are well-informed, Mademoiselle, about the material aspects but at the same time you may be poorly informed of the emotional component of my life. I don't mind telling you, although it is very unusual for me to be talking about this with a perfect stranger, and I do exhort you to total silence, but I get no satisfaction from my relationship with my wife, The Countess. She is belligerent, she shouts at the domestic staff and she makes my life a misery. But I should not be boring you with this Mademoiselle.'

'Please feel free to do so, Monsieur Le Directeur. I feel we have a rapport which goes beyond our business together. Furthermore, in the business environment, the current thinking is that colleagues should be there to help in many ways including what is called pastoral care; some mutual contact; some understanding of issues which are not just a Profit & Loss account.'

'Oh yes, the modern methods; all this that they teach you. Is it not human nature? Maybe not in the workplace. I certainly am in favour of the human touch, which I think you demonstrate most ably. There are several people in the senior staff who are very serious about their work and maybe find it difficult to relax. I may be one of them.'

'One would hope that they relax outside office hours, Monsieur. I'm sure everyone has his way of doing so, or her way.' He was silent for a moment. Natalie plunged. 'I am sorry to hear you get little satisfaction in your marriage, Monsieur le Directeur. Such situations are always most regrettable and can have serious consequences.'

'She knows whereof she speaks, the business school diplomée?'

'Yes, sir, forgive me for speaking personally, but I never knew my father. He died in action just before Metz. I know whereof I speak in this respect'. She smiled.

He smiled. 'I am sorry to hear that. I had no idea. So you have lived with your mother for some 20 years, she has got you through school, and here you are, making your own way in life, with already a certain measure of success if I may say so.'

'Thank you sir. You may. To be exact, 22 years, sir. I was 22 last month.'

'Extraordinary. You have wisdom way beyond your age, and a depth of character and warmth which is that of a more mature person. And yet you have youth on your side.'

'Thank you sir.'

'Thank you Mademoiselle.' He touched his mouth and

looked at her again. Did she see longing in the look? Was there a question mark?

He couldn't help giving the usual signal for the end of a meeting. 'That will be all.'

২

Chapter 24 – Cécile: turmoil

My emotions since my birthday dinner had been in turmoil and in limbo at the same time; six weeks or so.

The turmoil had been the excitement of getting the job at Daum and looking forward to getting stuck in. There was also some turmoil in my little heart because I had not found the opportunity to connect with Duchien properly. I wanted him to be impressed with this big step forward in my life, but on the three occasions I went to the atelier on my rounds for Daum he seemed tense, preoccupied with his work, leaning over his drawing table, a cigarette in his mouth. Twice he hardly raised his eyes. On the third, I told him nonetheless that I had been offered a full-time job with Daum; he acknowledged with an affirmative grunt that I had spoken, but that was it. I got the feeling I would have to find another opportunity like the conversation in the Place Thiers with the accordionist to be able to make progress.

So the feeling of being in limbo was for the same two reasons. I had six weeks to wait between being offered the job and starting.

My sentiments for Duchien were also on hold for the moment.

Natalie knew about my vague feelings for Duchien, both from my letters and from our heart-to-hearts. But when we got together for coffee at the Hôtel de la Poste on the Sunday before I started at Daum, I wanted to offload all of this on her at length. Also, it was only a few days till I took up the job at Daum, so our coffee cups were empty by the time I had finished talking about myself.

I asked if Natalie was looking forward to the gala for Mama's statue two weeks hence; I then learnt that Natalie had not been invited and wondered why. She did not proffer an explanation.

Maybe Mama had not taken to her and had leant on the Count not to include her; but she had been invited to my birthday party.

In fact I realised Natalie was being rather quiet about herself. I knew her well enough that the occasional sideways glance, or a glazing-over of the eyes, told me that she was thinking of something else. Why did her cheeks flush from time to time? Clearly not because of what I was telling her.

What made me believe that she was thinking about a man?

ঽ

Chapter 25 – In the Count's office

The Count usually had lunch in the directors' dining room with a few of his top people or with a client. Natalie never saw him in the canteen. On the Monday after seeing Cécile she passed him in the corridor and his eyes perked up when he saw her. He stopped so she stopped. He looked at the ground and then up at her and said 'Mademoiselle, good morning. I wonder if you would have a moment to drop by my office in, say, five minutes?'

'But of course Monsieur Le Directeur.'

She armed herself with some additional work that she had done on two of the departments and knocked on the door as bid.

'Oh yes, Mademoiselle, do please come in and sit down.' She did so, smoothing her dress closely over her waist enough to be able to sit down respectfully. She put her hands on her lap with her papers. He continued 'Now, clients for the Metal Casting department. Did you think further of your ideas?'

'I have been thinking about this since last week, as you asked, Monsieur Le Directeur. My analysis would be that it is not suitable to spend money on marketing in the sense of advertising. Your business is one which does not address itself to the public but to others in the iron industry or those requiring specialist cast metal parts for construction projects.' She took a breath, watching his eyes, noting against her better judgement how intelligent and kind he looked.

'Pray continue.'

'But an attention-getting device might be beneficial. I am aware that the 'art' sector is not part of your present product offering, but Nancy and the whole of France is so alive to the new art and so much money being spent on painting, ceramics and sculpture, that you could consider use of the casting facilities for making the bronze reproduction of sculptures. Some beautiful human bodies were cast in bronze, full size, by the ancient Greeks and the Chinese of the Shang dynasty. Today a wave of appreciation of art is joined by the wealth created by the industrial revolution, of which, you, Monsieur, are such a shining example. To lead the way, in the little dream I projected for myself, if it pleases you Monsieur Le Directeur, you could even have a quarter- or half-size bronze sculpture cast by the department on a speculative basis. You could display it alongside the full-size statue of you in stone in the foyer of the management offices. If the subject or the artist were of sufficient interest, you could invite the press to another unveiling. It is certain that potential clients on an industrial level would see the use of your facilities for other purposes and could consider for the first time using casting by La Fonderie for their own requirements.'

'This is most interesting Mademoiselle. Let me think about this. The subject is new as is your way of thinking in a new dimension. I must, like you, think of my facilities here as just that; facilities for clients to get what they need even if it is not one of my current product offerings. What... let me see now... you said a bronze sculpture which we would cast on a speculative basis? I see. But what on earth would the sculpture be? Who or what would it be of?'

'Why, a sculpture of you sir. You personify this company, the iron industry in the north-east and, in general, the riches and culture enabled by the industrial revolution.'

Me? Why. How very flattering Mademoiselle. Yes, interesting.'

'There might be some people, influenced by the fashions in art, who might suggest a female figure, a nude even, but in the case of your position in the company and your industry, it might not be well thought of.'

'I do agree. Very wise advice. Do you have other ideas on stimulating clients for the casting operation?'

'The sculpture proposal is one which I have developed in my mind. Permit me to consider some other avenues, knowing your predisposition to innovation, with a view to talking at some time in the near future. I am honoured by your attention but I would not like to waste your time with partly formed thoughts.'

'Good. Very well, you are quite right.'

'And if it is not presumptuous to add, my interviews with you are a refreshing antidote to working with the figures all day and attending to my mother in my spare time.' Natalie was consciously over-egging the pudding of her quiet home life; this may not have been the moment to tell him of her active social life in Paris for the last year.

'Presumptuous, yes, attractively so. And entirely suitable, and reciprocated. Thank you very much. Permit me to offer you my cordial compliments and the hope that we can talk again soon. In the meantime I wish you a good day Mademoiselle.'

ঽ

Two days later

As the days progressed, Natalie became aware that the boss's interest in her was more than their business discussions. At the same time she began thinking about him as a human being, and then as a man. For reasons which she could not pinpoint, he became for her a potential conquest. She could not imagine how a man 23 years her senior could be physically and emotional attractive to her; but that is what was happening. She felt a thrill in the way he smiled at her, in the way he accidentally went out of his way to bump into her in the corridor, the way he coyly asked for some totally irrelevant detail of the company's performance which he probably knew anyway.

At the same time she found slim pickings on whatever scene in Nancy she could summon up the will to mingle with. There was certainly no man of her age in her sights and she did consciously yearn for somebody who had maturity, poise and strength. Nor was she, with or without the complicity of Cécile at her side, throwing out the net of prospection. In her greedy moments she wondered whether money was an advantage in a man, but she did her best to put that out of her mind. She wondered also whether her career would suffer if others in the company suspected that she had eyes for the boss. Certainly her own direct superior, Schmidt the finance director, would find it unacceptable if his junior were engaged in frequent conversations (or extra-mural relations) with the owner and president of the company, whether for genuine business reasons or for personal ones. But when the heat rose in her blood she began daydreaming about the count as a man, as a lover, as someone with maturity to take her to the next stage in her own life. She had been so attuned to sexual relationships while in Paris that she found it hard having no such satisfaction back in Nancy... for half a year now. In fact Cécile was beginning to tease her about it and telling her she should get out more; but where? There were some teatime dances on a regular basis which she found deadly boring and there was none of the nightclub scene that she had experienced in Paris.

The Count as a conquest would present another complication. This was a secret she would have to keep from her Cécile; for the first time in their long friendship. How would she react? Would it be the end of the world for her if her best friend were engaged in an affair with her father? How would she feel about the age difference? But with the passage of time and when he started touching her hand or her arm gently and briefly, her lust and her excitement overtook any prudishness or consideration for Cécile. This could be her man, a long-term man. Even though it was clear to Natalie that the Count had very strong affections for her, and probably more, she felt he might not take the first step. She knew from Cécile that the relationship with his wife was impossible for him. She said that they had slept in separate rooms since Cécile was a kid. And that was not out of propriety but because there was no desire for sexual relations between the two and that they were very much out of love. What is a man to do, even one with everything in the world that money could buy, and a darling daughter and son? She was convinced that every human has lust, men and women alike. She did not feel she would be breaking up a marriage because their marriage had been over long ago. She convinced herself that in that way Cécile might be less antagonistic.

The Count got more and more friendly with the passage of days and with each conversation. Some of the executives and staff were on summer vacation so there were fewer people around. It was easier to know who was still in the office come five o'clock. Natalie was aware of some infernal acceleration; of her tumbling towards something significant with her boss's boss; of an emotional coupling which seemed now inevitable. It was exciting not daunting. She was also clear in her mind that she was in control and that she was exercising her right as a woman to choose.

On the Tuesday, after a brief chat in his office, as she took her leave, he took her hand in his and kissed it; formally, but it was a kiss all the same. She felt a girlish thrill and thought how long she could manage not to wash the back of that hand. As for the way in which she accidentally-on-purpose bumped into him in the corridor, he may not have realised initially that her desk opposite the finance director and two others was situated so that she could see through a gap in the door, habitually left ajar, enabling her to spot him on his way to the gents' cloakroom. It was relatively easy to time the gathering up of some outgoing mail so that she could intercept him on his way back. On the Wednesday afternoon she got a bit more daring and followed him back into his office. As he sat down, Natalie perched one leg on his desk with her dress riding up to the knee; only briefly, so as neither to jeopardise the budding frisson nor to risk being seen by a member of staff. She saw him gaze at the leg, withhold a gesture of shock and smile coyly. She mentioned some fabricated issue about figures, standing up again. Her point was made, and he accepted it. She knew he welcomed it.

২

On the Friday two days later, when intercepted, the Count said to Natalie immediately 'Oh Mademoiselle, I wonder; I have to stay in the office a little bit tonight. If you also happen to be delayed in the office, or had no pressing engagement to leave at five pm punctually, might it be useful to get together then?'

Her libido jumped to attention and she smiled broadly at him. 'Certainly, Monsieur Le Directeur, I am but your humble servant in these matters and would be delighted to make myself available to you later today.' She enjoyed the words she had chosen. She could see he did too. 'Shall I bring the interim half month results?'

'Err, yes, of course.' He looked up and down the corridor to check then smiled broadly at her impudence, squeezed her hand very briefly and went to his office.

Some other bespectacled and intense middle-aged employee in an office in the corridor also stayed on after five o'clock, much to her annoyance. What drove her mad was not knowing what the Count's intentions were, or indeed whether they were innocent, friendly, lonely or lust-driven. Natalie hoped that his intentions were anything but innocent. She resolved to move the conversation away from finance and marketing, immediately. An eternal half-hour later the management offices were deserted. The second shift of the day on the shop-floor still hummed in the background. Natalie left her desk, gathered up her coat and bag then walked through to the first floor reception, the access point to the management offices. No-one there. She turned her pass key in the glass door to the main stairs and went back to the office of the President Director-General. She knocked as if she were an employee seeking an audience, quite loudly. He bade her come in and smiled in a way which she found both attractive and a 'come on'. She felt brazen. She felt emboldened by his smile. She did not know what came over her, and it would have been most embarrassing if she had been reading the signals incorrectly, but she turned to lock the door to the director's office from the inside. She drew the curtain against the window to the corridor, to ensure privacy. The light on his desk and a distant glow from the workshop, through the windows from which he could look down on his factory, gave a romantic light to the room.

She went further in her fast-moving assessment of the situation. She knew of course that the Count found her attractive. She knew the feeling was mutual. She cared not whether he was seducing her or she him. She knew that this was leading somewhere; whether for a moment in time or for a lifetime, she did not contemplate for a second. But she did know that she wanted to remember every moment of the tryst which was unfolding. She would want to replay every detail. She would probably want to tell Cécile... no, wait a minute, he is her father. She committed every move, every button, every wisp of hair, every touch of flesh... to memory.

She waited as he walked towards her without speaking and took her hands in his. In a moment he was in her arms and she in his. He clearly was not in the mood to hurry things; maybe as a result of decades of abstinence, she did not know. Some men would be rushing at it, struggling with the buttons and pushing their lips grotesquely against hers. He smiled again and said 'Good evening Mademoiselle'.

'Good evening Monsieur Le Directeur '

The pressure from his hand on her back increased and she felt her face approaching his. Then the touch of his hand on her cheek sent electricity through her body and she felt him respond to her little shiver of anticipation. As his lips approached, he turned her head to the side and kissed her first on the same cheek, then on the ear, then on the neck. He pulled away enough to make eyes which asked whether he could go further. Her eyes and a quiver of the lips said yes; so he kissed her fully, on the lips, wet lips. She returned the kiss, and kissed him again. She found the tingle of his moustache and beard more arousing than off-putting. He released himself to his instincts and she felt him give himself up to satiating his pent-up need for physical contact and carnal love.

There was no couch in the office and the table was decked with two candelabra, a jug, glasses, writing pads and a vase; uninviting. The carpet was plush and clean. They dragged each other down to the floor without releasing each other. He continued the kissing, including over her body through her dress until he stopped and looked again into her eyes. He hesitated. Natalie was not in the mood for hesitation. She wanted this man, and now.

'Make love to me. Take me, Monsieur Le Directeur, for I am your humble servant in these matters.'

'No, Mademoiselle, you are not my servant. You are my muse. You are a goddess of beauty and youth. You are my intellectual superior. You are my stimulus and my future. And it is I who am in rapture of you, at your knees, drinking from your lips. It is I who am your servant...' She did not wait for the end of this romantic and stirring monologue. She raised herself on one elbow, and he, still flowering her with compliments, watched in delight as she very slowly undid her top button at the collar; and then the second; and then the others, all of them. He did at least take off his tie. Natalie's long dark blue dress, pleated as required to fit her form, had buttons all the way from the collar to the waist and to the ankle. She undid the belt.

As the dress fell away she saw his look of astonishment; she was wearing no corset. Good. The lithe body she knew he watched every day was hers and hers alone, without the support of bone-reinforced underclothing. Now he caressed her breasts, girlish and soft but not too small, her bare stomach, flat and inviting above her white cotton drawers, and her legs, bare down to the socks and shoes. Maintaining the tantalising slow pace of the seduction, he kissed her stomach then progressed down her legs. The feeling was sensational and much more acute then the inexperienced fumbling of the many younger men she had known. He unbuckled her shoes and took them and her socks off. He then kissed his way back all the way to her breasts and on to her lips. He lifted her shoulders off the ground enough to slide the dress off her arms. He rolled her over onto her stomach, put his fingers into the hem of her drawers and pulled them down her legs and off. He caressed the backs of her legs, her buttocks, then her back and her neck before turning her over and attending to her sensitive and aching breasts. As he kissed them his hand went down between her legs, stroking her pubic hair and the lips to her most secret parts. She had not expected this sensuous and apparently experienced performance from a man who had not been with a woman for 20 years, but she quickly returned to the matter in hand. In his hand, that is.

Without speaking he got up and looked down at her totally naked body, white, languorous but shimmering, on the floor. He took off his jacket, shirt, belt, trousers, under-clothes, socks and shoes, the lot. The President Director-General was standing above her totally naked and, from what Natalie could clearly see, ready. He dropped to his knees, spread her legs wide and stroked her where it mattered. Then he was inside her; with a few strokes she was in that heaven of sensation and pleasure. At this stage in her ecstasy she started to fail in her concentration on remembering all the details; her passion was too intense. As his arousal drove him forward into a mounting rhythm, she thought momentarily of the risk she had discussed with Cécile. As he drove to his climax, Natalie only needed to apply a hand under his groin to signal him to pull out. He acted as a true gentleman and did so. With the same hand she stimulated him through his final moments; his fervour was accompanied by passionate grunts and cries. He collapsed in tears of joy.

They lay on their backs, kissing and fondling. His continued passion and tenderness for her took his lips around her head, neck and shoulders, then all over her body. When he relaxed on his back Natalie returned him the gestures, pampering his body all over with tenderness and affection. They lay arm in arm, head to head, his hand on her breast, hers on his stomach, savouring the moment. They took their time. There was not a lot of serious talk; mostly sweet nothings. He said her name again and again, getting used to the sound of it and the impact she made on him. The important dialogue was said in the ultimate act they had just performed. They dressed and took leave without talking practicalities, and without making future arrangements. It did not seem necessary. They both knew the commitment they had made to each other, that this was not just a moment of sexual gratification on the office floor but the beginning of greater things. Both were confident of the sincerity of their affection and that the affair would take its course.

He gave her a pass key, went out first, got in to the waiting landau and drove off. The Count's coachman looked over his shoulder. She waited in the shadows of the entrance lobby till they had gone, locked up and set off in the dark on foot towards the village of Pompey, home, as she always did.

They each went on their way in the cool night air knowing that this was not the last such encounter.

২

Chapter 26 – The Countess unveils statue and plans

It was the day of the unveiling of the statue of the Countess at the Château. According to Duchien's invitation card, handwritten in black ink, it would be a formal-dress 'gala' with palm-court dancing, champagne and food.

The unveiling of the statue of the Count, their first Duchien commission, at his factory on 18th May, had passed satisfactorily. It had been business-like and, with just 80 people, almost low-key. But the gala at the Château would be a different kettle of fish. Antoinette had told him about some of the 250 people on the guest list, many of whom he knew were the slavish false-aristocrat friends the Countess cultivated. The thought of an evening in their company made him shiver. Duchien was not really a shy man but he was so much happier in his own company and with his own thoughts, certainly since the death of Émilie. He seemed to be happiest in the atelier working on a sculpture. In the last two years Duchien had seldom gone out. He dressed up to go out even less.

His thoughts turned to the patronage of the Count. Was it irresistible? The fee for doing his statue and that of his wife each brought in about six months' worth of his present income – designs for Daum and furniture carving for Louis Majorelle's manufacturing company – and he felt grateful for the positive bank balance. He also felt that the Count's industrial and city connections could lead to other such work. He felt obliged to go, both for his clients and for his future. Duchien accepted, against his instincts, that he could not refuse the invitation to be present at the unveiling of another Orlowski statue he himself had sculpted. He was also going for himself in the hope that events and socialising might be steps towards getting out of his depressions.

He had taken a bath in the copper tub in the downstairs garden room which he used as his bathroom. He had shaved his face, sideburns quite short, as usual. In the looking glass he thought he looked quite fine. Over his plain white linen shirt, top button done up, he adjusted his dark blue cravat; no patterns; no tie pin. He put on a light grey waistcoat then his best dark grey suit in cotton and wool, a tunic-style jacket with eight buttons. He left the two top ones undone to show the cravat... and to let him breathe. Even in a brighter mood he disdained accessories, which he thought of as fineries for people who wanted to give a more elevated impression of their rank or character than reality. He preferred the plain look: no tie pin, no watch-chain, no silver-knobbed cane, no carnation in his button hole and no hat. At half past six, dreading the obligation to be sociable with one and all, he stubbed out his cigarette, walked to the cab rank in the Place Thiers for the journey north into the hills above the Meurthe.

The cab drove up the west bank of the river six kilometres to the weir at Le Renclos to cross over to the east. From there it was only a couple of kilometres uphill northeast into the folds of the hills. The Château de Lay-Saint-Christophe was in its own domain beyond the village of Lay-Saint-Christophe, further to the east in the valley of the Amezule, approached through grazing farmland and backing on to the Forêt de la Taye.

Now he could see the broad rectangle of the château's facade, constructed quite recently by the Count around a 13th century castle-priory. The sunlight was fading and torches were lit as the guests gathered on the steps to enter the reception. The construction of the new mansion was of white sandstone from Lorraine, the sort Duchien preferred for stone carving, with tall windows and little ornamentation, but he found the tortoise-shell clay tiles and the lines of metal fleurs-de-lys pointing skyward at the peak of each roof rather showy, even nouveau riche.

As they approached, Duchien turned to admire the view through the back window to the city of Nancy, clear in the distance. He took a deep breath and prepared himself.

All the guests seemed to be arriving at the same time, and the various carriages, landaus, fiacres and hansom cabs were backed up all the way round the drive back into the single track road. Horses and drivers were getting impatient. After five minutes waiting, Duchien gave up, paid the driver and walked the last fifty metres up the gravel of the drive. The uniformed doorman looked down his nose at him, but let him past.

The statue of the Countess stood in pride of place in the atrium hall between the two curved flights of stairs. The plinth was chest high and the sculpture, covered by a burgundy red velvet drape ready for the unveiling, rose another metre and a half or more. He cast his mind back to the two sittings when the Countess came to his atelier and the two when she demanded that he came to the château. She managed to make the atmosphere very unpleasant on each occasion and seemed to be angry at everything, not least her husband, her servants including Antoinette, her circle of friends, French politics and art. She got angry at the slightest provocation; an annoying fly one day, an uncomfortable seat another.

Duchien, taking a glass of champagne from the silver tray proffered by a servant, saw quite a few people that he knew about but who did not immediately acknowledge him. Why not? Did they think of him of the crazed sculptor who spent more time with his demons than with people? As soon as the Count saw him, he was shepherded into the throng to be introduced to some important guests. Feeling like a prize filly being paraded in the ring, he pretended to be interested in each of the personalities that the Count introduced him to and drank his champagne slightly more quickly than he would have wished.

Duchien found it frustrating that the guests took an eternity to negotiate the queue up the drive and get their first drink. At last he master of ceremonies (Raphaël Guidon, Nancy's undertaker, taking an incongruous but regular moonlighting role) called everyone to order from the main stairway and introduced, with flowery words and his full name, Le Comte Geoffroi Orlowski. The Count then held forth. Duchien knew from the last time that he'd be good at saying the right thing; but it contained nothing but platitudes. He wondered how many present could have detected the false tone of his fulsome praise for his wife; a more vacuous speech Duchien could not have imagined. However, when the Count introduced his wife and she started speaking, all such records were broken, and by a margin. Duchien felt the will to live sapping away, revived only slightly when the repetitive clichéd remarks included praise for the sculptor's skill and diligence. By contrast, the Count looked like a man with plenty of will to live. His ego and his joy after the speeches surprised even his wife as much as Duchien.

Guidon then announced the names of the triumvirate, the Count's usual eminent pals, appointed to unveil the statue. There was Aristide Majorelle (Director of the Musée des Beaux-Arts) and Léon Goulette, the owner/editor of the regional daily paper L'Est Républicain, both of whom had been supportive to Duchien over the years. He hardly knew Nicolas-Émile Adam (Mayor of Nancy). The Count and Countess pulled a string to release the drape, which snagged predictably on an orb in the Countess's stone hand, an orb which Duchien had been told was a priceless insignia of her proud family. Once the statue had been fully unveiled, Duchien, to his horror, saw the Mayor step forward to speak. Indeed, each of the three VIPs wanted to hear the sound of his own voice. As soon as the brief round of light applause for the last had finished, the hubbub and drinking recommenced. The white sandstone sculpture of the Countess towered above the throng of guests holding their glasses of champagne. None of them seemed to be looking at his work, Duchien noticed. They gossiped busily among themselves.

Mercifully, some good food was being handed round. He ate. A small orchestra started playing in the orangerie. To get away from the people talking to him, he made the music his excuse and walked through. Several couples were dancing already, a polka, looking quite fine. Duchien was content to watch them for a moment. Nancy certainly did not lack beautiful women, beautifully dressed in a variety of pastel robes. The men, in contrast, looked drab and characterless in their reglementary black frock suits. Duchien touched his cravat, realising that he looked just like them, indistinguishable apart from his choice of dark grey. He was wondering how long he had to stay with the polite company at the soirée before he could escape through the orangerie windows, and return home.

২

Mother ignored me. Papa was busy introducing selected guests to each other even though they were in most cases already well acquainted.

I was looking forward to seeing Duchien in a different

environment and to springing a surprise on him. I would have been missing Natalie except that I found myself the centre of attention early in the evening, mostly with the Méli family. The Professor was quite proud of me, his star pupil, for securing the job with Daum. His wife Sophie had been at my birthday dinner and had shared in the excitement of the announcement; I sensed that her fine bloodline pre-disposed her to Mama's posh friends and to a formal gathering with them. Jacqueline, their daughter, was complimentary from the point of view of women making their way in the world and I spent a good moment talking about the new art, Natalie's time in Paris, her job with the Count and her influence on me. I wanted to talk to her about Duchien because she liked his work so much and had included him in two exhibitions, but I was uncertain of my footing and where the conversation would go; so we stayed on the theme of women and art. Easy; she wanted more women in art. We were welcomed into the circle of Louis Majorelle and his family; Jacqueline rated him highly and featured his work, mostly furniture, in her art exhibitions. Majorelle's wife Jika was delightfully intellectual and acerbic; her insights into the people at the party were memorable.

Antonin Daum was attentive; he thought I had made a good start. He wanted to introduce me properly to his elder brother Augustin who I had hardly spoken to at work. A bit later I found myself feeling flattered when Émile Friant made a bee-line to engage me in conversation... flattered until I realised he was making hints about his fascination with the nude in art, and with me, in short order. I was rescued by the pushy and colourfully-dressed art dealer Jean-Christoffe de Platigny who, at an event featuring a sculpture by his commercial partner Duchien, was working the floor ostentatiously.

I spotted Duchien once or twice, either trying to look enthusiastic about the compliments people were paying him or on his own, looking as though he did not belong. He looked tense, in a Duchien sort of way. His face said that whatever reverie he was having was self-deprecating. I had completed the list of people I knew I wanted to speak to (Natalie had instilled in me the need to cultivate business contacts at social events) when I saw him at the far end of the orangerie, lifting the curtain of a French window aside to look out into the garden courtyard and fountain.

I was drawn to him. I determined to insert myself in his thoughts, now in the gaiety and music of the gala, like in the Place Thiers in the spring sun. I approached him from behind. He recognised my voice as soon as the words left my lips.

'Good evening Monsieur Duchien'.

'My goodness. Mademoiselle Cécile. What a pleasure to see you and may I say, forgive me, a surprise.'

'Ah, did you not think that I frequented such exalted circles, hob-nobbing with the important people of Nancy. Strangely enough, I feel quite at home here.' Duchien entirely missed the reference to 'home'. I realised instantly, and with secret pleasure, that Duchien still did not know that I was the Count's daughter.

'No, well, I had not given it any thought. I did not expect to see you. I imagine your relationship with the Daum ceramics enterprise is a possible entrée to such an event.'

'Indeed, something like that. It certainly would be if I needed one.' I was thinking on my feet. To steer him away from the reason for her being there, and towards something more pleasurable, I made a bold suggestion. Nothing to lose. 'Thinking back to that pleasant interlude in the park, and the pleasure I saw in your eyes, would it please Monsieur to invite the girl from Daum to dance?'

Duchien was momentarily flustered, mostly because he had not danced for three years; and that was with his wife, his late wife. But it turned out he did not dislike dancing; his foot-to-music coordination was almost as good as his sculptor's eye-to-hand coordination. I saw his face light up and pleasure come to his eyes.

'Why, Mademoiselle Cécile, I was just thinking the same thing myself. Would you do me the honour of the next dance please.'

'It would be my pleasure sir, and may I say, an honour to take the first dance with the author of the splendid sculpture which I see in the hall.'

Within moments Duchien and I were as harmonious a couple as any other. I had been well trained in the art of the ballroom dance and initially held Duchien with one hand, the other holding my dress off the floor. Halfway through the leisurely *Skater's Waltz*, a new and popular piece by Parisian Émile Waldteufel, Duchien permitted himself a small smile, a grin even, and took me more firmly, his right hand around the small of my back and his left hand firmly in my right hand at shoulder height. I smiled back at him, intentionally a bit coyly, inclining my head downwards and looking at him out of the tops of my eyes. I held my lower lip between my teeth. Duchien found this very amusing and returned the gesture with a nod of the chin and a discreet lick of the lips. He dropped his hand to my waist and pressed once briefly. I thrilled to the touch.

We paused after that first dance. It was a moment to relish this new intensity of contact.

'Cécile, did you tell me the other day that you have been offered a job at Daum, full time? I am so pleased for you, and impressed of course. Forgive me for not being more responsive when you told me; I have been quite intent on my work recently.'

'I told you that a month ago Monsieur Duchien! And now I have taken up my post; I started Thursday ten days ago.'

'Oh my goodness, that must be exciting for you. Will I continue to see you when you come to the atelier with a letter or for a pick-up?'

'Of course you will' I added with a cheeky smile.' I might even drop in to see you on Saturdays even if there is nothing scheduled.'

'That would be welcomed Cécile. To celebrate, shall we dance again?'

'If it pleases you Monsieur, it pleases me.'

Our relaxed partnership continued through Tchaikovsky's *Swan Lake*, also composed only ten years ago. As it finished he held me warmly and looked deep into my eyes. I thought he was going to kiss me. My heart fluttered. I tightened my grip on his shoulder and on his hand. His smile was one of new-found love but also of respect and patience; an intoxicating cocktail. He was not in a hurry but I was certainly he had strong feelings for me. The orchestra struck up Strauss's *Blue Danube* and my heart sank; I was urging them silently for a slow dance but it was not to be. Our dancing was obligatorily more active for the third dance, but we both enjoyed it immensely and wheeled round the floor with the other couples. My thoughts were about how unseemly sweat must be on a well-brought-up girl but not about the tender moment of a kiss. As we stopped to catch our breath, hesitating whether to reach for the champagne glasses or have another dance, the Count was there. Damn. I would have preferred to continue in the arms of my sculptor.

'Dear Duchien, my dear friend, the hero of the evening, the creator of artistic works that will last an eternity.' Duchien released me to listen 'I'm so glad to see you enjoying the music, especially in the company of such a fine lady as my daughter.'

If he had been holding a champagne glass, Duchien would have dropped it. I could tell that he was kicking himself for not putting two and two together, neither at any time during the months when I had come by the atelier on the regular pick-ups for Daum, nor when we had been talking earlier. He really should have pressed me to find out how I came to be invited tonight.

'Yes, of course, Monsieur Le Comte, I... indeed... yes... I have been enjoying the music and dancing with this intelligent young lady whom I have had the pleasure to know for some time in her professional activities. Monsieur Le Comte can be very proud of... his... err... his offspring.' Duchien gathered himself together. I suppressed a giggle. I felt like throwing an arm around Duchien and kissing him, but judged it would be the better move to throw myself round my father and kiss him instead. Which is what I did.

'Thank you Papa for such a wonderful party for the unveiling of the statue of Mama, and for inviting such an interesting person to make the sculpture. He dances quite well also.'

'Well, well, excellent, I must say, well, very well, Duchien. If it pleases you, may I beg of your company a moment to meet some more of the guests who are determined to shake hands with you, the maestro.'

'Of course sir, it would be my pleasure although, Mademoiselle, the pleasure of dancing with you was a comparable pleasure,' and bowing his head to take my hand and kiss it in a formal way while murmuring into my ear in complicity, out of earshot of my father, 'in fact, certainly far superior. I would have liked to have danced for much longer. I hope I have another such occasion in the future'. I gave him the coy look again and said nothing.

Duchien continued with the Count to do his rounds of the VIPs, looking much more cheerful.

ॐ

I was in a dreamlike daze. I liked the beautiful sculptor a lot. He made me feel so... wanted. I found myself wandering away from the dancing and into the salon. Damn it. I was unable to avoid the eyes of my mother, who beckoned me over. She was surrounded by the more doting of her friends of whom two ladies, I knew, were divorcees or people living separate lives to their spouses. A brutally ugly man, overdressed and with an opinionated body-language, was haranguing my mother. He held firmly on to a matron-like and over-dressed middle-aged lady, good looking by comparison.

'My daughter, where have you been. I have been looking for you all evening. At last I can introduce you to the Baron Günter Ménard von Auersperg, his wife the Baroness Clementina and their son Maximillian.' She shepherded the three von Auerspergs away from the other friends so that they surrounded me. Trapped. Maximillian, probably early 20s, over-dressed, had the disdain and haughtiness of his father but luckily some of the better looks of his mother. The Countess continued 'I know you have been looking forward so much to meeting him.'

I was dumbfounded. I posed myself an internal question mark? What was Mama talking about? I had not the faintest idea who Maximillian was, nor why I should be looking forward to meeting him. But I proceeded to curtsy to each one, in a correct, maybe even polite, way, wishing them good evening.

'Yes' said the Baron, emitting a fine spray with each tonguey consonant 'and we have been looking forward to meeting you Cécile'. His wife added an echo 'Yes, haven't we.' The Baron took the lead. 'We hear you celebrated your 21st birthday a few months ago...'

I trod carefully. 'Indeed. My parents organised a splendid

dinner in Nancy for the family and one or two friends.' Where is my father when I need him?

'... and that you are working for a glass factory.'

'Well, the Cristallerie Daum is not just a glass factory, it is one of France's foremost...'

The Baron had his agenda. 'It must be so tedious working in a factory...'

'No not at all. Actually, I ...'

'... that you must be looking forward to finding the right husband and settling down to you place in society and making a family.'

'You are so pretty Mademoiselle, if you permit me the compliment; isn't she Maximillian' bubbled the Baroness. The son remained aloof even if he agreed.

I went on the defensive again. 'I do not think that my present plans include finding the right husband and settling down when I have just secured the job of my dreams in the world of fine arts for which I have studied so ardently.'

'Oh but your mother tells us you do really want to settle down and that this is just a little phase after leaving college, is it not.' The Baroness shot a glance at my mother.

'Yes indeed my dear Baroness. Cécile will be most keen to get to know Maximillian better, and, I must say, a better match cannot exist. We are most excited. Why don't you two have some time together? Shall we leave them my dear Baroness, my dear Baron?'

I could have no doubt now that my mother had suggested, or even proposed, the marriage of Maximillian Ménard von Auersperg to some chattel of hers, me, Cécile Orlowski. I was so shocked by this turn of events that I did not have the audacity there and then to denounce the idea; I could hardly believe my ears.

I managed to exchange a few words with the young man, speaking French, asking him what he did in life. He replied in German 'Ich bin ein Gentleman' using the English word, but he turned rapidly to his mother, his language skills having run out, and asked

'Mutti, entschuldigen Sie bitte, wie sagt Man das auf Französisch, ein Gentleman?'.

I knew perfectly what he meant by 'a Gentleman' and presently the consensus was that one would use the English word in French as in German.

For my part I chose to interpret his statement as meaning that he did nothing in life.

My heart sank further. I had learnt enough.

To my dismay, presently, her mother said to the von Auersperg parents 'Excellent, thank you so much for the invitation. Cécile, the Count and I will travel to Marsal next Saturday for the weekend with the intention of progressing this most commodious matter.'

I made an excuse and left the group as soon as was acceptable.

I looked around for Duchien. I couldn't find him so I asked Monsieur Guidon who had been the master of ceremonies if he had seen him. Duchien had left a few moments ago. I went to the front door and looked down the steps to the drive; indeed, I could hear one hansom, maybe his, going away down the drive.

I needed some fresh air so I walked down to the stables and sat on the stone mounting block. Jean-Marc was sitting against the wall. He smiled at me. Hubert came over and gave me a touch of the nose and a wag. I lifted my eyes to the clear night sky.

If I was looking for a sign I didn't get one.

২

Duchien was happy to get away from the party, not so much to be distant from the Countess's friends and the noise but to have a moment on his own to digest the emotions of his encounter with Cecile.

During the dancing, an unfamiliar but welcome sensation came to him, one which he recollected from deep in his psyche, sometime in the past.

His arm round the waist of this young lady, although still a girl, he guessed late teens, felt familiar and pleasant to him. As the little coach swayed down the drive, Duchien puts his arms round his own chest. He could smell a light eau de cologne and the distinctive aroma of her coiffured hair which had been so close to his nose. Her hair was beautifully done up in a shapely flat bun which was so fashionable; a wide bun like a big circular flat loaf of bread. He couldn't see a single wisp of hair not properly contained within the narrow black ribbon which secured it, a detail which appealed to Duchien's love of organisation. The girl in his arms felt totally relaxed and at ease. She had the same effect on him.

He recalled the detail of the delightful being in his arms; the artist in him had committed this detail for memory in case he wanted later to make a sketch of her.

She wore a similar style of dress to most of the ladies in the room; a long evening dress in a colourful mix of silk and satin, with a plunging but semi-circular neck-line, a wasp waist descending to a modest bustle to add fullness at the back and the un-pleated skirting down to just above the ankle. Where the elder women would cover the arms all the way to a full-length glove, Cécile bucked the fashion of her elders with a dress suspended by 2-inch wide ribbons between the neck and the shoulders. Duchien could admire the full length of each arm, the delicacy of two white gloveless hands (the hands of an artist, he knew), the thrust of her collar bone and the turn of each shoulder. Unlike the heaving bosoms of some of the ladies, constrained and supported by a bodice, the pure line of Cécile's chest struck him... and it was her own. She wore a beautiful silver necklace suspending one pearl and matching ear-rings with no ornamentation. Her ivory white satin dress had hem detail in off-white lace; she needed no flashy colouring. While many of the ladies looked, in Duchien's eyes, gross and overdone with their colours, embroidery, ornate hems in contrasting colours, falbalas, fanfreluches and jewellery, Cécile gave the image of modest perfection.

Duchien revelled in the feeling of his hand round her waist where the form was her own; he could feel no stays and no corset. He felt warmth. He permitted his mind to wander fleetingly to the inner being, even the animal nature, of this delightful young woman. Was the notion of love playing with his psyche?

It occurred to him that this was the first time since his wife's death that he had felt like this, so at ease with a woman. He even gave a thought to Bernheim, the psychiatrist and hypnotist who told him that something would occur in his life to reinstate him on the path to happiness and possibly even a relationship.

He recalled looking down at the human he was holding. He was pleased.

ॐ

Chapter 27 – Cécile resists her mother

Pompey, the day after

I had agreed with Natalie in advance to meet the day after the gala, at three o'clock, in the Hôtel de la Poste. We found it a place where we could talk in discretion but with some openness.

'Thank you Natalie. You're the only friend I've got that I can talk to about this. I think what has just happened could be the worst thing that's ever happened in my life; and could jeopardise my entire future.'

'Tell me. Tell me Cécile. What could be so awful?'

'My mother has fixed me up for an arranged marriage. She introduced me to this lanky Prussian with a long name. I could tell in a moment, from first glance, that he was obsessive, introverted, lacking social skills, quirky, pedantic and unattractive. From what was being said I was expected to know all about him in advance and this was to be my husband. I haven't seen my mother yet today, but I shall tell her what I think.'

'But that's impossible. People don't do arranged marriages anymore.'

'Tell that to my mother. She lives in a world of some ancient époque of 40 years ago. I can't help feeling that there is even a price on this. Doesn't the bride's family have to put a huge amount of money into her dowry to get rid of their daughter? What value is put on me for heaven's sake? All she wants is to increase her own status in this imaginary aristocratic society she subscribes to.'

'And if that's true she must have discussed it with your Papa to make some arrangement for whatever the money is. What has he said?'

'He wasn't there when Mama introduced me to Maximilian von rubbish and his family so I don't know. Nor have I seen him this morning. Money might not be the problem; I asked the boy what he does for a living and he said he's a gentleman i.e. a lay-about.'

'This is totally unacceptable. Your mother's treatment of you, as a bit of flesh, some item number in a cattle market, is disrespectful of you. It's insulting. You have rights, Cécile, as an individual. Also as you can see from what I've written and said, there is this new wave of female emancipation. We have the right to decide our own lives.'

'Yes but tell that to my mother. I can't bear it. I'm so unhappy.'

'I'm thinking aloud here. You cannot let this happen. The first imperative is to talk to your father about this.'

In the back of her mind Natalie was assessing the impact of her asking the Count, when she next saw him, discreetly and confidentially. But as Cécile did not know about Natalie's affair with the Count, she could not mention that. Her clandestine meetings with him were mostly on Friday evenings after work. She would find the moment to ask the Count about this arranged marriage. Then she would have to find the right moment to tell Cécile about her affair with her father.

'Yes, but what do I tell him?'

'Tell him what I have just told you. You have the right to decide your destiny. Women nowadays cannot be treated like cattle. If he loves you, he must persuade your mother to let you decide. You think, as I do, that you have to be in love to marry someone, to commit to them for the whole of your life.'

'Well, yes, of course I do darling sister. You're right. But it is going to be hard work, both with Papa and with Mama.'

I paused, then moved on. 'Can I ask your advice on something else, maybe just as important?'

'Something else? Oh my goodness. You're on fire today. What secrets have you got for me?'

'Well, not really a secret. I wrote to you about Duchien some time ago. But every time I see him I think I like him better. Then last night...'

'Go on, I can't bear it.'

'Duchien was at the gala of course, the honoured sculptor. Remember, he still didn't know that I am the daughter of a Count so when I contrived to bump into him I was still just the girl from Daum. I know he likes me like that. Just simple me. Just Cécile. Anyway I got him to dance with me.'

'Can he dance? Did he hold you tight? Go on, please, do.'

'Yes, he can dance. Yes, he held me tight. When he put his arm around my waist I felt like I was being transported into another world, on a cloud, part of him. It was difficult to express. I know in the slow dances he was enjoying taking in the scent of my hair and the perfume round my bare neck. At the same time we were jokey and teasy and sort of, dare I say it, loving. We talk easily. He seems so relaxed but at the same time in charge of what's going on.'

'Well, you have got a thing for him haven't you? And he certainly has an eye for the women if his nude sculptures are anything to go by.'

'Yes, but that's the point. I don't want to be one of his muses. I don't want to just be some tart who takes her clothes off and poses for him in the studio. I don't want him seeing me naked, lusting after my body. Not like that. I want him to like me. At the end of the dance my father talked to us, so now Duchien knows I am the daughter of the Count Orlowski. That stunned him momentarily!'

'Well, then, my dear Cécile, the die is cast. Your father has not pronounced on the arranged marriage but he does know that you like the company of men... of another man. The sculptor you danced with.'

'Yes, but...'

'No buts. Duchien likes you. He might even love you in the future. If you like him and you think you might love him, then you, Cécile, are the person in control. You will make certain that the option of being with Duchien is open to you. That is not an issue for your parents; ignore them right now. Ignore the German boy. It is Cécile that decides. As far as the path to Duchien's heart is concerned, you will hold him at arms-length and lead him up the path that you think is the right one. You are in control. If you don't want to be a muse, tell him. You have that right. And, if you to fall in love so be it and to hell with Max; to hell with oppression; to hell with your mother's schemes.'

'You make it sound so simple... but exciting at the same time. Did you think Duchien is too old? And what about him being married before?'

'Too old? No. You, like me, have become bored with the clumsy, immature, gushing, awkward boys of our age. Married before? He is a man of experience. I bet he knows how to make love to a woman. He's been through to hell and back since the death of his wife and daughter and I think you would find him a great person.'

I thought of the child he lost and wondered whether he would like to have children again. Something deep inside me said I hoped he would.

Natalie concluded 'In fact you would probably <u>make</u> of him a great person. You might be the person that turns his life around.' I wiped away a tear. I got out of the chair, moved round to Natalie's side of the table, knelt on the floor and hugged her as warmly as I knew how. As I got up I held her head and kissed her noisily on both cheeks. Then I sat down again and burst into tears of joy.

ॐ

I returned home fired up with the support from Natalie and determined to express and enforce my own wishes on my affairs of the heart. As I walked up the hill in the dusk the thoughts whirled around. Talking to Natalie about myself, it hit me that I was extremely attracted to Duchien. I had seen him, on and off, for over a year and was fond of him. I found him intelligent, sexy and very good-looking. I liked his creativity and I shared his interest in the new art and the Nancy 'school' of creative people.

Natalie's self-confidence empowered me. Even the slight streak of jealousy I had for her, and some distaste at her lifestyle, were part of the package that made me want to compete and improve myself. At the same time I wanted to avoid being quite as free with men; I preferred to think of myself as someone who would find a solid life partner; a lover yes, but someone permanent. I looked back at the conversations over the years with my best friend; we had the same cultural roots, we were living the same revolution in the woman's role in society; we each had the right in this new world to decide our own lives... and lovers. I believed it was not my fate to wait for my parents to name me a husband.

I got home in time for supper with, exceptionally, the whole family. Before we sat down to eat my mother took me into the salon and sat me down.

'Now, it's all arranged we shall go next weekend to Baron and Baroness von Auersperg and we will start making the arrangements. It is so exciting don't you think Cécile?'

'Don't you think I have a say in this, mother?'

'Stuff and nonsense. That's hardly relevant. It's all arranged, and what a wonderful match for my dearest.'

I knew that I had to pluck up courage now. 'It is I who will decide who I marry, mother. If I am to marry, I will marry somebody that I am in love with; someone with interests in common; someone I have chosen.'

I watched my mother's face suffuse with rage. 'Now listen to me. You are too young to have any knowledge about what is best for you and it is your mother who will make these decisions for you. You must be more respectful of your position in society and your debt to your family. I would ask you to talk to me in more convivial and cooperative terms. It is decided. You will find everything will work out perfectly. You could not hope for a better husband.'

'This is as convivial as a young lady can get when she is being forced to a momentous decision in her life by a third party' I retorted. 'There may have been a time when parents could arrange a marriage, but those times are past. The emancipation of women affirms our right to decide. Woman's abilities give us the competence to make our way in life.'

Just as the Countess started off with 'Bah, humbug, where do you hear this emancipation rubbish, who from and...' the Count came in wondering why we were not coming to table. 'Ah, I see you must be talking about the marriage. Very well.'

'It is not 'very well', Papa. Please tell Mama that I'm not going to be forced into marrying somebody I do not love and whom I only met yesterday for the first time, without even being warned of the arrangement or of his invitation to the gala. Please tell Mama now that this is not going to happen.'

'Nonsense' screamed the Countess. 'Your father will not intervene in this issue. He has no knowledge of these matters and no finesse in the social arena. We leave on Saturday morning at ten o'clock to stay with them at Marsal and that is final. Now we should eat supper.'

The Count gave me a shrug of the shoulders and a weak smile. I held back the tears and calmed myself to fight another day.

'Where on earth is Marsal?' asked Papa.

'It's their estate, near Dieuze. East from here off the Saarbrucken road. It will be a most diverting weekend.'

We went through for dinner. Jean-Marc must have heard the shouting and was already looking nervous. Even though he was with us and a maid serving, the Countess did not slacken the pressure on me. At moments she sounded like a Baptist preacher haranguing sinners from the pulpit. The Count could not raise his eyes to look at her. She laid out in some detail how a perfect life should be constructed; how a young lady should behave; how adults know better. As the main course arrived she was starting to shout at her husband for not giving her more support in persuading me to marry Maximillian. She emphasised a point by stabbing her fork on the table; Jean-Marc couldn't take it. He got up with his plate and went to eat in the kitchen with Antoinette.

I was disappointed that my father made no effort to support me. I would have been angry even, but I guessed what was in in his mind. I could see he was angry but that he did not want a confrontation on this issue. He had told me he did not support my mother's stance on a forced marriage. He knew me better. He respected my opinions, my career and my personality. He had seen me waltzing joyfully close in the arms of an attractive man. He felt I would exercise good judgement in my life. All of this I knew in my heart. But this was apparently not an opinion which he was prepared to share with the Countess, in this mood or ever. It did cross my mind that there might be some other reason why he did not want to be telling people what to do in their love lives.

I cried myself to sleep that Sunday night, racked by emotion. I realised that the way I felt when Duchien held me could be a turning point. I was fully aware of how strong my feelings were for him.

⚘

Chapter 28 – Antoinette recounts the gala

Antoinette was at Bernard's café on the Monday evening after the gala for the Countess's statue. She bubbled with enthusiasm to recount what had happened and she ordered a Cognac along with her petit café. Franz and Marcel leaned closer along the bar, as did Bernard from the service side, drying some glasses. Mimi craned her neck into the group whenever she was not serving one of the three or four tables with customers.

'My God, my goodness, you have never seen such a ball at the weekend. The Count and Countess hosted an event which even by their own standards was an extravagant and magnificent evening. A string quartet welcomed the guests where the new sculpture of the Countess is mounted on a big plinth a metre high. The sculpture is of stone and shows her in a highly decorated ballroom gown and her hair in a wonderful bouquet. Champagne flowed and food was served individually on little plates to 250 guests. I had to bring in extra staff from Nancy, did I not, Mimi? After dinner, there was dancing to a dance-hall orchestra in the orangerie. Oh yes, I forgot, there were speeches. The Count congratulated his wife and the sculptor and his wife made a warm response. Anyone would think they were a happily married couple.'

Franz interjected 'Why, what is the problem between them now. Something more than her maltreating that son of theirs?'

'They sleep in separate rooms. This is absolutely confidential and you must not breathe a word of it to anybody otherwise I'm out of a job. They hate each other. I have no idea why they make this show of living together. Would not such a couple separate or get divorced, even if they are eminent aristocrats? It has been legal in France for several years now.'

'Yes but they have so much to live for in the way they are seen as a married couple. The status of the count alone, as owner and head of the steel mill is such that he could not for a moment be involved in salacious gossip or a broken marriage'. That was Bernard, in a surprisingly wise mood.

Marcel added 'There are those that think they are not real aristocrats anyway, but we will never know'.

'Marcel, your tongue' reproached Antoinette. She continued. 'They might also be considering the children. Cécile has finished her diploma and has been offered a full-time job with Daum, but still living at home. Jean-Marc is 19, but with all the difficulties of his personality and education he must be particularly susceptible to the damage that a broken home would cause. The father is also patently aware of how much the mother hates Jean-Marc and does what he can to make his life bearable.'

'And from what I can see,' said Marcel 'Cécile is wonderful to him. Just seeing the way they are when they arrive on the trap; their body language. They are not just friends and siblings but they are complicit in their own world and depending very much on each other. Oh yes, and the dog; Bernard, you can congratulate yourself on being a vital link in the chain of survival for the boy that you provide a small dish of water for the dog when they're waiting outside. You will surely go to heaven.'

'Jean-Marc just watched the comings and goings from outside his rooms in the stable block. Cécile was not allowed to bring a young gentleman, although I don't know if she has a boyfriend at the moment. She can be quite discreet.' Antoinette had clearly not seen Cécile dancing with Duchien nor was she aware, as she was not serving at dinner on Sunday, of the introduction of Cécile to the Prussian suitor.

They continued to listen to Antoinette with amusement and interest as she continued with as much of the list as she could remember of the eminent guests, what they wore and who spoke or danced with whom.

☙

Chapter 29 – Duchien: a shoulder for Cécile

On the Monday after the gala, I got up alternating between total joy and total misery from one minute to the next. I got into work at Daum and, mercifully, was rushed off my feet with the pressures of meetings, designing, managing, selling and delivering the wonderful glassware by the Daum brothers. I hesitated before contacting Duchien. I wondered, after the dancing at the gala, whether he had feelings for me; whether or not I had stirred the embers of love in his heart; whether I was dreaming it all. I wondered if I should wait for him to contact me.

It was not until Wednesday after work that I plucked up the courage to go round to his atelier, only a few blocks walk from the Daum workshop in the centre of town. I knocked on the front door but as was my habit when picking up work from him, I walked on through to the atelier saying 'Good evening Monsieur Duchien' in a bright voice to warn him of my presence. Since the first time I came, having seen the sculptures round the place, I was aware of the risk of coming in upon him hard at work with a lady with no clothes on. I did give that some thought today, knowing that I wanted something different to the other girls; wondering how to communicate that to the sculptor. My concern was given visual form by the sight of a full size limestone statue of a nude lady, the small of her back, her derrière and the backs of her thighs in finished form, but the rest in rough-hewn rock. How strange that he starts at the rear, I thought, my mind wandering to other related fantasies.

Duchien was clearly very pleased to see me. He was working on wooden furniture doors. He dropped his mallet and wood-chisel immediately and came towards me.

'My God Cécile, I thought I done something wrong and that I would never see you again. It goes without saying, I'm very glad you have come.'

I was relieved, happy, excited, all in one. He had the same feelings as I. The emotion of our dance was for real.

I didn't have time to say anything before he took me in his arms and held me warmly. I rested my head on his shoulder and let out a big sigh; a sigh of relief; a sigh of being comforted; a sigh which leads to something else. His arms were strong yet the embrace was light. His torso was hard as rock but it felt soft against me. I looked up into his eyes and touched his cheek. He needed no further invitation. He inclined his head with one hand behind my neck and kissed me on each cheek and then gently on the lips.

I whispered very quietly 'Good evening Monsieur Duchien.'

He whispered back 'Good evening Cécile, the girl from Daum, the daughter of The Count and Countess Orlowski. I think you were never going to tell me, were you...?'

'For you I just want to be Cécile from Daum. I'm just a girl in the arms of a sculptor.'

'Yes, that I know. You are welcome Cécile. I welcome you into my embrace.'

'Monsieur Duchien. We need to talk. I'd like to talk, not here please, with all the statues listening; somewhere where we can look each other in the eye and talk seriously.'

'Yes, alright. I would like that. Let us... let us go to the new Tea Rooms in the Magasins Réunis. It is quiet there and we could find an alcove table.'

'That would be good. I have heard it's nice there but I haven't been.' Not cheap either. I wondered if Duchien would offer to pay.

Duchien did not put on a coat for the two-block walk. He steered me with a hand to the small of my back out onto the street and locked his place up behind him. As we walked alongside each other I wondered what it would be like to walk arm in arm with this man. We did find an alcove table with partitions between them and the neighbouring tables. It was as intimate setting as we could imagine, but not one which would trigger enthusiastic chatter if anybody saw us there. Anyway the Tea Rooms were slightly above the station of Antoinette and her friends at Bernard's so we could reasonably expect not to see any of them there.

I poured out the whole story of the arranged marriage and the confrontation with my mother... well, almost the whole story; I did not mention my chat with Natalie. I adopted all my friend's advice as my own.

Duchien was flabbergasted. When I finished there was silence. The tea - Earl Grey scented with orange blossom, the new

Russian Blend from Dammann, Paris - had come with cucumber sandwiches, brown bread, announced on the printed menu 'à l'anglaise' and there passed a moment of selecting a lump of sugar, the right amount of milk – just a dash – and the right amount of stirring. Duchien liked the detail of a process like this.

'Unbelievable. I, like you, thought that arranged marriages were a thing of the past. But your mother is a redoubtable person as I know from the sittings, and not one to take no for an answer.'

Then he sat in silence again, his eyes doing the speaking. I could clearly see the glistening of the eyes which spoke of some unsaid emotion welling up inside this fragile but beautiful man. I could tell that he was wrestling with his feelings for me and how to express them. I cast my mind back to his failure to attend the opening of his exhibition at the Beaux-Arts the year before, and the reasons. I had picked up from Antoinette that his depressions were serious and that he was seeing someone about them.

I left the space for him to express his feelings for me. No words came for the present. But his hand advanced across the white tablecloth, caressed my fingers and then clasped my hand firmly. The way he held it communicated not only warmth and desire but also hesitation and, maybe I was kidding myself, the fear of losing me.

I took my tea in the other hand and drank from it purposefully. With each tilt of the cup I looked up and into his eyes with my coy half smile. Each look was a question mark. I was willing him on.

'You're right' he said at last. 'I must organise my thoughts and help you assess what decisions to make before the weekend when you go to meet this Prussian lord. Would you like me to speak now, the thoughts that come to mind, jumbled and unfinished, like a sculpture where I have only hewn out the outline of the subject?'

'Yes. If it pleases you, Monsieur Duchien, tell me your jumbled thoughts.' My mind flitted back to Antoinette telling me about the professional help he got; I wondered how a psychiatrist would have eased the real Duchien out of himself.

He hesitated, smiled briefly at me, took a deep breath and reverted to a serious face. 'First, I must tell you, although I think you know some of it, that since the death of my wife I have been a broken man. I have sought medical help for my depressions, with, happily, some measure of success. Here in Nancy is a world-renowned mad-doctor - that's what people call them - who put me under hypnosis to help me release the trauma and its on-going effect on me. I have a strange but welcome feeling that I am on a path to recovery. Your arrival on the scene, now in my feelings not just your work visits, comes at a time, therefore, when I am not sure where I am putting my feet, and where I should put them.' He paused.

Cécile took in the features of his face; a friendly face; such intelligent eyes; such a knowing look. She noted the scar running from above his right eye into the hairline, and thought of his suffering from the accident.

'You must also be clear that I am a man of limited means, that is to say I don't earn a huge salary nor do I have the patrimoine and wealth to be certain of a future. I am a man below your social station and I would not be happy if you felt you were to allow yourself into a relationship with somebody inferior. But I do find myself moved when I'm with you. I sense the positive parts of my inner workings returning to the surface. I know in my heart that you, Cécile, the girl from Daum, could be part of the solution; a path which leads to my reinstating myself; my reason for living; my creative instincts; my life.

'I must be fifteen years older than you and I do not feel it's right that I impose myself on you. It is not right that I insert myself into your thoughts or into your heart by abusing this opportunity - you being forced into marriage with somebody else.'

'Thank you Monsieur Duchien. Thank you for being so honest. You are in no way inferior and that has not even crossed my mind. For me you have great qualities, the creativity which I so respect, the single-mindedness which makes you so successful in your career as a sculptor, the very essence of you as a man. I should turn the question around by asking whether you would be happy in a relationship with somebody with fewer skills than you. Yes I can draw, but I am an amateur in comparison. If we come together, we do so as equals, as two human beings.' I warmed to my subject and felt a flush on my neck and face. I glanced to the side to see if anyone might be cocking an ear in our direction. There was not.

I continued. 'You can imagine that I have feelings for you which are difficult to express because I know them not myself. My resolve to resist the forced marriage must be related to my affection for you, but I do not think for a moment that you are abusing this conjuncture. In any case, I do know that I must take a stand against a forced marriage. There is something evil about my mother and I am not going to permit that evil to prevail and dominate my life. But I think I will not be able to avoid making the trip to Maximilian's family at the weekend. I just need to be anchored to the hope that you are there for me when I come back, whatever the outcome.'

He leant forward, lifted my hand and kissed it. 'I will be your rock. I am your rock now. I am as solid as my sandstone of Alsace. Later you will know what form to chisel out of the rock which I am. You will do the chiselling. You will sculpt the future Duchien. Until then, because we are rational human beings, let us see what happens over the next few days. I must be frank; if you come back from the weekend betrothed to another then of course we will have nothing to say. Please make sure that is not the case. My heart is open, Cécile. I would like to spend some more time together like this. I would be so happy to get to know you better. I would like to find what grows between us.'

One part of me hoped that he would express undying love for me but the rational part knew that he was right. There would be time for this to develop. I did know how seriously he felt about me. But he had kissed so tenderly on arrival. He had even had the courage to talk about his own mental state and I knew I was happy to work with that. I relished the idea of being the one to bring him alive again.

But another thought occurred to me. 'We are laying our cards on the table. This is a good time to be doing this. I hope you don't take it badly when I say that I do not think I want to be one of your muses. I don't want to be one of those girls of the statues of yours in the Musée des Beaux-Arts and around your atelier. I'm not certain I want you to think of me first by the shape of my breasts – or my derrière even, thinking of the half-done female nude back there. Forgive me, I mean, I do not want to be merely a muse. There is something which tells me I offer you more. If we find a relationship it will be one which starts on a higher plane; more personal; more ours...' I paused, my voice fading to a whisper, looking downwards, 'more permanent.'

He continued to caress my hand and paused before answering. 'Thank you Cécile. You are wonderful. You are quite brave to be so open but, yes, these are serious issues for me as for you. I reciprocate everything you say. Leave me a tiny bit of space to collect my thoughts and interrogate my psyche.'

'What can I call you Monsieur Duchien. I think we have left behind us the regime of total formality. May I use your first name?'

'I hate it. And it brings back bad memories of my childhood and my schooldays. My first name is Gaël. Would you like... would you call me Duchien please, no Monsieur, just Duchien. That is what my wife called me. But I would be pleased if we could tutoyer each other.' Duchien had moved from using the second person plural, vous, the formal, and had started using the second person singular, tu, reserved for family members and close friends.

'You honour me, Duchien...' I also used the second person singular for him. There was a pause. 'Do you have bad memories of childhood?'

Duchien hesitated and wrung his hands. 'Yes. Bad memories. Is now the time to tell you?' I nodded. 'My father Armand was a wheelwright and blacksmith in Arnay-le-Duc, not far from here. He was good with his hands and turned wood for chairs. My mother was from Brittany originally, baptised Maiwenn, but everyone called her Marie. She must have won the battle over my name, because Gaël is also a Breton name. The trouble was, they had not thought about how my school friends might say my first name and second name together, Gaël Duchien, which quickly become 'Gueule Du Chien'; a dog's mouth, or a 'hang-dog expression'. So I was bullied at school, mostly about my name but also because I was a bit of a softy. My mother was quite supportive but there was nothing she could do about the taunts in the school yard. I never had any real friends.

'I think life was modest but survivable for them until 1853-55 when three years of floods in the winter and droughts in spring and summer brought the farmers to their knees. They could not even keep their horses shoed. Many of them were killed for food.

There was no work in the Reims region either because philoxera had ravaged the vineyards. My parents moved to Paris where he had been offered a job helping to look after the army's horses. That was in 1857. I must have been two years old. They worried about disease in Paris and left me in Arnay-le-Duc with my sister Marie-Angèle, nine years older than me, and some neighbours who agreed to look after us. My parents were right to be worried; they both died of croup in 1859. I don't know much about it except that it is associated with diphtheria. Flaubert described it in *L'Education Sentimentale*; it makes for a very painful end. I would not be here today if they had taken me with them to Paris. But I was a burden for my sister who had no means of support as far as I can remember. I had to scavenge for my own food. She was taken on as a domestique here in Nancy at age 17 and we moved here when I was 8. That was not too bad through my teens. Just as I started work with a carpentry shop off the rue Grandville she met a man and moved to Ussel near Clermont-Ferrand in the Massif-Central – a world away. The man died I think and she stayed there. No children. We were never in contact much; she didn't come to the funeral. I have not seen her since then, 1872 maybe. No other family.'

'I'm sorry. And then...' I dried up because I knew it was not the moment to mention the death of his wife and daughter. So I changed tack. 'You have been so productive and creative with your own work, your sculpture. You can be very proud. And let's hope we, I mean you, are at the dawn of a new life of happiness.' My lower lip was between my teeth and my head inclined. He smiled, raised my chin with a finger and touched the said lower lip. 'My heart leaps for you when you do that.'

I sensed the jerk of a tear but held it back and wiped it with the knuckle of my index finger. There was silence. I glanced at the carriage clock on the mantelpiece in the tea room. 'Oh my goodness I must go. 'Walk me to the station please, before I cry.'

Duchien left money for the tea, thanked the waitress and shepherded Cécile to the door and down the main stairs of the Magasins Réunis into the Place Thiers. I put on my coat, scarf and hat against the cool of the evening and we made our way across the square to the station.

'Duchien. Goodbye until the next time which, if you permit, will be soon. May I drop by again please?'

Duchien broke into a huge smile and his eyes sparkled. I had never seen him like this. It gave me great joy.

&

Chapter 30 – I am sorry Maximillian

Marsal, near Dieuze, north-west of Nancy, Saturday 17th September 1892

Pressure of work and arrangements prepared by my mother conspired to make it difficult for me to find the time to get back to Duchien before the weekend. I had caved in. I had decided to accept to make the trip with my mother to visit the Von Auersperg family, but I was intent on resisting a forced marriage. My mother had bullied the Count to come with us and we drove mostly in silence in the coach for the hour and a half it took us to get to Marsal, this side of Dieuze, a town in the foothills of the Vosges to the north-west of Nancy. Papa had confided in me that he did not support his wife in forcing me to marry Maximillian but he wanted to find the right moment to show open support for me if needed. I felt he loved me enough for this to be true.

We had not even been shown our rooms when we were offered a light lunch. As soon as coffee had been taken I was ushered out of the house with Maximillian and told in no uncertain terms to go for a walk. This was the walk which Mama and his parents expected would result in love, common sense and a proposal of marriage. Papa remained silent. I could tell from his eyes that he knew I would do the right thing, whichever way I decided, and that he hoped I would follow my heart.

I felt sorry for the boy. I thought of him as a boy because he was so immature, certainly compared to what an adult I considered myself. He was expecting our hearts to come together or, at least, a productive conversation about getting married. I think he was primed by his parents to be ready to propose to me and to arrive back at the house triumphant.

We got over the platitudes about the gala at our place and how nice his was. Within twenty minutes I had plucked up the courage and got to the point.

'Maximilian. Do you mind terribly if I use your first name?'

'No, of course, please do.'

'I will not be marrying you. I have a strong heart and it is leading me in a different direction. There is a man in my life of which my mother is not aware. I am not betrothed to him but our mutual affection and my commitment to him are such that I cannot bring myself to consider another man, certainly not an old-fashioned marriage of convenience. Society has moved on from those times. Women can determine their own futures, in their careers, in their lives and in their loves.'

'My goodness...'

'I am so sorry that my mother did not consult me in advance, which would have avoided this embarrassment. I apologise for any misunderstandings between our families. And I apologise to you if you suffer disappointment at the position I take.'

'My goodness. Yes. This is a surprise, although I recall, I did not get a very positive response from you when we met at your house.'

'I am sorry Maximillian. But then maybe I have liberated you from the millstone of a marriage to a stranger; maybe you will find someone not just to marry but to love as well. I wish you happiness in your future.'

I did it. I said it. We walked back, mostly in silence. I went to my room, lay on the bed and reflected. I stilled myself, breathed and readied myself for an evening with these people and for the reaction of my mother.

Every element of the evening was an onslaught on my sensibilities. The home of Baron Günter Ménard von Auersperg and his wife Baroness Clementina was huge, even bigger than ours at Le Lay-Saint-Christophe. It was older and more dilapidated except for the reception rooms; there was not a bath I could use and the plaster in my bedroom was beginning to crumble. The service from the house staff was over formalised and lugubrious.

The family paid more attention to how one dressed for dinner and the time of entry into the salon than on the food and conversation. The parents were extremely boring and had nothing to say except on the rights of the Prussians to have invaded Metz in 1870; I was alerted by this point of view and by the accompanying silence from my parents, who I think came from Metz in the first place, that the Von Auerspergs cannot have been in this house very long; it was in France up to 1870. They probably were not nobility either. But then I sometimes posed the same questions about my parents. The rest of the dinner talk was tittle-tattle about friends in common.

Maximillian sat glumly at the dinner table, so much so that his mother asked him if he was alright. He had not plucked up the courage to tell his parents of our conversation. Despite the enquiring looks from my mother, I had said nothing. There must have been some consensus among the parents that they would not, initially, push us too hard.

Over breakfast on Sunday the truth was out. In response to the unsubtle jibing from his mother, Maximillian could not hold back the truth... 'Mademoiselle has turned me down. She told me yesterday she did not wish to marry me.'

My mother contained her rage because, in front of the Von Auersperg family, that would make things even worse. Instead she repeated endlessly her apologies and her resolve to get me to see sense. After breakfast, when she could get me on my own, she went through the whole set of arguments again, in a most acrimonious confrontation, which reduced me to floods of tears and heaving sobs; I was quite enjoying my acting skills and there was no harm in showing extreme distress. I was also enjoying the decisiveness with which I had undertaken my task.

'What do you mean, there is another man. How dare you? How dare you entertain such ideas without even telling me?'

'You don't even know me mother. You never talk to me. You have no interest in my affairs. You have no respect for my fine arts qualifications and you are disdainful of the work I do. You're not a mother to me. I have no obligation to tell you who I love, who I do not love. I am not going to participate in an arranged marriage.'

My inner Cécile was beaming with pride at my courage in holding my ground and speaking like this to the ogre who could not believe that her daughter was refusing her. I thought of Natalie, with her stern, friendly and beautiful face; so I took resolve that I was exercising my rights. I thought of Duchien, his calm voice, has clean shaven face, his twinkly eyes and his hand on mine. I knew I was deciding for the right man.

Presently the Count was so embarrassed by the noise emanating from the salon that he came through to break up us two women. Within moments we had agreed to head back to Nancy and regroup.

The coach ride back home was even more painfully silent than the outbound.

꿍

Chapter 31 – Duchien and Cécile on the footbridge

We got back on Sunday at lunchtime and I thought of going to see Duchien then and there. I was emotionally exhausted and Mama wanted to have another round of shouting at me. So I resigned myself to seeing Duchien on Monday in my lunch break. I knew he would be patient till then because he knew we would not normally have got back till Sunday night. I was hoping fervently that he was missing me and keen to see me.

On Monday at lunchtime I came in the front door of the atelier, called out 'Good afternoon Monsieur Duchien' as usual and walked into the back. Duchien got up and couldn't resist, in his dirty cotton work tunic, embracing me and kissing me softly on each cheek and then the lips.

'Bonjour Duchien' I murmured into his ear, dropping the Monsieur for the first time. 'Bonjour Duchien' I repeated into the other ear, kissing him, touching him, just to make sure he knew I was there and giving him some hope that my news was good news.

'Bonjour Cécile' he whispered. He continued to hold me and kiss me gently. I reciprocated with kisses for a moment then put my hands on his chest and said 'Not now my dearest Duchien. Can I come back later? I am not permitted the time now in my lunch break.'

'Yes of course but I will die if you do not tell me what happened at the weekend.'

'I turned him down. I had a blazing row with my mother. We came home early.'

'Oh my goodness, I am so pleased. My heart leaps with delight.' He paused to see the fervour in my eyes. He continued 'I have missed you terribly. There has been a vacuum in this place and in my heart since Wednesday. It felt like months. I was half hoping you would visit me again before the weekend but clearly you could not. I feared there might be a reason you did not come again last week. My heart has been aching like it did when I was a teenager first in love.'

He was holding me close enough that I could sense the stirring in his loins which told me that he wanted me as a partner not just a friend. We had gone beyond that.

'I have decided. I have resolved to do everything possible to win you over. My heart tells me I will love you Cécile. It would have broken my heart if I had lost you to the German aristocrat. '

Then he realised what my smoky smile and the lift of the eyebrows meant. 'I mean, I am so sorry that you have such a disagreement with your mother and that you have lost such an eminent suitor' he added with a smile as I gave him a playful slap on the cheek.

'I must hurry back to Daum. I'll be back later. Don't go away.'

'I will be counting the minutes.'

&

I was in an emotional turmoil all afternoon. Everything was happening too quickly. This felt like such an important moment in my life, a turning point. I did not want to make the wrong decision. I did not want to be bounced out of my rejection of Maximillian into the arms of Duchien, but as far as my sculptor was concerned, his path to happiness with me was clear. I had hardly been able to concentrate on work.

I found I could get away from Daum a bit earlier than usual. I was with Duchien at 5. I was terribly nervous, uncertain. I had resolved to say all this to Duchien, to tell him the issues which still made me nervous; my misgivings, my hesitations. I wanted to replay the conversation of the Tea Rooms to make sure he was still true to me and what we had talked about then. We embraced warmly; well no, he embraced passionately. I tried to keep him controlled. I put my hand on his chest and a finger on his lips and asked 'Have you got time to walk with me Duchien? Please? It's such a beautiful evening; I just want to be with you, and close to you, with my hand in your hand.'

He quietened. 'Of course Cécile. I would like nothing better.'

We walked. We walked and talked. We went across the Place Carnot, to the Parc de la Pépinière, across the canal and all the way to the river. We held hands or walked arm in arm. We never stopped talking. We stood, leaning over the foot bridge across the Meurthe, looking back towards the city. If there were birds or other people we didn't notice them. We both enjoyed each other's company; minute by minute we were inescapably falling in love.

'I cannot take my eyes off you; even in your working clothes, your long dark blue dress and your wide burgundy belt, you are the image of perfection and beauty. I want you to be with me. I love you.'

I blushed and lowered my eyes. But I relished the platitudes. No; that's unfair of me to have thought of his declarations of love as platitudes but I wanted first to talk about him. I wanted to know every detail of his life, of the scars, of his hopes and aspirations; I wanted to know that before I made further commitment. Was I being selfish? Or was it a mature act by a relatively inexperienced 21-year-old confronted by a 37-year-old once-married-and-widowed artist? Were these moments of discussion a better basis for a long-term relationship than a head-over-heels affair?

I asked him about his politics, about realist art and art nouveau, about Paris. I asked him to tell me about the rhythm of his day, the balance of work with relaxation, his sleep patterns, what he ate, the people he knew, his family. I raised the issue of his sculptures and asked if he could bear it if I turned out to be something other than a muse, something other than a nude statue for him. Of course he agreed. I mentioned, indiscreetly, the foul-smelling cigarettes he sometime smoked. Without further prompting, he said he would give up smoking and that he had been wanting a reason to do so. Therefore I put my arm round his shoulder, touched his cheek and kissed him gently on the lips.

The intensity of the discussion and its importance to my future brought a glow to my cheeks; I could feel the tremors of passion coupled with such a rational approach to the most important commitment a person can make. My intellect continued, as he spoke, to seek him out. My eyes continued to look into his eyes and deep into his inner self. I liked what I saw. I was with a wonderful man whose every word seemed instilled with wisdom. He had no pretensions. His clothing was simple. He had put a grey cotton and serge jacket over his work trousers and shirt and had grabbed his felt hat with a wide rim turned up at the edges.

Everything about him seemed true. I felt safe with him. I felt much safer with him than I did around my mother. I didn't want the moment to end, but at the same time I wanted a little bit more time. We walked back to the station with the talk turning to me, my art, my job, my family, and my aspirations. He soaked up everything about me.

Best of all, he said how important it was to find out about each other now. He respected me for wanting to have the discussion of the previous week and today. We both felt enriched by the process.

Outside his atelier, his home, I asked him to let me go. I promised to come back tomorrow after work. I did not know what my agenda was, but I promised.

As soon as I left Duchien and got on the train to Pompey, I was on my own, in my own good company. Two thoughts came to me. Firstly, I was lonely the moment I left him. Secondly, I knew I had decided. I had decided in his favour. As I went to sleep that night I could feel my heart thumping; it said my heart ached for him. Even so I was happy, smiling, satisfied with the way love was coming, the way I was leading myself to the commitment. I felt in control, as if the empowerment of women included the right to say no... or, in this case, yes.

⅋

Les Amoureux (Soir d'automne, Idylle sur la passerelle)
The Lovers (Autumn Evening) (1888)
Émile Friant (1863-1932)

On Tuesday I dressed in a mid-length dark blue dress but with short sleeves and, for me, quite a low neckline. It was warm; a late summer in Nancy. During the day I wore a light long-sleeve shirt over it for propriety at the office

When I got to Duchien's place, at about half past four, I was flushed as if I'd been hurrying back to him, running. But I had been walking quite slowly. My heart thumped. I took off the shirt as I walked through to the atelier.

When Duchien wrapped his arms round me, an excited, pink-faced, lovable 21-year-old female, he must have guessed that I had decided; that I wanted to give myself to him. He told me yesterday that he had no second thoughts about our age difference; he was excited that my youth made me all the more attractive to him. He wanted to respect the serious nature of my feelings for him, but the way I presented myself to him now was a red rag to a bull. I could not help putting my lower lip between my teeth while looking into his eyes. Duchien could not tell if I did it intentionally to arouse him, but arouse him it did.

'My god, when you do that, my loins erupt. You make yourself even more desirable. Une femme fatale but adorable and innocent at the same time. I cannot escape you. You awaken some primeval urges deep within me.'

There was no controlling our rush of hormones. As his hands wandered urgently around my form, we could think of nothing but possessing each other, of being one, of being insolubly united. I didn't resist as he kissed my bare arms and my neck, then lower, towards my chest. He then started unbuttoning my dress. The moment he could slide the straps off my shoulders he kissed them slowly and then over my collar bone to the dip of my breasts. As he kissed lower his hands lifted the hem of my dress so that he could stroke the backs of my thighs, his fingers under my culottes, now feeling the shape of my bottom. My hips reciprocated in a dance of their own, out of my control. I caressed his back and his hair. Our animal heat was getting intense; he broke off momentarily to make a signal with a lift of the head towards the stairs going up to the bedroom. I agreed with smallest of nods of the head.

We walked up the stairs to the inner sanctum, Duchien's bedroom, a place which, I imagined, no woman had seen since the death of his wife. I was not certain of that, but I felt privileged and excited to be there. I was excited by the passion Duchien showed me because in the back of my mind I wondered whether he still had it in him, whether he had moved on from the years of trauma to a full expression of his libido; I was excited by the urges I had aroused in him; I was excited by what I felt within me too, passion I had never experienced.

Any fears disappeared as he gently but firmly undressed me. Before I was fully naked he pulled back the cover of the bed and lay down with me there. I found the luxurious pace entrancing, erotic, all-enveloping; such a contrast to schoolboys' awkward fumbling. I enjoyed being submissive to Duchien at that moment while still feeling in control of myself. I enjoyed deciding to cede to him. So I lay happily in his arms kissing him, my hands wandering over him. I put my fingers round the muscles of his arm. I felt the sinews of his stomach. I purposefully moved a hand to his trousers, took off his belt, unbuttoned him and insinuated that hand. Duchien was ready. No libido problem there. Now he raised me to sitting while he removed my slip. He lay me down, raised my hips and he slid my pants down my legs and off. He hardly paused kissing me from the breasts down to my legs, not missing a single part of me. At the same time he finished removing his own clothes, then lay alongside me and pressed himself warmly and urgently against me. I was in raptures of heat for this man, a feeling I'd never had before. When Duchien paused for a moment and looked me in the eyes, stroking me between my legs, I gave a tiny nod and whispered 'Yes, please, Duchien.' I had not expected the ultimate act so quickly in our burgeoning relationship but it was my decision to come to him. There was nothing here I didn't want.

Our love making was so intense that I was barely conscious of what was happening. He took me to the heights. Our communion was total.

We relaxed and separated, our hands wandering over each other. We let the silence speak.

'Good God, Cécile, that was unbelievable. Sublime.' He paused and took a big intake of breath. 'Thank you so much. Thank you for being you. Thank you for finding me and persisting. You make me feel like a young man again.'

'I love you Duchien. I thank you too. I have loved your spirit for some time. Now I think I love your, umm, your body.' With a cheeky smile in my voice, I asked 'Do you think your libido has returned?'

He laughed. 'That's funny. What have you just experienced, Cécile my dearest? Was that a man lacking libido? I don't think so.'

'No. I agree. Not that I have much to compare you to. I just love what you are and what you've done to me.' I paused. 'In the end, this has all come quite quickly hasn't it? I expected us to come together at some stage, but this...'

'Quickly? You made me hang on for weeks. Then there was the threat in the form of a German aristocrat. I had an awful feeling you would choose against me.'

'There was never any doubt in my mind. But I did want to make certain that I was not going to just be one of your muses. I was scared of being taken by you and then discarded. But in the last few days, as I've got to know you, I think of you already as a life partner, something solid in my life, a rock. Am I going too far?'

'You are not going too far. You must have guessed, if you did not know for certain, that before I got married there might have been the occasional fling with a girl; on the spur of the moment. Nude art arouses passions which are not easy to escape. But that seems an age ago. Maybe it is because I am a bit older, or what I have been through in the last few years, I contemplate the joys of being faithful. And, I would not want to lose you.'

I didn't have to answer. I leant over to give Duchien some soft kisses, my hand in the hair of his chest.

'Goodness, I could do with a cigarette right now. But I have promised...'

'You don't need a cigarette Duchien. If you want something between your lips, put them round the nipple of my breast, here.' I moved his head with my hand so that he could do so. 'If you want to inhale, take a deep breath of me; of my hair; my mouth; my armpit; my toes; of what I smell of, for good or for bad.' He breathed in at my armpit with a huge sigh of happiness and a rueful chuckle at the list of options I had given him.

'You missed one out Cécile.' I gave him a play spank and continued. 'If you want a rush of adrenalin, Duchien, make love to me again. If you want relaxation, just hold me in your arms. But I warn you, I, like tobacco, could be addictive for you. You don't need a cigarette. You have me.' I flattened his head on the bed with a forceful and succulent kiss.

'Cécile, my heart is bursting with joy. Thank you, thank you.'

We went on talking in this half dream, with the realisation of what we had just achieved, the rapport we had made, enveloping us.

'I feel I am reborn, Cécile. The man with depression, the hollow man, the nobody man, has gone. He is no more. This is me the real Duchien. You have made me new again and I am yours.' He paused 'You remember the doctor, the 'mad-doctor', Bernheim? He said that I might find a person, or a person might find me, who cures me, who reinstates my sense of manhood, my urges and my will to live. It seems that he was right. You are witness to all of that. Maybe I'll tell him one day.'

We went on talking. We went over all that had gone before, all that we had said, here, in the Team rooms, walking by the river. We talked in detail for the first time about all that could come in the future.

We had been lying side-by-side, he on his back and I leaning against him, for about half an hour. I raised myself to admire his body. I ran my hands quietly through the hair of his chest and across the muscles of his thighs. I felt the pangs of eagerness, a sensation I had never experienced before. I was wondering; and my hand was wandering, not so aimlessly now. I ruffled the hairs round his tummy button and continued downwards, very gently, teasingly. In a few moments my fingers triggered a delicious response. I watched with pleasure and some amazement as I saw the evidence that Duchien's heart was working just fine, pumping blood, proud and strong. Duchien was rearing and ready to go.

I could not resist. I rolled over and sat on him, my legs each side of his midriff. Laughingly and lovingly I sank onto him, slowly. I wanted to state my authority and take a lead role in the proceedings even at the moment of my surrender. He laughed and groaned with pleasure, caressing my breasts, pulling my face towards him for more kissing. My upper hand was short-lived; after a few of my strokes he said 'Oh no you don't. Get off and lie on your front.' I did so. My mind flashed to the unfinished statue downstairs and I imagined what he was looking at. He must have liked it. He stroked the cheeks of my bottom and between my legs until it was almost too nice to bear. He extended my arms above my head at full stretch and my hands round two uprights of the metal bedstead. Then he lay down on me, with all his weight, and rammed himself into me quite forcefully. The feeling was exquisite. His bearing down on my most sensitive points worked me up into another ecstasy of passion as he mounted to his second climax of the evening. I cried out in joy. I could not imagine how love making could be so wonderful.

Afterwards, my romantic mind dwelt on this moment as the beginning of the rest of my life. I could not think how anything would be the same again. My practical mind? Well, here I was, naked and sweaty in bedroom of a man who had been a stranger till recently. No, that's not fair to either of us; I had first met him more than a year before, during my summer job, and our fondness had grown steadily. I liked the sensation that this might be the first of many times here, in his bed, with him in his life, the beginning of a new life together. I could have stayed all night. But my instinct was telling me to get dressed and to get back to the station and home. Did I feel some duty to my parents? Did I owe Duchien some space?

I started making tender goodbyes to my lover. He was almost tearful with delight and would hardly let me go. All of a sudden I noticed the clock said nine and I had to rush to get the last stopping train for Pompey from where I could walk home. I quite often missed dinner with my parents so there would be no embarrassment today coming home late - sometimes work demanded it - as long as I came home.

❧

Chapter 32 – The statue of the mistress

The Count had an assignment in town which he preferred to do after dark; a Monday evening. He had his man stop the trap a block short of the Place Thiers and walked past Bernard's, then turned left to Duchien's atelier. Normally it would be perfectly innocent to commission a sculpture especially if one had the eminence and wealth of the Count. But given the subject matter, the intrigue, and the fact that his wife knew nothing about his extra-marital relation, the Count felt it better to act with discretion.

He asked himself again, as he walked, why he wanted a statue of his lover. His mistress. He knew he would not be able to display it at home; well maybe, as if it were an artistic piece or some muse of the sculptor. But the Countess would be furious, especially as she had made such an effort to get equal with her husband by commissioning one of her to match the one of him. Will it ever end, he thought. What he really wanted was to preserve this moment in time, and the girl, his lover, in stone... for ever. It did not really matter where the statue was as long as it existed. The statue would have the merit of existing.

He was also excited in a boyish and voyeuristic way about Natalie's response to his idea, which he communicated when they were lying naked, wrapped round each other, on the floor of his office. She laughingly said she wouldn't mind having a statue done of herself, especially if the artistic process meant she could strip naked and stand motionless in front of a good-looking male sculptor. She admitted to a taste for exhibitionism and to the idea that her lover could see her as nature intended, for ever. The Count had hardly dare consider a statue of her in the nude, but suddenly the frisson was unstoppable. She became very aroused and initiated an erotic round of love-making. She did promise not to seduce the sculptor. He reciprocated and decided definitively for a nude statue, which made the need for discretion all the greater.

'Duchien, good evening Monsieur.' The Count, having been several times in the past for his own sittings and twice to bring his wife there, had taken to the habit of walking straight through to the atelier.

Duchien was shocked. He felt as if he was in one of his nightmares and that the ground was about to open up and swallow him up. He could only think that the Count had found out, within six days, about his affair with Cécile his daughter. Why, only on Saturday had they renewed their ardour, here in his home, and he was totally in love with the girl. How could the Count have found out?

'Err, yes, good evening indeed, Monsieur Le Comte. I am... what a pleasure to see you again.'

'Yes, and I think the pleasure you experience will be even greater when you hear that I would like to make a third commission, on the same terms. It is one which will, I think, knowing something about the theme of many of your previous great sculpture works, interest you even more than the extraordinary work you did on the statues of my wife and me; a sculpture of my... of a... of a young lady. '

Duchien let out an audible sigh of relief and his head dropped on his shoulders.

'My dear man, is this not an attractive proposition I make?' Duchien lifted his head and made a joyful face, gathering himself up. 'No, sir, I mean yes, indeed, very attractive. How could I, given the two aspects of this commission, the fee and the subject, turn you down dear sir? The young lady... someone I know?' The count brushed past the question. 'She is available in the evenings after work, say half past five?'

'I see you have this quite well planned already sir. And when is it you schedule the sitting to commence?'

'This Wednesday. This Wednesday at half past five then.'

The Count reached into his tunic pocket, took out a bulging envelope and thrust into Duchien's hand. 'Here is 1600 francs, the complete payment. I am sure you will enjoy the assignment and, equally, I am hoping for the highest quality in the work. This one is particularly important to me. Is that acceptable?'

'Indeed thank you. Yes. It is most attractive to us humble artisans that we can benefit from such generous patronage from the champions of our industrial revolution.'

'Indeed. I wish you a good day and productive interludes with the young lady.'

As he got to the door between the atelier and the front office, the Count hesitated and wheeled round. 'Ah yes, Duchien, discretion. Discretion. I forgot to mention that this is a secret from my wife. A surprise shall we say. Most important. And therefore a secret from Antoinette who speaks often and, I regret, quite openly, with the Countess. In fact it is a secret from everyone. It will be a surprise.'

'I understand Monsieur. My lips are sealed.'

❧

On leaving Duchien's studio after commissioning the sculpture of Natalie, the Count walked a different way back to his transport, turning left and left again. In the main road, in the window of a Papeterie Tabac, he saw a board of notices and items for sale, hand written. He knew that he might have a need for something that would be displayed there, and he stopped there for a moment to look through them. He read in the pale gas light; somebody willing to walk your dog; four-poster bed for sale; business for sale; ah, this was more like it... two or three cards announcing apartments for rent or sale. He got out his pocket notebook and wrote the details of one which said 'separate entrance'. The address was No.2 rue Victor Poirel, within two blocks of here. Perfect.

This was how he came to find the apartment where he discreetly installed his mistress. It turned out to be on the first and second floor, above a jewellers shop. The entrance to the apartment was down the side of the building and accessible of course even when the shop was closed. Discretion assured.

The urgency was only because of the thrill in his body, because of the passion with which he craved Natalie and the inconvenience of conducting a love affair in the office; for three or four weeks now; sometimes twice a week, sometimes thrice. A bit sordid, he thought, and a bit risky. It would be much nicer to provide her a place to live where he could visit her on occasions. Often.

The day after seeing the advert, the Count contacted the agency. He completed the rental paperwork by the Thursday. Then on Saturday 1st October, Natalie packed two bags and installed herself in the apartment. It was left furnished so there was little to add except some touches of luxury like crystal glasses, a couple of oil landscapes, some lighting and top quality bedclothes and towels. She had lied to her mother. She told her she was going away for the weekend and she left the bulk of her clothes and things at home in Pompey. Foremost in her mind, apart from the lust she had for her (rich) elder man, was the inconvenience of the commute from Nancy centre out to Pompey. She planned to walk to work as normal most weekdays and to find a modus operandi with the Count to establish the dates and times to meet at No.2, which is how they immediately starting referring to the apartment.

The Count and Natalie celebrated the creation of this love nest within minutes of her getting there with her things on Saturday at lunchtime. He was meant to be at work as far as the Countess was concerned. He was unconcerned about how few clothes she had brought because he was more interested in removing the ones she was wearing. Within minutes she was running naked between the bedroom and living room giggling and teasing him. She let him catch her immediately and they proceeded to a house-warming party of the carnal kind. Their love-making could now be unfettered, with total abandon and with no risk of being caught. The neighbouring buildings and the space below were all commercial properties, offices, where there were few or no people on evenings or weekends to hear their joy. Over the next weeks, the Count dropped in twice a week to pay his respects to his mistress - although some people, if they knew, might think of it more as his exercising his droit de seigneur – often on a Wednesday evening if Natalie made the trip into town, and on Saturday in the middle of the day. She went home every time to avoid alerting her mother.

The only aspect the phantom couple couldn't conclude on was Natalie's transport from her job at La Fonderie, which continued positively and above-board, to the apartment in town. It seemed a shame that the Count came so often but that they could not share transport; they would be seen together immediately of course. In the end Natalie found an ordinary fiacre for hire when she was going in to town. Nobody at La Fonderie were any the wiser. Natalie and the count were over the moon with their sexual and emotional fulfilment. Satisfactory practical arrangements – the apartment and how to get there – were in place.

The Mistress (2020)
Robert Butcher (born 1961), as if by Duchien

Two days later, on the Wednesday evening, Natalie appeared at Duchien's address. As instructed she entered the front office, closed the front door and walked through to the atelier.

'Excuse me, Monsieur Duchien. I believe you are expecting me.'

'Good evening, Mademoiselle. What a pleasure to see you here and so punctually.'

Duchien took in the simple but stunning beauty of the young lady, wearing a long dress (her working clothes, not that he knew that) and a light shoulder cloak, brunette hair nicely tied up into a flat bun, in the style of the moment, and a twinkle of the eye. Creating the image of this person would not require Duchien to know her identity. In fact, the abstraction of any identity gave him some frisson, some intrigue, some excitement. Despite his two-year depression, he remembered how he adored female models. This one was beautiful enough that Duchien thought it a pity to be sculpting her fully clothed – she could hardly be out of her teens. He pointed out the raised podium with the chair and a stool where she could pose and went for a large cartridge paper drawing book and some charcoal to start preliminary sketches.

He did not immediately realise what she was doing. In a moment, out of the corner of his eye, he saw that the girl had taken off her cloak and was methodically undoing the buttons of her dress, all the way to the bottom. She took off her belt and let the dress slide off her arms. As Duchien watched, with a mixture of surprise and supressed desire, she folded it neatly and put it on the top of the chest of drawers next to the podium. She did not stop there. She leant against the stool while she took off her black lace-up shoes and stockings, stood up and undid the laces of her one piece undergarment. In a moment she was totally nude and unabashed, standing full frontal in the sightline of an astounded sculptor, with her hands on her hips. She fixed him with her intent gaze and the very slightest of smiles.

'Mademoiselle, I think ... Is it...' stammered Duchien, '...Was it the Count's intention that the statue be of Mademoiselle in the nude? Naked?'

'Yes of course Monsieur Duchien. What is more beautiful than the female body?'

Now Duchien felt some embarrassment. What kind of a married man would commission in secret a sculpture of a girl in the nude?. He recollected that the Count had mentioned that the commission should be a secret from Madame la Comtesse. He alighted briefly on the idea that she was his mistress but discarded it at once; if their affair was a secret he would not want to have a sculpture made It also crossed his mind that the count could be some kind of obsessive who wanted to feast his eyes on the naked body; but would he have the statue at the works, in his private apartment at home, or... he thought as laterally as possible... directly donated to the Musée des Beaux-Arts?'

'Monsieur Duchien is hesitating. I hope there is no problem.'

'No, no, Mademoiselle. I beg you to forgive me. I was just reflecting on where such a statue could be displayed and whether some of the gossips in our community might find it odd to think of the Count commissioning a statue of a young lady in the nude.'

'Yes, Monsieur, but he has sworn you to secrecy I think. I can assure you that the finished work will not be displayed in public and not even to prying eyes. In the fullness of time I think he will be able to tell you the purpose of this work of art.'

'I understand. So... So may I ask your name? The Count did not inform me.'

'I'm sure he will in due course.'

Natalie enjoyed watching him wrestle with her identity and her relationship with the Count.

'Very well. Do please then put yourself fully at ease. May I suggest initially sitting on the stool with your side towards me. I do have some experience of sittings with ladies and I'm sure we can keep in the ill-at-ease to a minimum.'

As he said this, Duchien realised that this young woman was not ill-at-ease at all. She sat on the stool on the podium with one foot still on the floor and one foot dangling. She made no effort to hide her breasts or her sex. She gave the impression it was the most natural thing in the world, to parade herself. So much so that Duchien was aware of the beginnings of the pangs of the hunger that precedes lust as he looked at her scintillating body. He had to remind himself that Cécile, his new-found love, was fully satiating his desires.

Therefore, and as a matter of decorum, he picked up a wooden pole on a stand and put it between her legs (but not touching). An exotic waft of woman delighted his nostrils. He trailed a strand of artificial leaves round the pole, giving an art nouveau feel to the composition.

He went to his sketch pad, extinguished his cigarette – two left in the last packet, having promised Cécile he would give it up – picked up a stick of black charcoal and got to work.

&

Duchien felt a fundamental change in himself, in his attitude and in his physique.

Being able to express himself at the psychologist and to unburden himself of so much of what he had been hiding about the trauma and the loss of his wife and daughter had made him feel more positive. Now he was undertaking a female nude for the first time for three or four years during which he not seen a woman nude, had not touched one, had not kissed one, had not made love. But now when Natalie sat, of course he felt forces stirring within him, as he did when younger.

But even more significant was the affect Cécile was having on him. The strength of his feelings for her gave him to believe he had found a new partner, someone he could love. At the same time, the tender and passionate physical love they had together told him his libido was back.

&

The girl is with me in the atelier. She was stone and now she is real. She has come alive. I know that she is something to do with the Count. Is she his wife? Is she his lover? Is she his daughter? I find this perplexing but it does not worry me. It does not worry the girl. She undresses herself and gives herself to me. She takes me upstairs and I find I have lust for her, for her touching me, for my touching her body, everywhere. She tells me I am erect. She shows me; she makes me look down then and she kisses me there. She takes me in her mouth. I hold her head and marvel with amazement at myself, and at her, at her love for me, at the love-making she wants to give me. My wife and my daughter were in the atelier but I hear them leaving by the door to the street. The girl and I lie naked on the bed having made love. Her face and neck are flushed. My manhood is flaccid now but I'm not embarrassed. The blind accordion-player in the Place Thiers is now Mimi, the waitress at Bernard's café; she smiles at me while she plays. She can see me and she approves. There is a glass of pastis on the bench beside her. She glances at it then at me to offer it to me.

Chapter 33 – Another key in the door

Nancy town centre, Friday 7th October 1892

Natalie had sent me a message to meet after work on Friday, at Bernard's.

I had been Duchien's lover for a couple of weeks and everything pointed to it being the real thing. But I felt so love-struck, tender, vulnerable even, that I had chosen to put off telling my friend. I hoped I could spend an evening with her without it all coming pouring out.

At just a few minutes after five I was at Bernard's, inside against a chilly autumn wind, smart in my working clothes. My work, the Daum glass atelier, was only five minutes' walk away. To my dismay, within moments, an old school friend Thierry Neuville brought his glass and sat down with me. He was a pal of my boyfriend in the middle of last year, Jean-François de la Haye, and his leery and cocky attitude gave the unwanted impression that he thought he knew everything about me and the boyfriend. And what we did.

Natalie was a bit late because of some panic in the office. I could see the dismay in her face when she saw the boy sitting with me, someone she didn't know. She settled into a glass of Moselle white like the two of us and listened into our one-sided conversation. Thierry had to get away from talk of my personal affairs but his presence was nonetheless unwanted. I tried sending Natalie subliminal messages that I wanted rescuing. I saw her eyes lift as if she was attentive. After a few moments I had to resort to tapping the toe of my boot against her heel.

Natalie got the message and interrupted; 'Excuse me, I'm sorry to butt in to your conversation, but I have something so exciting I can't wait. Cécile, I have moved out of my parents' house and I have my own apartment in town.'

'Oh my goodness Natalie, that is so exciting. When did this happen?'

'So recently, just last weekend. I did not have time to tell you yet. I was thinking, it might not be convenient, I was wondering would you like to come and see it? You don't mind do you, Thierry, if I steal Cécile away?' she said, giving him no option to come with us.

'Of course, I would love to.' I jumped to my feet, spilling the boy's wine, grabbed my bag and took Natalie by the arm. She smiled brilliantly with the satisfaction of having read my mind so well. Thierry was left to pay for the drinks.

'This way'. She marched briskly away from the café initially towards Duchien's atelier in the rue Gambetta.

'Was that just a lie? I hope you are not just taking me to Duchien's place for some reason are you?' I had an awful feeling that Natalie was going to crowbar my big Duchien secret out of me by accident. 'Anyway, thank you so much for getting rid of that boy for me.'

'No problem. No, I really do have a new place to live. And that is where we are going.'

Natalie took my hand. My mind whirled with questions. We left Duchien's workshop on the left and turned right into rue Victor Poirel. At number 2 there was a jeweller's shop which had closed as normal at four o'clock on a Friday. The side passage was open to the street, leading to a solid wooden door to which Natalie applied one of the three keys on her green-tassled key ring. The front door gave onto a narrow staircase going up; I followed with bated breath. Another locked door at the top opened into a luxuriously appointed living room with the door to the kitchen and another staircase up to what must have been the bedroom and bathroom. I was as much shocked as impressed.

'How can you afford this. Heavens.'

'Well, I have been earning quite well and my mother helped' said Natalie slightly unconvincingly as she went to the drinks cupboard to pour herself a large glass of Macon, superior to the Moselle they had been drinking at Bernard's. She offered me the sofa then knelt and lit the fire with kindling that had been prepared there in advance. We kept our coats on while the room warmed up.

'This is so amazing. I had no idea that this sort of thing would happen at your young age. Has your Mama got much more money than I ever dreamed?'

'Well, not really but we got a good deal.'

'Yes, trust you Natalie. The one with the business brain.'

We two girls continued enjoying our wine and each other's company. We shared stories about work and plans for the weekend although I was curious as to Natalie's plans in this luxurious apartment. I could not, or did not want to, talk about Duchien.

Something in Natalie nagged me that she was not telling me all.

Indeed, after a quarter of an hour there came the sound that made Natalie blush to the roots and hide her head in her hands. The noise was that of another key turning in the door at the bottom of the stairs. It was clear to me she knew who it would be. Moments later a bearded, well-dressed distinguished-looking man carrying a small valise, breathing deeply, appeared round the door at the top of the stairs and looked round the corner into the room where we were sitting.

It was my father.

Silence.

I was flabbergasted; the surprise was so complete that it hurt. I was angry. I was the butt of a deceit by Natalie in bringing me here without telling me... what? I was confused; what was going on here? What was going on between my father and my best friend? I could not bring myself to make acknowledge the obvious.

I was conscious of my jaw dropping. My father's jaw dropped; then opened to release some stuttering words.

'Good evening Cécile, my dear. Good evening Natalie, err Mademoiselle...' The Count could not even remember her surname. 'Duhamel' said Natalie. 'Yes, Duhamel. Thank you. Natalie Duhamel.' There was another silence except for the whirring of my brain trying to analyse what was going on here. No-one moved.

The silence forced me to ask. 'Tell me, please, that I what I think is happening here is not happening' I blurted, choking back a sob.

'Well, Cécile, sorry about the surprise, and you know that your father is my employer; it's true, he very generously helped me get this apartment.'

'My father...' I retorted. I was angry. 'More like your Père Noël you mean, and if I am guessing right, your paramour... and you cannot even remember each other's names'.

Natalie put her head back in her hands. I had never seen

her blush but now she was crimson red. The deceit of bringing me here was apparently tiny compared to her having an affair, clearly quite a solid one, with my father, her boss.

As the reality hit me, I was red in the face, but with anger. I was angry that my best friend was having an affair with my father. I was angry she had not told me. I was angry I found out accidentally. I was angry that their affair was a slightly sordid juxtaposition with my burgeoning and true love for my sculptor.

My father closed the door and came to sit by the fire. After a moment of inspecting the carpet he asked 'What do I have to do to get a drink around here?' Natalie got up to pour him some Macon.

'Anything stronger?' Natalie poured him a glass of Bourbon whiskey, imported from America at great expense. It was apparent to me that Natalie was in the habit of offering him this tipple. I sat expectantly, red-faced, oscillating between curiosity and fury, staring at my father.

'Well?'

'I'm sorry Cécile. I apologise. I did not want to let you know this way. How shall I put it?' Le Comte Geoffroi Orlowski started off hesitantly, searching for words and hesitating before the start of each thought. 'Your mother and I, Cécile, well I know you have noticed, do not have a relationship which one could call warm. It may be cordial, yes, but Leonora, your mother, is now a difficult person to get on with, to like. I know you feel the same because you mentioned only at Christmas and several times since. Difficult to get on with, difficult to like, and impossible to love. I can tell you, my daughter, a mature young lady of 21 years of age, that it has been many years since the love between your mother and me has extended as far as the bedroom. Every man has urges. He has to love and he has to be loved, I mean, also, in the … in the sense other than Platonic. Many women have the same urges. I have had the honour and pleasure to be exposed...' I coughed '...yes, sorry, I will chose another word, to be able to work alongside such an intelligent and beautiful woman as your good friend Natalie, Natalie Duhamel.'

Natalie's eyes stayed fixed on the floor, avoiding contact with mine. But she might have noticed, from my tone, that I was giving the first signs of beginning to enjoy, sadistically, my father's embarrassment.

I was actually still furious at the deception but the fury was being mollified by the thought of my own romps with the sculptor, fifteen years my senior. There was a risk of the pot having black thoughts about the kettle.

When Natalie at last raised her eyes to meet mine I could tell that she was hoping that I was beginning to accept the idea of she and her father being lovers; I could just about handle the distasteful idea of my father having sex... but with Natalie?

The Count continued 'It has been some moments now that Natalie and I have had a relationship of, how shall I say, of love and intimacy, of true friendship and mutual respect...' '...Of lust' I interrupted, glancing at Natalie with distaste. She lifted her head a bit to see my expression. There was the slightest of twinkles. I did not twinkle her back but I think the grimace of distaste evaporated from my mouth as we looked at each other.

The Count was still flustered and red.

'So, this is the right time to explain further, to you my dearest daughter, my faithful, bright and beautiful daughter, whom I would never want to hurt in any way, that it is now my intention to spend as much time as possible with Natalie. While respecting my honourable duties to my wife, your mother, and my household, I have been studying with the counsel of professionals experienced in these matters what can be done about my marriage and whether there is a way to, shall we say, in the present conjuncture, all things being equal, to terminate it equably. It is slightly difficult for Natalie and me to find out that the door is not all the way open to such a solution but we will be patient.'

'Papa, how long do you think you could have kept this a secret? This is such a shock. Does Mama know?'

'No, I must tell her presently. The upcoming dinner with Monsieur and Madame Prevost and the Daum brothers and their families makes it impossible to get her attention. I will tell her as soon as possible. Only then will I know what can be done about a divorce. In the meantime I have Natalie, to whom I am devoted, by my side.' He got up, sat on the couch with her and put a large ill-at-ease arm round her.

'How long has this been going on?'

'A month. Five weeks.'

'Well you don't hang about do you. City-centre love nest already.' Natalie flushed with indignation but thought better of saying anything. She knew it was true.

My mind was racing. I thought further for a moment, then asked 'Papa; what makes you think that Mama will permit a divorce?'

'Well, that is a question which is as perspicacious as any question my perspicacious daughter has ever asked. Natalie knows that I, for the moment, have not been able to judge the moment when the Countess might be pre-disposed to agreeing. This is the reason why I have not told her about Natalie. We seem to be committed to the long grind of a double life unless some miracle comes to pass and we find that your mother has a generous and forgiving side after all.'

'A generous side? Mama?'

Natalie drew a long breath and faced me. 'I had not intended to show you the new apartment yet. My rational self told me I should wait till my relationship with your father and the arrangements at the apartment had settled. But when the situation with the boy in the café presented itself, the easiest way to get you away from him was to give in to my emotional self which was screaming to show you the apartment immediately. Geoffroi said he was travelling today and would come on Saturday morning, tomorrow. I am so sorry about this unhappy turn of events, believe me.'

'Yes, but it does not change the facts. You and my father are having an affair. This is quite a shock'.

Of course I thought of Duchien again. I let the image of his body on mine, and the places our spirits visited together, wash through my mind. When I transposed those thoughts to Natalie and my father, the image was not quite so alluring. I could not think that their love was so romantic or so passionate. Or was it? Natalie was not one for accepting the banal, certainly not in bed.

A further problem presented itself: when was I going to tell Natalie about me and Duchien? When was I going to tell my parents? With this in mind it was easier to forgive these two curious love birds sitting with me.

I thought I would leave them to it. I made my farewells, with brief kisses on both cheeks of friend and of father, and set off for the station.

Where the rue Victor Poirel meets the rue Gambetta, Duchien's place was straight ahead. I stopped and look at my reflection in an office window. I looked well. I looked beautiful. I looked fervent, as if my life depended on my every act. I was looking in on myself from outside. I wondered what Duchien saw in me; what he would see in me now, this evening, this very moment.

I crossed the road, entered his front door, locked it from the inside and called out 'Duchien, it's me.'

I walk confidently down the road from my bedroom to the workshop. The statues are all there. My women of stone are unmoving, waiting, respectful and beautiful. They are all female, luscious, smiling and encouraging me. I cannot choose the one I want to have. They come to me and take it in turns so I must take each of them one after the other. As each act is finished the girl floats away and disappears. Then there is nobody left. I feel a rampant desire. My libido is pulsating in me and round my body. The winding road, the hill and the stones on the road retreat into the distance. I have finished my sculpture of Cécile, full size in bronze, cast by the hand of the Count himself, her father, at La Fonderie. The statue is alive. It is the white flesh and the sweet lips of Cécile. I take her. I take her for mine. The Count is there with us and he smiles benignly before leaving with Natalie through the office to the street.

Chapter 34 – Jean-Marc and a friend of mine

As most Saturdays, I had taken breakfast at seven with Jean-Marc. That gave us a slightly more leisurely moment than on weekdays, to be ready for our usual trip to Nancy for my errands. Even though I was working the whole week at Daum, Saturdays were still the errand days, by habit. Today I had something extra in mind. My secret was safe. I had seen my father only at meals when my mother was also present, so there had been no talk. Natalie and I had made no contact.

Jean-Marc and I got into the trap with Hubert and were on the road before eight. We went initially to Daum in the town centre where I had to spend a couple of hours or more organising some files and filling out the day ledger for sub-contractors, mostly the incoming work from designer contractors like Duchien. I also had to keep the suppliers' book written up, mostly about shipments from the suppliers of raw goods including silica sand, vitrification materials and colouring agents like limestone and soda ash. More recently we bought clay and the iron oxide needed to make faïence, pottery glazed so that the painted decoration could be detailed and brilliant; Daum had purchased a very-high-temperature firing oven to give this result. My weekend tasks were not the creative ones except for the stimulus of meeting the freelance artists and peeking into their work to see how the new styles developed. I continued to do watercolours at home to record what I saw in the factory and in the artists' work. On the weekdays there was time for me to create my own designs for Daum.

Jean-Marc was perfectly attuned to waiting patiently while I visited the Daum office, usually sitting on the seat of the two-wheeled trap, whittling a stick with a penknife or watching the world go by. He was happy with his own company – but also with mine. If Hubert was not with him he was running his territory-marking patrol round the entrance to the factory gate, sniffing and marking his territory with a pee here and there, normally within sight of his master.

At about 11 o'clock I jumped up beside Jean-Marc with a packet to deliver, giving him a big smile. He was pleased to get the sense that I was happy. Hubert lolloped back, jumped up and added to the sense of friendship by pushing his way to sit between the two of us; he gave me an affectionate push on the thigh with his nose. I gave him a pat. So I gave Jean-Marc a pat too, and a brief hug.

'Next, my dear brother, this vase to La Maison de la Verrerie, then to Sebastian Memère for a pick up.'

As the pony trotted merrily through the streets, I enjoyed feeling the joy Jean-Marc had in driving and in being with me. Although I had decided not to tell Natalie about my love for Duchien, and certainly not my father who would be obliged to tell my mother, I wanted to let my brother in on my excitement. I leaned in a friendly way towards him.

'After that, would you like to meet a new friend of mine? Somebody I think you will like.'

Jean-Marc grunted, keeping his eyes on the road. That was his way of expressing agreement. 'Go on brother, say yes'.

'Alright then sister, yes, if you want' said Jean-Marc in his usual hesitant and wayward voice. 'But tell me who this person is.'

'He's a man, dear brother, and he is a sculptor. I have met him through the work with Daum because he supplies designs for them. I have known him since June last year. His workshop is behind Bernard's so that is where I go sometimes when you are waiting there.'

'So?'

'Yes, well, indeed. I think have fallen in love with him. This is very recent and I find it overwhelming. My feelings are so strong. I have never felt this before. And I do not know what the future holds except that my heart is jumping for joy.'

'Jumping for joy, ay, sister? I see you sitting perfectly still.'

I laughed. 'Are you happy for me?'

'Yes, I suppose I'm happy for you, depending on whether I like him. I'm not happy for me.'

'Oh, dearest brother, I should have thought of that. I will adore you with all my heart as I always have done and always will do until death us do part. I promise promise promise.'

I knew what Jean-Marc was thinking. His best friend in the whole world (except Hubert, who did not speak in the normal sense) was me. I had just told him that another man had stolen my affections. Having overheard on more than one occasion the way in which I spoke to my friend Natalie, Jean-Marc could imagine that this new relationship might go as far as the cuddling, kissing and touching activity which left him struggling with his emotions in the dark of his mind. Whether or not I and this man had progressed to that stage he did not know. What exercised him was the fact that I would have less affection left for him. Somebody was stealing his place in my heart. But this was not something he could express easily, certainly not right now with the news so fresh. He put a brave face on it.

'What is he called?'

'Duchien.'

'Duchien the sculptor, I know about him. Did he not do the statue of Papa for the office and Mama for the Château?'

'Yes, exactly that. It's him.'

'That's a funny name. What is his family name?'

'No, Duchien is his family name. He is only ever known as Duchien. He lost his wife and daughter in a road accident a few years ago.'

'I know that. Antoinette went to the funeral.'

'How do you remember these things? You are special.'

'Do you kiss him?'

'Ah... yes. I do. Well... I have.'

'I won't like him until I know his first name.'

And so it was that Jean-Marc, Hubert and I parked up outside Bernard's sometime after 11:30 to walk round the little street to see Duchien. I made certain to pop into the café to salute everybody. There were already quite a few clients so Mimi bustled around. Franz and Marcel stood at the bar and Bernard himself, as seemed to be always the case, was drying a glass with a white serviette. They acknowledged me with a wave or a 'good morning Cécile'. The little Saturday family went on its way to meet my lover. We were unaware of what was unfolding at the Château.

Chapter 35 – The Countess: retribution

Château de Lay-Saint-Christophe, the same day

The Countess enjoyed inviting some of her better friends to coffee at her stately home. That is to say, the friends who had not yet abandoned her for her arriviste attitudes, her bad manners, her Eastern European accent and her outbursts of rage.

On this very-same Saturday, when her two children were together in Nancy with the dog, she had nine ladies round. At the end of the coffee morning, as the graceful ladies walked out of the hall to their waiting carriages, Ursula Poniatowski, the self-styled Princess Poniatowski, lingered. She took the Countess by the arm and turned her back towards the salon.

'I did want to say, my dear, out of earshot of our other friends, how dreadfully sorry I am to hear the news. You must be feeling terrible, that mixture of rage and sadness.'

The Countess Leonora Orlowski stopped and turned to face the source of this incongruous comment.

'Yes, quite, my dear. But forgive me, what on earth are you talking about?'

'Yes,' continued the Princess, 'I remember so well the weeks I was in denial before I knew that everybody else knew and that all there was for it was to call my lawyer. Of course in my case, I cannot speak for yours, the facts of the matter were so clear that my husband did not even contest the divorce proceedings and I have lived, as you will, a fruitful new life after the separation.'

Of course the hostess felt obliged to play dumb. As the blood boiled in her head at the realisation of what she was learning, she was having to rationalise what to say in response. This lady, almost a stranger, was apparently telling her that she knew her husband was being unfaithful; was... having an affair; was cheating on her, while she, his wife, was not the slightest bit aware of any facts. Yes, some late nights at the office, once or twice an unscheduled trip into town, and some noticeable improvement recently in his choice of clothing and in the care he took with dressing for work.

This was terrible; somebody somewhere was talking about her husband having an affair and she was the last to know. The shame of the ignorance was almost as bad as the anger at her husband's behaviour.

When she had dismissed Poniatowski with some 'Yes, yes thank you my dear, I am handling this promptly and in my own way - I do wish you a good day', she closed the front door quietly and contained her rage until she got back into the orangerie. Then she took the one remaining tray of tea things. Screaming and red-faced, she hurled it through the window.

Now she continued to let her fury stoke up. She was stoking it up herself.

She paced up and down for a few moments tussling with the evidence and with decisions about her next steps. This was unacceptable. This was the beginning of the unravelling of her oh so perfect life. This was certainly the end of her marriage to the Count as she knew it. She had maybe thought in vague terms about what infidelity on his part would mean, but now that it was upon them she was at a total loss.

What a stupid man. So arrogant. So full of his own insignificant success in business. And yet he seemed incapable of looking after the element of his life the most dear to him and the most important: his wife. He would not even support her in her plans for Cécile's marriage. She now doubted his blood line and took the opinion that all he had done for her was to sire a son who was clearly backward. She could not countenance for a second that Jean-Marc's handicaps could have been the product of her own family's genes. She felt ignored and betrayed.

All these thoughts ran through her mind as her temper rose uncontrollably.

She stomped in her fury through to the kitchen, cursing, swearing and shouting for Antoinette at the top of her voice.

The housekeeper had wisely taken shelter in the kitchen and was cowering against the hob with the cook and the maid. She had enough experience of the Countess's violent tantrums to want to keep out of it, but here was her ladyship in full flight and in full fury.

'Antoinette, you snivelling cur. Come here and play your role in bringing the Count to his senses ... or to justice. You, of all people, you who knows everything that goes on in this house and in town, why did you fail to tell me that the Count has taken a mistress? Why? Tell me.'

'Oh, I...Madame...' started Antoinette.

'Spit it out woman. Of course you know.'

Antoinette feared that she could not deny that only last Monday Franz and Marcel had been telling her in the bar about a young and good-looking dark-haired lady who had been seen with the Count on foot walking along the pavement past Bernard's. Then of course they asked Antoinette what she knew about this mysterious lady. The fact that they had seen her more than a couple of times gave rise to the suspicion that the Count was in a relationship. Antoinette, knowing the parlous state of their marriage over the last 19 years, since Jean-Marc was born, could not summon up any criticism of the Count. From the human point of view, and as she preferred him infinitely to the Countess, she found herself warm towards the idea of his extra-marital relationship, possibly even jealous. Antoinette had never been married but she appreciated that all men had lust, or indeed the need for love. She certainly did not find it un-natural on his part.

'I, yes, well Madame la Comtesse, I have heard recently from friends in town that Monsieur Le Comte has been seen with a young lady. I am so sorry Madame. This information is so recent and so vague that I have not taken it upon myself to mention it to your good self. I'm sure that, if I were to see anything with my own eyes, I would immediately have informed you.'

'A young lady! My God, woman, and you didn't even tell me. And I thought of you as a faithful servant. You are despicable and treasonous. You have sided with the enemy and you will pay for this.'

'No, Madame, I...'

'Where is the Count this morning?'

'He, I think, did he not go to Metz with Monsieur Schmidt and Monsieur Turcat from the company to meet the iron-ore providers? He certainly left the house after breakfast. He was picked up by the coach of one of the two gentlemen.'

'Ah, the scheming bastard. I shall have him later upon his return. Now, about the woman. You will tell me now where she is. I will go immediately and settle this once and for all. The count is not going to have extra-marital relations. I will not have it. It is not legal. It is not what he vowed to do on his wedding day. It is demeaning to me. I will not have it. Now tell me where I can find her.'

'I do not even know her name, Madame. I know that she has been seen near Bernard's and the Place Thiers, and I think my friend said they had seen her there on her own. Maybe she lives in the neighbourhood?'

'Go on. Go on, and maybe you will keep your job.'

'More than that, Madame , I... Let me think now. Was there not talk of Duchien as a destination for the young lady. Does she maybe know him. The sculptor?

'I know who he is, in the name of God. I sat for him you stupid vagrant. Go on.'

'I, I don't know what to suggest, Madame. We could, I mean you could go there and make enquiries.'

'Get the driver, harness the horses. You are coming with me you snivelling little insect, and we leave in five minutes.

&

The Countess screamed abuse at the driver and Antoinette all the way from home to the centre of Nancy; ten kilometres of misery and fear for her employees. For her they were totally complicit in this savage crime by the Count. She went as far as to accuse them of procuring the woman for him and of aiding and abetting their secret relationship. Neither could deny the fact that there was a relationship, but they tried to defend themselves against the accusations of putting them together in the first place. This drove the Countess to further rage. Her face was puffed up, her breathing heavy and her eyes watering with tears and fury.

Antoinette offered a further piece of information which, if she had kept it in, would cast on her further blame when the Countess found out. 'Madame la Comtesse, there is one further piece of information which might be useful to you. It is not impossible that you might have seen the young lady from a distance. I am told that she works in the finance department at La Fonderie. She might have been at the opening of Monsieur Le Comte's statue at the works. I think she also was also at the Château once or twice by cab to deliver financial papers to the Président Directeur Général.'

'Why did you not tell me this immediately you lying treasonous wretch? Yes, now I know exactly who she is. Quite tall, dark hair the face of a harlot and a body to match. It takes a hollow and classless man to fall for a bitch like that. This will not continue. I will not have it. I will find her and I will deal with it.' Antoinette and the driver shuddered at the thought of what might happen but said nothing.

Presently they arrived at the Place Thiers where there was some extra parking space opposite Bernard's. Antoinette spotted the empty trap in which Jean-Marc and his sister would be doing the Saturday rounds but she didn't mention it to the Countess.

The Countess marched straight across the road, making a two-horse cab shy and change direction at the last moment, towards the café. She shouted belligerently as she lurched into the café to the surprise of and horror of the staff and the clientele.

'Where is that man? Tell me you stupid people, where is the man who thinks he's my husband, and where is the whore that he has taken to his bed? May the devil take the both of them. Tell me where they are.'

Marcel and Franz glanced at each other then quickly at Bernard. They probably knew more then they wanted at this moment in time. Mimi had a big tray of dirty crockery and continued to the back minding her own business. Marcel had the least to lose and was the first to summon up the courage to speak.

'Good morning Madame La Comtesse. I wish we could help but we have seen neither Monsieur Le Comte this morning, nor the person you might be seeking.'

'So, you atrocious piece of trash, are you admitting that you have seen them at other times and that you know that they are complicit in an illegal and sordid relationship. And don't say 'person' when you know full well it's a woman; it is a she. She is a prostitute, a common whore, a female of no class who has no role in the life of my husband. Where are they then?'

Franz was as bewildered as he was insulted. 'I can only inform Madame what I just said; they have not been here today. We have seen neither of them.'

'Well, I see that deceit and lies are spread across the whole of the town. I'm going to the atelier of Duchien, the sculptor, and if I find you are lying I will come back and beat you myself, call the police and have you prosecuted for obstructing the course of justice; and aiding and abetting a criminal act.'

The Countess, blathering, built herself up into an orgasm of rage, her body shaking and her hands uncontrollable. She was perspiring from the face, under her armpits and down her back. She wheeled round, barged a chair out of the way, headed out of the door and turned left down the rue Gambetta; the Countess knew exactly where Duchien's atelier was because she had been there twice for sittings. Antoinette followed at a safe distance, followed by Franz and Marcel at another half a block. Marcel still had his cognac glass, now empty, in his hand. Mimi and Bernard were following.

She crashed open the door of the front office, screaming abuse at Duchien, my father and 'his prostitute', none of whom she could see. Her dishevelled hair stuck to her forehead and eyes making it difficult for her to see clearly.

This was just a couple of minutes after my brother and I, with the dog, had arrived to introduce Jean-Marc to my sculptor. Duchien had nipped upstairs at the back to put on a presentable shirt. For this reason I was standing at the desk leafing through some dinner plate designs by Duchien to show Jean-Marc. Despite having heard my mother coming through the door, I misjudged the reason for her mood. I thought she might be having a go at me again for choosing Duchien over the arranged marriage, even though I could not think how she knew it was Duchien. I turned briefly to glance at her but immediately, as a gesture of disdain, moved my attention back to the designs. I had totally misunderstood what was going on. The Countess saw through her bulging, manic, sweaty eyes the back of a young brunette, hair in a bun, slender, medium-build, long dark blue dress – exactly how she remembered the girl from La Fonderie. She did not for a moment realise it was me. Her rage coming to a climax, she picked up off the table at the entrance a one-quarter size bronze of a nude woman on a weighty plinth, and raised it behind her head as she lurched towards the woman at the desk, me. As she swung it forward with both hands, aiming at the head of the person she thought was her husband's mistress, Jean-Marc screamed in horror and threw himself towards his mother to protect me.

The 15 kilogram lump of bronze hit Jean-Marc on the left temple with a sickening crunch of shattering bone. He slumped to the desk then slid to the floor. I turned to face the onslaught too late to alert my mother to the mistaken identity. I saw only the impact and then my brother in a pool of his own blood on the floor. The blow had killed him instantaneously. I fell to my knees and in a futile gesture tried to revive him by shaking his shoulders and calling his name. The dog waited till I had stopped shaking him then, in his turn, nudged his master's thigh with his nose.

The Countess, aware now that it was me, had dropped to her knees with her head lowered and the murder weapon on the floor in both her hands. She sobbed in heaving sighs of agony. Antoinette had seen everything; she put a hand on the Countess's shoulder and said her name but she appeared to be comatose and unresponsive.

Franz, Marcel and the driver Binder, had now caught up Antoinette and tried to take in the situation. They could not immediately understand what had happened. Franz cried 'Jean-Marc, is he dead? Why has the Countess killed her own son? What is this travesty? What have you done, you insane woman?'

Antoinette said simply, in a voice full of pain, 'She mistook her own daughter for her husband's mistress. In her fury she swung the statuette to kill the woman. Jean-Marc saw his mother coming, jumped towards her to prevent her attacking and took the blow to his own head. History will relate that he saved his sister's life.' Antoinette then put her arm round me, said that my brother must be dead and quietly expressed her condolences and her regrets. There did not seem to be much else to say.

France and Marcel were stupefied but they had to jump into action because the Countess got to her feet and started staggering to the door to make her escape.

'Stop her, Marcel. Stop her, Franz. Hold the Countess.' Antoinette then called to Binder and the half dozen people who had assembled outside, straining their necks, on hearing the commotion. Bernard and Mimi were there. 'Call the Gendarmes. Call the police. Get somebody here and an ambulance for Jean-Marc in case he can be saved.'

Two of the onlookers and Bernard wheeled round and ran up to the Place Thiers. There was always a gendarme on duty round the station. Franz and Marcel took the Countess by the arms. Antoinette got a chair and sat her down on it. I was still kneeling, sobbing, wailing and calling my brother's name. Blood was soaking into the knees of my dress. It was warm, clammy and sticky. The dog joined me, whimpering at first and then howling when my wailing was pitched higher.

Duchien was as confused and horrified as everyone to come downstairs to this scene of death and desolation in his own workshop office. Luckily he had got the gist of Antoinette's explanation. He went down on his knees and put his arms round me. I was so glad he was there. My rock. I raised my head enough to put my tearful face into his neck, holding on tight. He held me tight in a warm bear-hug and kissed my face and neck despite the full force of my wailing in his ears. When we looked back at this moment, we realised that this was the definitive act of bonding, the moment at which our lives became inseparable, the moment at which he was able to save me from a life of solitude, damnation and guilt; Jean-Marc had died saving my life. I had been the main force in overcoming Duchien's demons; he now would be able to return me the favour.

All he could do at the time was to console me. He did have to shuffle me back from Jean-Marc's body because the copious blood from his head was pooling towards my knees. There was obviously nothing that could be done for him.

The police arrived in a couple of minutes. They only needed to glance round the office and hear the initial reports from Franz and Bernard to know what had happened. Without hesitation they handcuffed the Countess and started walking her away to custody.

Binder had walked quietly back to check on the horses.

The ambulance did not come quickly. After a quarter of an hour, I felt Duchien shifting as his knees got numb; he got up and helped me to my feet. He encouraged the dog to move away from the pool of blood because further bloody footsteps, that is, paw-prints, round the office would be one more thing to have to clean up. When the ambulance did arrive after half an hour the medics confirmed the absence of pulse and that they would be taking Jean-Marc to the mortuary.

My father only found out about all this that evening when he returned from Metz. Natalie was in Paris for the weekend for a reunion and did not find out till she got to her office at La Fonderie on Monday morning. She still did not know, even then, about me and Duchien.

☙

Chapter 36 – The Countess: outpouring

Château de Lay-Saint-Christophe, Sunday 11th December 1892

The death of my brother two months ago, the savage act by my mother and her imprisonment awaiting trial weighed heavily. I cried myself to sleep. I cried on Natalie's shoulder. I looked down at my hands when talking quietly with my father.

I cried naked in Duchien's arms. I was delirious with love for Duchien. Everything about the tenderness of his spirit; his kindness to me; the body of the man; his passion. Our affair was red hot and tender at the same time.

Ah, Duchien. He saved me. He saved me from succumbing totally to grief. He always found the mot juste, the way of saying something which supported me and brought me closer to him. Lying alongside him one morning before getting up, my hand wandering across his chest, he wanted to know about the dog. Hubert, at the age of only nine years, died of a broken heart on the morning of the funeral of Jean-Marc his master, on the 31st of October, only ten days after the tragic and fatal attack by the Countess. He was asleep in his bed, dead, in Jean-Marc's room in the stables when Antoinette went looking for him. They buried him with Jean-Marc. My brother had been inseparable from his dog in life, and it was so to be in death. When I thought of one I thought of the other so I missed Hubert too.

Duchien was curious about Jean-Marc and whether he could have had any medical or psychiatric help for his introverted character and learning difficulties. Did he have depressions? Duchien knew what a positive effect Bernheim had had on his life, but he did not know whether it would have been applicable to my dear brother who he never met properly. He asked me whether his parents had ever asked for professional help. My answer was of course a wistful no.

All my self-pity, my crying and my leaning on Papa, Natalie and Duchien for support had an upside as well. I did not cry myself to sleep alone much because I was with Duchien so often. Crying in Duchien's arms released tangible emotional energy from him in my favour, triggered not just by his love for me but also by the miseries of death in the family he had been through. I felt my heart supported by him and our love-making was all the more intense. We had a standing joke for a while that if I wanted some rousing sex, all I had to do was have a quick blub in his presence. I felt close to Natalie and respected her counsel. My father did everything he could to assuage my pain and I began to find out more about his past and my mother's. I had a job I loved, in a great company, in my chosen profession. I realised with the passage of time that I had every reason to be delighted about my life.

I was at the Duchien's place as often as possible. Because he was walking distance from Daum, my employer, it was more convenient to stay there on weekday nights. My father was quick to understand my need to be with my man even if he did not broadcast widely the fact that I was effectively living with him out of wedlock; but he did not really have a leg to stand on as his affair with Natalie was such that she was of course sleeping at the Château with him, probably most of the time. It could have been embarrassing when I was at home, with the thought of her in my father's bed, but I loved her enough to see that she had found happiness in the man she had chosen, whether or not she would be able to marry him in the future. The shock of finding out about their affair was allayed by the warmth of their relationship now and the conniving winks she would send discreetly but often in my direction in the presence of the Count. The winks said my father was the real thing as far as she was concerned, and not just emotionally; our intimate conversations confirmed this. My father was clearly very happy, even motivated in his new life. He seemed ten years younger. Natalie agreed.

I quite often stayed Saturday night back at home. Duchien was not somebody to go out dancing regularly or to go out drinking in the bars, so I had no obligation to him at the weekend; only desire! Duchien was fine with giving me some space and he did not want to be overnight in the Château. I was happy to go back home alone, get my clothes washed, eat some proper meals, rest my body, pamper myself, sit, read, talk.... and bathe.

The new bath room was particularly appealing to me, part of my parents' suite of rooms. With my mother locked away and out of the picture, Papa invited me to use it whenever I wanted. He had recently had a big white metal and ceramic bath fitted with running hot and cold water from two fitted taps. The water was heated by the cooker in the kitchen, which was kept alight all day with wood, and stored in an insulated copper tank in the attic; the warm water flowed up into the tank of its own accord, warm water being lighter than cold. He always liked to have the latest luxury although we did not have electricity yet because we were too far from the mains supply in the valley and Papa did not want the noise and smell of our own generator. Anyway, the hot water was a spectacular luxury as far as I was concerned. Lying in a warm bath, water up to my neck, I felt my troubles ebb way. I enjoyed the touch of the flannel and the suds of the soap even if the sensations made me yearn to be back with Duchien again; I felt the smile on my lips and the warmth in my heart. Natalie understood those sensations and encouraged me to bathe often, sometimes twice in a weekend.

I was up for breakfast one Sunday and happy to be with Papa and Natalie. The talk came round to my mother. 'I was at the prison in town on Wednesday with the avocat to see your mother. I cannot say she sent you her love but she does think of you.'

I did not have an answer to that. I thought of her every day, with mixed feelings. I knew I did not love her but she was my mother nonetheless. My father continued. 'I have explained to her how you and Jean-Marc happened to be in Duchien's front office that day and how close you are now to the sculptor.' I wondered, but did not ask, whether she had demanded to know about his affair with Natalie, which of course was the cause of her outburst which ended with her son's death. 'She has been denied bail again. Her avocat is warning us that she might not get let off lightly.'

That thought troubled me deeply. 'What would that mean in practice?'

'We cannot be sure, my dearest, but of course it's worrying. Murder carries the death penalty, as it does in many parts of the world, unless there are clear attenuating circumstances. Even then manslaughter is punishable with life imprisonment in most cases, sometimes without the possibility of release.'

I glanced at Natalie. She had lowered her head and her eyes appeared to be closed. This meant for her that the Count would remain legally bound to his wife even when she was shut away in prison. Natalie would be tied to a life of living with him out of wedlock; the thoughts of the legal issues, the status of their children, if they had any, and their emotional well-being troubled her.

'That's terrible' was all I could say.

'Would you like to come and visit her next time I go?'

I let the question hang.

'Forgive me, dearest, but I think maybe you should.'

'Yes. Maybe I should.'

I had no idea what could be said. I found my feelings towards her so conflicted and mixed up. Was I meant to show her some warmth? Was I meant to forgive her the atrocious crime, the murder, killing her own son? What could she tell me I didn't know? What could she say that gave me any peace with what happened? But I was her daughter. I was worried by the fact that I had her genes. I had seen no evidence during my life that I had her anger gene, thank God, but maybe it would emerge at some time in the future. The thought horrified me. It was a great comfort that Duchien often said to me that he would never hurt me and that he would protect me from any harm. But would I sometime hurt someone else?

There was much I did not know about my mother's early story. I wondered whether she would open up and tell me about her childhood and how she got to be in Metz when war broke out. I wondered whether she would show any remorse. My curiosity was a factor in the decision to go. I glanced at Natalie for support. She inclined her head to give me a nod.

'I will come, Papa. I am frightened at the thought of such a meeting, but I think I should come.'

He smiled weakly.

෪

Execution outside Charles II Prison, Nancy, 1890

Light snow was falling. We drove slowly, just my father and me, in the covered coach to the prison in the northern part of Nancy so not too far from Lay-Saint-Christophe. Binder was driving and he seemed competent and inscrutable as always. The Charles III Prison was dilapidated and dirty. It had a reputation for the worst conditions of hygiene and a high mortality rate among inmates. Luckily my mother was in a cell of her own in the wing for women and she was living in sparse but clean conditions. We were allowed into her cell. Chairs had been provided. We were obliged to be with the avocat. Papa let me bring her up-to-date with what had happened in my life since October. I found myself telling her I was in love with Duchien and spending as much time with him as possible. Her body language and her face showed revulsion and anger, but she held her tongue. I told her how much I missed Jean-Marc. I had the courage to say I thought she had committed an awful, awful act. I told her Hubert had died. Then, because I had related the death of a four-legged friend, I started sobbing.

She leant towards me from her bed where she was sitting and put her hands round mine. I found it difficult to realise that she was going to be apologetic.

'I am sorry, Cécile. I am truly sorry. I cannot think what drove me to such a rage. I cannot say how it was that I came to kill your brother. The memory of the whole day is very vague and I find it difficult to understand my emotional state and what actually happened. I am sorry.'

There was silence. There was nothing I could say to that.

'There is so much I want to tell you about my early life and who I am. It does not give me any excuses for what I did but I want to give you the opportunity to know me as your father does.'

'Yes. I suppose I would like that. You are my mother. Knowing some more, related in your own voice, would help me come to terms with what has happened.'

'I have been thinking a lot about my childhood. I was called Blanca then, did you know? It means 'white'. You know I did not even have a proper home. We were always travelling. Both my parents would pick fruit or vegetables during the harvest season. At other times of the year we would be at markets working for farmers who had cattle, crops or vegetables to herd or transport to sales. The winter was the worst and we went back to my father's home village south of Prague where his brother let us use some rooms at the end of his house. My father Boguslaw was a ferocious man. He killed a labourer in a drunken brawl when I was eight. I saw him hit my mother from time to time as his frustrations and rage with his life boiled over. My mother Ludmila was beautiful. I think I must have taken her looks but his emotional make up. I must have been a mistake, an unwanted pregnancy, because I always felt like an unwanted child. I had no siblings. I had a cousin who I quite liked and she let me sleep in her room when we were there. I thought of nothing but getting away from my father and our terrible nomadic life. I did get away from my father but I failed to get away from the nomadic life.'

'What did I do? I survived. It was not easy. In my teens and early twenties you can imagine I was subject to all sorts of abuses and scrapes but I had enough aggression to look after myself. I worked at whatever came my way.'

It did not seem that she wanted to give details of her early life. I can only speculate what she did for all those years. Did she continue working on the land like her parents? I doubted it. With her good looks she could have been smiled on by a well-off gentleman and got employment with a family. She could have been a waitress, an artist's muse or, at the extreme, a courtesan. I found the latter idea neither surprised me nor disgusted me, in her case. How she ended up travelling with the army she didn't say.

'When the Prussian army mobilised I must have been near Königsberg; a regiment just marched into my life. I was 27. I was a cook's assistant for a while. At least I got something to eat and somewhere to sleep. When we started the march against the French in the spring of 1870 I just went with them. To free myself from the unwanted attention of this and that soldier I was not ungrateful for a relationship with a high-ranking General; Franz Von der Heyde. I was treated as his wife; life was good for a few months. I think it was him who came up with the idea of calling me Countess; it was good for appearances with his senior colleagues.

Prussian Soldiers Escorting French Prisoners of War,
Metz 1870 [1888]
Gaston Claris (1843-1899)

But war is brutal. He was killed in one of the battles with the French near Metz. His aide-de-camp and I had to get his body and bury it as the army moved on. That aide-de-camp? You know him, Cécile. That's Binder, your father's man, who still works for us.'

I was astonished. 'Binder? You knew him before father?'

'Yes. Without him I might not have survived. I realised I needed him to get out of the predicament, travelling with an army when my... when my General had just been killed. Binder felt some loyalty to me because I had saved him when he was arrested on some trumped-up charge, stealing some things which were ours already. There we were, in the middle of nowhere, the army having moved on. The horses had been taken so we walked according to Binder's sense of direction, east towards the Moselle then south away from Metz. Then I made a chance encounter which would set the course for the best 20 years of my life.'

'We arrived at an inn on the main road from Metz to Nancy. It is still there. The Relais du Nord at Arry. Several carriages were already there and a smell of food emanating from the inn. Travellers were coming from every direction. I was given the one remaining seat at a small table with a young gentleman. He was polite and welcoming.'

She smiled and paused. My father looked up momentarily and she addressed him.

'It's like yesterday. I chose the plat du jour which you had already started eating, lapin chasseur.'

Papa interjected '...with sauerkraut and potatoes'.

She continued. 'He had a gentile French accent and he spoke German too. He was Geoffroi of course, your father.' She continued looking at the Count and he returned her gaze with more pity than happiness. She looked back at me. I was speechless.

'Your father's real name was Marcel de Hénin-Liétard, born of a good family in Metz.'

'Marcel, Papa, Marcel? I never knew.'

'Yes. You know the Banque Commerciale Hénin de Metz, Cécile? That was founded by your grandfather. He was generous enough to make your father a modest loan to start up, with a business partner, a steel retailing and distribution business in a small warehouse at Montigny-lès-Metz by the southbound railway about two kilometres from the city walls. Seven years later when I met him, he was still only twenty-three but the business was profitable and expanding. Is that correct dearest?'

The Count, or Marcel, took up the story. 'Yes. But then the Franco-Prussian war came. The arrival of the Germans was a threat to any business in the area, especially a small one; at best we would be serving the interests of an occupying force and at worst we would be ex-appropriated and penniless. I had no confidence in the French repelling the superior invading army – it turned out I was right – so the thought of business as usual did not feature. I was in higher spirits than others in Metz because I knew how I could get out of Metz quickly and set up elsewhere; and I had a beautiful woman across the table from me. Very soon I was telling your mother about my business and that I had been on a four-day trip to clients to the south and west of Metz to deliver some orders and collect from them any outstanding monies. I had intended over the previous months to buy out my business partner and set up my own business, in the steel industry, elsewhere. The arrival of the Germans would give me ideal cover to collect my cash and assets from the business, with or without the cooperation of my disinterested sleeping partner, and depart for another part of France.'

The Countess returned to her story. 'He told me that he was heading back home to Metz before any further fighting flared up there. I asked, on the spur of the moment, if I could hitch a ride. He did get a bit of a surprise when leaving the inn because there was Binder in his Prussian army tunic, luckily faded and without insignia, sitting on a trunk with my bags. Quick as a flash, before your father could change his mind, he put the trunk on the back of the carriage and secured it with the leather straps. Binder offered to drive to make himself useful. Marcel seemed pleased to be relieved of the driving after four days at the reins. The horses had been fed and watered. Marcel tipped the stable boy and got into the carriage with me with a sigh of relief. Binder discarded his coat and trotted the horses on. Marcel and I got to know each other in the back, although after a few moments on the straight road along the river, where Binder and I had walked the opposite direction two hours before, Marcel was asleep with his head in my lap. Are you happy to hear all this Cécile?'

'Yes of course Mama. It's all so... so unbelievable. Go on, please.'

'There were no roadblocks but certain places where opposing traffic and people walking blocked the road. At the bridge where Binder and I had walked across earlier in the day, there was a long line of French soldiers and artillery crossing towards the west and we were in a line of carriages of various sorts waiting. It therefore took us two hours to get the 12 kilometres to Marcel's little house in a terrace block in the southern part of Metz, outside the city wall. There was every sign that the French army was preparing to defend the fort and we were lucky that no-one asked for our papers... Binder and I had German Army passes which would not have impressed the French. Marcel had his French passport.

'At Marcel's there was a ground floor store-room where Binder could sleep. He parked up the carriage and fed the horses, then went out for provisions. Marcel's kitchen and bedroom were on the upper floor. We lit the stove for hot water and cooking and I had a bath in the Sitzbad, a copper tub in which you could sit, the first for three months or so. We already had some affection for each other, or at least some complicity, and Marcel was talking about his plan for leaving Metz as if they included me.'

I wondered what 'complicity' meant.

'Marcel got up at dawn to go down to the yard and workshop of his business only a few hundred metres away. When they came back, Marcel had a large leather portefeuille on a shoulder strap which he then kept with him at all times; I presumed correctly that it contained money and valuables. It was time for him to implement his plan and leave Metz. Binder had kept some blank German laisser-passer forms. What names to put? Marcel wanted to use a different name anyway and we decided that travelling as a married couple, the Orlowskis, would be more convincing if we were stopped. The three of us round the table, Binder wrote out one for Marcel in his new name Count Geoffroi Orlowski and one for himself in his own name but with a birthplace in Lorraine and French nationality. My papers in the name of Countess Leonora Orlowski were fine.

'We loaded up the carriage with all the food and drink left in the house, the baggage and some materials from the workshop. First we drove into town so Marcel could visit his bank. As we left the city around half past ten, we heard the rumble of artillery to the west. Binder called down from the driver's seat to say they sounded like German guns at only about ten kilometres distance. We found out much later that the Battle of Gravelotte had started, when the French were finally beaten and driven back into Metz. We agreed to depart immediately before the roads were blocked by either the French or German military. We headed off southbound towards Nancy, in the opposite direction to the day before.

'We had no problems with roadblocks or people asking for our passes. We had a bigger problem coming. Thank goodness Binder was with us.

'After about ten kilometres trotting along the main road alongside the Meuse, the sound of artillery still rumbling over our right shoulder, we heard the clatter of galloping horses coming up behind. It seemed initially like two highway robbers. They made us stop the carriage and brandished their arms at us, one a flintlock pistol and the other just a rapier. Binder pulled out both two-barrel handguns which had belonged to the General. Without hesitating, and before either of the assailants had noticed his guns, he fired at the first who took the ball through the chest and fell to the ground. The one with the rapier turned his horse on its heels. Binder's second ball hit his arm and he screamed as he fell off the horse. Binder was extraordinary as you would expect from a hardened soldier. He was calm enough to think of gathering up both the horses, who did not seem frightened by the gunfire. He attached them by leading ropes to the back of the carriage. We drove on. Two bodies by the road, with the comings and goings of traffic and the threat of the advancing German and Russian troops, would not draw anybody's attention.

'I learnt later from your father that the assailant with the gun was his business partner and the other one was the partner's brother. Maybe the partner had thought Marcel was plundering the company and getting away with the cash. I don't know. The trauma of the death of his business partner never seemed to have affected the Count any more than the trauma of the escape from Metz and the end of his life there.'

She glanced at the Count who was studiously looking at the ground. I looked from one to the other wondering why the business partner would come after him if he had only taken his proper share of the money and assets. Mama continued.

'We continued past Pont-à-Mousson towards Nancy, but it was slow work... some of the traffic was ox-carts and farm rigs led at walking pace. Binder negotiated the traffic and people on the road as best he could. We didn't stop. We handed some bread, cheese and a drinking flask to Binder up on top. Marcel and I ate and talked.

'It took some ten hours to cover the 60 kilometres to Nancy. In fact we first arrived at the village of Pompey, a village you know well because we all live so close and you went to school there. The ironworks of Fould-Dupont moved down there from Metz within a few months, and the Count started his new firm La Fonderie there. How the business came to be based there was so fortuitous; on that day, at dusk, the Count happened to see between the railway and the road a 'for sale' sign on abandoned stables and farm buildings with 22 hectares of farmland. We pulled over. The sign also gave the name and address of the land agent in town which he noted. Light was failing. He was uncertain about where to spend the night but he had noticed the gate was unlocked as were the double doors to the drive-through stable. We drove our carriage, with the two spare horses trailing behind, all the way into the building, out of sight. That's where we spent the night.

'We were woken at seven by the sun streaming through the open stable door and a man shouting blue murder at us; the owner, an old farmer. The Count was impeccable, apologetic and efficient. I saw a coin go into the hand of the owner. The Count explained his intention to make the land agent his first point of call with a view to purchasing the property at a good price. So the old man agreed to let us leave the spare horses there while we went into town.

'We drove straight to the Count's bank in Nancy to check the balance of the accounts he had set up two days previously. His foresight was reaping rewards. I was impressed. '

Papa could not resist adding the details. 'To my delight, some of the funds were in already and they had notification of 1.5 million francs coming in a day from the Banque Commerciale Hénin de Metz. Armed with the funds I had brought with us, and those in the bank, we proceeded to the land agent who was not only able to sell me the farm building and its land for cash without delay but also propose to us several private houses for sale. The agent accompanied us back to Pompey in our carriage and had the owner, who lived alone in a little house opposite, sign the deeds. He gave him the money and retained his commission. I was from that moment the owner of the land on which the offices and factory of La Fonderie was built. You continue, dear, please; my apologies.'

'The next day we went into the village for provisions and a cup of coffee. At the café next to the shop there was a crowd of locals listening to a post-boy in uniform relating that the French had been defeated at Gravelotte and had retreated into the fortress of Metz.

'Then... well Cécile... I must confess I have not told you everything about your father and me in those first two days. The fact is, we were in love. The fantasy of travelling together as husband and wife turned into reality. We knew we could become very close even in the first night in Marcel's home in Metz. It just happened. Very suddenly. We also had reasons to want to get married and formalise our relationship, mostly to ease the process of settling down in a new place with our new identities... well, his in particular. I felt at ease with this wonderful and good-intentioned man. So it was that we drove into the centre of Nancy and parked a block away from the Place Stanislaw where a brasserie's stable boy was looking after some other carriages. We made the short walk to the Mairie where the Count sweet-talked the official into an immediate marriage ceremony given the circumstances of the invasion by the Germans. He was also able to change his name to Geoffroi Orlowski by deed poll. He was given a provisional passport in the new name. His German laisser-passer was destroyed in front of us. My German papers were acceptable even if frowned-upon. The marriage proceeded and the register, filled out in their new names, was witnessed and signed by Hermann Binder. By lunchtime, two days after we met, we were man and wife. 20th August 1890. A great day. Fortune was shining on us. We went to lunch in the brasserie where the boy was looking after our carriage and horses. Champagne for the happy couple and beer for Binder who we invited to join the celebration.'

'You got married. Just like that.'

'Yes, dear. That is how it happened. I wanted you to know. We visited all three of the houses on the agent's list. One of them was ideal (and empty) so we moved in a day later; that's the Château where we live now. The house where the new one was built was so dilapidated that we knocked it down and started again. We lived in the stable block where Binder and his wife live now. And Antoinette.'

She did not mention that Jean-Marc's rooms had been in the stable block too. My dear departed brother. He was happier close to the horses than close to his mother.

'Our new life in Nancy started off so perfectly, didn't it?'

My father couldn't resist chiming in 'I set up initially in the specialised metal work materials and equipment which I knew so well but, to protect my new identity, I did not want it to be too obvious that it was a replication of the business in Metz. Within a couple of months, I had spotted another market opportunity. Fould-Dupont did not get going in Nancy as quickly as me and could not supply all the demand for iron and steel for railways, bridges and construction. I also invested in foundry equipment including some specialist turning jigs to form by machine the ornamentation for metal gates. In another three months as the income from the foundry picked up, I invested in the rolling equipment to make rails, including those curved to a very precise radius. So was the successful business of La Fonderie created.'

'You see dearest, what a clever father you have. I played my part. I worked hard at establishing the household, helping Geoffroi set up the company and finding staff. Then my luck took a downturn three weeks after arriving here. One night in September I collapsed and was bleeding. Binder and Geoffroi managed to get me to the Central Hospital in Nancy. Afterwards they said I had been was pregnant, four or five months gone. The baby would have been General von der Heyde's. I look back and think that your father would have accepted the baby as his in our new life together.

But I had lost the baby of course.'

One large tear rolled down the Countess's cheek. Papa looked at the ground. She had probably never talked about this to anyone before – apart from him.

'I fared badly myself, getting out of hospital only after a week. I took a month to get back on my feet. Maybe I was never the same again. I was back supporting my husband, working in the business, setting up hospitality for clients to impress, organising dinners – in restaurants in Nancy before the Château was built – entertaining the men with a smile, leading a cheery conversation. Yes, life was wonderful for a while even if, in my quiet moments, I was devastated by the loss of my baby.

'You father and I were very much in love. You must have been something of a miracle because you must have been conceived in October already. Nature is remarkable. I think your birth, Cécile, in July '71, lifted my spirits somewhat. But Geoffroi worked late and was travelling all the time, so my life at the house was my own.'

She faltered.

'I found myself getting depressed, and a bit lifeless over the next couple of years.'

She stopped, unable to bring herself to say the next part of the story. Papa took over.

'Then our dear departed Jean-Marc was born two years after that; and he turned out to have bad health which led to severe difficulties with reading and writing, with school in general, as you know dearest.'

I did feel sorry for Mama I suppose. There were many difficult issues in her early life and, now to learn of the miscarriage was to help me put in perspective her vile temper and her apparent disdain for Jean-Marc and me. As any daughter would have done, I got up, sat on her bed and put my arm round her. I was shocked more than touched when she leant her head on my shoulder and burst into tears of grief, wailing loudly and moving her feet back and forward.

અ

Chapter 37 – Binder's story

Over Christmas I let this dramatic story unwind in my consciousness. I had to let bits of the narrative one at a time into my thoughts to be able to digest and understand them. It became apparent that there may have been parts of the story which Mama had not told me. I wondered what else there was to know, what the studious and distant reaction from my father meant, his eyes fixed to the floor as his wife spoke.

I felt I owed it to Natalie, as my friend and as my father's chosen partner, to recount everything I had learnt from my mother. I did so, in the long dark days over the holidays by the light of a little oil lamp. Natalie and I reclined on my bed to talk. It was clear Papa had not told her much so she wanted to know every detail. She, like me, found some pieces were missing.

She recounted some recent remarks by the Count. 'The other evening, we were particularly relaxed, in bed, forgive me Cécile...'

'It's alright, you are allowed to be in bed with my father as far as I am concerned. It's been a couple of months already! I am tempted to call you step-Mama to put you in your place' I teased.

'... and we were talking about this and that. I asked Geoffroi about Binder, implying that his driver must have guessed a long time ago, I mean, about your father and me. Back in September he must have seen me occasionally leaving La Fonderie late on evenings when the Count left late as well. He doesn't say a lot but you can tell that he notices everything and takes it all in. Your Papa said I was right and very perceptive as ever. He said Binder had been faithful to him ever since they met and he would never talk to anybody. Geoffroi said I could rest assured that he would remain discreet. Anyway he only speaks two words of French; he has never made the effort... or his brain cannot engage in a different language. Your Papa said he came from Silesia originally; a Prussian and a professional soldier. He would not even talk to his wife about anything that does not concern her; he is that kind of man. I asked if the wife was the German lady who works in the

227

kitchen. He confirmed that Ursula is indeed Ursula Binder.'

Natalie was intrigued by the coachman. So was I. He was a character you would imagine as fictional, from tales of Frankenstein. He had a slightly hunched back, no hair and a crooked jaw. When he smiled, which was very rare and usually not because he found something amusing, you could see some of his teeth were at crazy angles and others missing.

'I had never heard him speak to your father except to say 'Jawohl mein Herr' in acceptance of an order he gave, but he was always there, willing, responsive and doing the right thing.'

'Yes, I always saw him the same way. He looked after the horses beautifully and was very kind to my brother. His rooms were in the stable block and he loved sitting with Hubert on the straw in the stable of a grey mare called Jezebel. Binder put Jean-Marc to work as much as he liked, refilling hay racks and the water troughs, cleaning tack and bigger projects like re-shoeing horses or re-varnishing the two carriages.'

'I wonder whether Binder would ever talk about what happened. Would he add any detail that your mother did not reveal? I can't understand why your parents have stayed married; clearly there was little love left after your brother's birth. I suppose Geoffroi knew her secrets, possibly a misspent youth, taking on the title Countess. If Geoffroi had tried to take more of his share out of the business in Metz then she knew that secret. Binder knew both your parents' secrets but must have been happy to keep them to himself as long as he was in their employment. I just wonder if what your mother told you in jail before Christmas has gaps remaining.'

જ

Friday, 13th January 1893

Natalie spoke fluent German. It was her Mama's mother tongue, as it was that of her Papa who she had never met. He died in a few days before she was born. When she and her mother came to Nancy, Angela made every effort to have Natalie speak perfect French and without an accent if possible. So at age five she integrated easily into the village school and continued to improve her French accent and vocabulary.

When leaving work, Natalie often saw the patient coachman Binder waiting for the Count in the office coach park. It was natural for Natalie to greet him and asked the time of day, in German. He responded well, whether or not, more recently, he knew her relationship with his boss. After the death of Jean-Marc and the Countess's incarceration, Natalie and the Count saw each other more openly, certainly as far as the driver was concerned. When he took the Count into town, he had seen Natalie entering the apartment at the same time as he arrived on one occasion and had seen her at the first floor window on another. He knew it was Natalie Duhamel from the finance department of La Fonderie of course. On other occasions, when she went on foot up to the Château , Binder could see her perfectly from his window seat in the stables where he quietly took in all the comings and goings. But he did not seem to abuse his knowledge of the affair nor were there any leering looks or any behaviour of his which made her feel uncomfortable.

On the second Friday of January, it was bitterly cold, just above freezing point and with driving rain. Natalie left the office at about six, the typical departure time on a Friday, by force of habit now, to meet her lover the Count. She knew he had been away on business and would be waiting for her in the warmth of the Château. She wrapped herself up snuggly in her scarf and hat and walked across the drive of the factory.

'Fräulein Natalie, guten Abend' called the Count's coachman.

Surprised, she asked him why he and the carriage were there. 'Guten Abend, Herr Binder. Was machen Sie dann hier, darf Ich fragen?'

Binder had got a message at lunchtime from the Count – the post boy had walked up to the Château with a telegraph - to go and pick Natalie up because of the weather. He gave her now a wry but polite smile, all toothy, jumped down to open the door and gave her a hand up. In five minutes they got back at the Château. Binder accompanied Natalie up the stairs to the front door. A fire had been lit in the sitting room but the rest of the house was cold. It was clear the Count was not back.

Binder hesitated as if he wanted to say something. Natalie took off her hat and scarf and hung them on the rack behind the door. It struck that he might have been thinking of talking to her about the Count's history. Or could she broach the questions? She turned to ask him but he had gone.

Natalie stood in front of the fire and rubbed her hands to get the blood flowing. Binder returned. It was still raining so he had been to get the carriage under cover, to stable and to feed the horses. Binder said the Count should have been on the Paris train arriving 17:15 or the 18:15 in which case he should be here. The next one did not arrive until 10:15, three and a half hours away. The Count would take a hansom cab whenever he arrived. Then Binder asked Natalie whether she would like to come to his rooms in the stable block. It was much warmer there and his wife was about to serve something to eat; she was welcome to join them. Natalie was pleased and accepted immediately; she was intrigued whether Binder had something on his mind.

᠖

As work came to an end this cold Friday I was looking forward to the creature comforts and warmth of the Château. I popped in on Duchien for a while; warm embracing, catching up on his day, a glass of wine, and his assurance that he would not mind if I went off till Sunday night. I jumped in a hansom with the idea of getting back for dinner.

I arrived just as Binder in his rain gear and Natalie under her umbrella stepped down the front door stairs to walk to Binder's rooms in the stable block. As we embraced, Binder hovered, then ushered Natalie and me towards his rooms. 'Komm Kind. Kommen Sie beide.'

'What's going on?' I asked.

'I think he wants to talk. About your Papa and all the history. Your father will be home much later. Come with us. It'll be warmer and there might be something to eat' said Natalie.

'Absolutely. Good idea. I guess Papa is not back.'

The coachman's rooms were small but homely. Frau Binder, Ursula, was a bustling apron-wearing, taciturn wife. She had laid for three people and within moments made it four place settings and was serving a delicious stew which she called Eintopf. I could tell Natalie was well tuned into Binder's German vernacular, even if she was getting to know him for the first time. He didn't bother to wait until he had finished a mouthful before starting each sentence he spoke and the collection of teeth that he had could not prevent the occasional splattering of stew escaping from his excited mouth.

He liked Natalie. He had always liked me, for some reason. As he spoke he made it clear that he thought Natalie was not just a good person but the right person for the Count, whom he respected immensely... even if, like every man, he had his weaknesses. He expressed regrets that Natalie and he couldn't formalise their relationship while he was married but something in his choice of words gave us to wonder whether he was hinting at something we did not know. He also made it clear that the Count deserved better than Leonora; a marriage without love must be a millstone. Binder's wife clucked, like a pleased chicken.

I had been plunged into this German-speaking discourse without warning, but my school German was good enough to understand most of what was being said. I was fully aware, since our New Year's Eve conversation, that Natalie thought Binder might know more. I was keen to listen in.

Natalie began to probe to see if Binder would open up and tell us more about how the Orlowskis got together, where and when. She asked him to elaborate on the Count's weaknesses. He shook off a laugh and said he must have told her everything in his past. Natalie was surprised he thought that; she said that the Count had never accepted to talk about the past. She looked at me then told Binder that I had relayed to her much of what the Countess had said to her in jail before Christmas.

Now Binder began to warm to the subject.

He wished well to Natalie, and to her future with the Count; he felt she should know everything. He imagined I knew most of it from the meeting with my mother. Frau Binder cleared the dishes away and refilled our wine glasses.

Binder spoke deliberately, in his German vernacular, with

hardly an interruption. Natalie and I were spell-bound.

'The Countess would not be inclined to tell you everything Fraulein Cécile, would she? Tell me, do you know much about the Franco-Prussian War of 1870?'

I replied in French. 'Yes, I know the history quite well.' It was difficult to have been to school in northeast France without knowing that that the French Army retreated in August 1870 into the Metz fortress after its defeat by the Germans and Prussians at the Battle of Gravelotte. The German forces had laid siege to Metz until the French ran out of food in October and surrendered. Most of Alsace and Lorraine, but not Nancy, was ceded to the Germans.

The amount of further detail given by Binder was surprising given how taciturn and uncultured he normally seemed.

'A few days before Gravelotte and Metz, on the 16th of August, a Prussian force – we must have been 30,000 men – under General Constantin von Alvensleben and General Franz Von der Heyde attacked the huge French army at Mars-la-Tour, west of Metz. We won it but we had massive casualties. General Von der Heyde died on the battlefield.'

Binder hesitated and wiped his mouth on his napkin. He wanted to give emphasis to his own role, even if I had heard it from my mother.

'My name is and was Hermann Binder. Unlike some in this story, I have always had the same name. I had been General Von der Heyde's Ordonnanzoffizier...', my mother had said aide-de-camp, '... for eight years. It was I that had to take charge of getting his body back to camp.

'A beautiful and sexually-precocious lady in her late twenties named Leonora, assumed to be General Von der Heyde's wife, mourned his death. He had certainly treated her as his wife. She lived and travelled with him, with us, on the long campaign. I knew he, the General, was married and that his real wife was back in Silesia, near Breslau, with three children.

'Did the Countess tell you that, Fraulein Cécile? Did she? '

I shook my head, but it did not surprise me that the General was a married man.

Heinrich XVII, Prince Reuß,on the side of the 5th Squadron:
Guards Dragoon Regiment at Mars-la-Tour, 16 August 1870.
Emil Hünten (1827-1902)

'After an hour sobbing on his body in the field tent Leonora realised the imperatives of ensuring her own survival and welfare. She knew I could be the means of her getting to safety and away from the battlefield. She also quite liked me, and knew I could be discreet.

'Matters were made worse when I was I was arrested by three warrant officers on General von Alvensleben's staff. The army was de-camping and was about to move on so they were looking round the officers' tents as they were being dismantled to make sure there was no pilfering. I had been caught coming out of my dead general's mess tent, with a leather hold-all containing two silver goblets, his pocket watch, some jewellery, his personal papers, a pair of twin-barrelled hand guns, powder and ammunition. The officers had no time for an enquiry or a court-martial; justice was going to be immediate. I was on my knees with a pistol to my head when Leonora intervened. She pulled rank on the officers, stating that she had asked me to pick up certain items on her account, as the general's widow. How could they expect her to ensure her own safety without weapons? And without me? How could they deny her the right to repatriate his personal belongings? Then a bugle sounded from close by and a Korporal Unteroffizier shouted instructions. The senior warrant officer swore in frustration, holstered his weapon and ran off with the others to the remaining General to assure the departure.

'I was shaking like a rag doll as Leonora untied me and gave me to drink. I thanked her a dozen times for saving my life. I feel forever in her debt despite the sour turn her character has taken in the last 15 years or so and how despicable she is to my wife and me. Leonora helped me dig a grave. It became clear to both of us that neither had the desire to continue in the battlefield. Leonora was free to make her way home; an unpleasant thought as she then had no family that she knew of. I had never been presented with such a plausible opportunity for leaving the army after 22 years' service; a deserter yes, but until I was a long way from the action I could always argue that I was doing the right thing by the general's widow. In the back of my mind was getting back to my wife and children near Breslau or setting up home somewhere else. Then I noticed the leather hold-all was where I had left it. There was money among the papers. We could survive if Leonora stayed together with me.

'With two hours of light left we said prayers for Leonora's dead lover and set out. I decided to get to the main road running down the valley south of Metz. The only horses left were dead. We started walking east through wide forest paths; I pulled Leonora's trunk on a wooden four-wheel baggage trolley whose missing wheel I had found and patched up. We had some water, bread and cheese.

'At night fall we sheltered under my canvas sheet erected in the lee of a pile of felled and trimmed pine trees. By half past ten the next morning we crossed the railway and the Moselle river at Ars. There were carriages and people walking, all of them going to the south on the Metz-Nancy road, away from Metz, so we joined them. Before we got to Pont-à-Mousson, at about midday, we arrived at a tavern. I suggested she go and sit down to eat in case she met anyone who could be useful to us. I sat with the trunk near the carriages and ate some bread and cheese. When I next saw her, an hour had passed, and she was in the company of a bearded, well built, properly dressed gentleman, a bit younger than her maybe, called Marcel. Now named Geoffroi.'

Natalie turned to me and said quickly 'Your Mama told you about the tavern didn't she, and meeting your father?' I nodded in affirmation and let Binder carry on.

'She had introduced herself to him as the Countess Leonora Orlowski. When I heard it I was surprised because I had never heard that family name before nor had she explained it. She had been using the name Leonora Von der Heyde. Maybe Orlowski was her real name. Maybe she was a Countess. Maybe she had kept it unsaid so that she could play the role of the wife of General Von der Heyde not his mistress.

'Leonora and Geoffroi clicked immediately. They seemed like more than good friends even just in the back of the coach from the tavern to Metz. By that evening they were behaving like a couple as far as I could hear; the wooden floor of Geoffroi's three rooms upstairs was not at all soundproof and I could tell by the giggles that the Countess, as I now began thinking of her, was using the Sitzbad and that the Frenchman was there with her helping with jugs of water. I could only imagine the intimacy of the scene.

In fact, after we ate and I retired, my ears were witness to the fact that she did not sleep in the spare bedroom but with him. Surprising in one way; she had been faithful to the general and he had only been dead a day and a half. Unsurprising in other ways; if she had decided Marcel was the escape route then she needed to cement the relationship. Furthermore, I do remember she and the general had showed their affection for each other in a most active way most evenings so she was not averse to the attentions of a gentleman. Forgive me ladies, both of you, I should not be going into such detail.

'I made out new papers for them. He was happy to change his identity on leaving Metz because it seemed propitious to be able to claim, if stopped by the Germans, to be man and wife, the Orlowskis, and because he needed to make himself untraceable in his new life. I think the title of Count suited his ambitions in business and society. The surname sounded to him like Jewish money and industrial power. Maybe he thought he would be able to revert to his real name at some time in the future if necessary. He never did of course.

'On the way out of Metz, I saved their fortune and probably their lives. Did you hear that from your mother?'

I nodded.

'I was right about them falling for each other. Just like that. Whether for love or convenience, it made little difference; they got married the day after we arrived in Metz. I signed at the Town Hall as the witness to the Count changing his name and to the marriage. They invited me to a proper lunch after the formalities. This was looking good. It was the moment for them to offer me a permanent post in their future household or in the business, to my choosing. Turned out to be both and I have never left them.

'You can see that we were now an eternal triangle of debt, gratitude and the need to keep certain secrets. For my part, Leonora had saved my life. Then the pair of them had given me the way out of the army and the inevitable court martial. I was keen to keep that secret. I was entering into a new life outside the military which probably suited my advancing age. I am 69 now, so I was 46 then, finding the going quite tough.

'Leonora, for her part, had lost a lover and found another

one within a day and a half. She had found an attractive young man, evidently with business skills, and a bag full of money. She had found her escape route; a path to a new life. She never spoke to me about where she came from and I have the feeling she never wanted to divulge that; I have some reason to believe she had a simple birth and upbringing in eastern Europe somewhere – not in Prussia because her German was very coarse – and, if she had been a real Countess, there would have been family heirlooms, letters from her relations and slavish behaviour by officers.'

'She was in my debt because I saved her bacon getting away from Mars-la-Tour, probably saved her life from the attackers on the road from Metz and because she knew I would have realised she was not a Countess.

'As for the Count, he knew, and knows to this day, that I was with him on the last morning in Metz when he pulled all the money together; that I was with him on the road when his partner came after him. But, ladies, I save you from doubts about the Count because it is perfectly possible he was acting out of the interests of the business in the face of the advancing enemy or that he took only his share. The Count did not know whether his partner was out just get some money or to kill him. He has always been clear that my use of the guns was a turning point in his life and that he would be forever grateful.

On top of that, I knew he was not a real Count and that he had a French name until August 1870. Anyone could have checked at the town hall registry that he had changed it by deed poll and adopted the title Count, but no-one ever has. His clients, colleagues and society were happy in the company of a wealth-creating Count with an exotic name, and he asked me early on not to divulge his change of name.

'Certainly his debt to me has been sufficient to ensure good employment for me; as his coachman; stable lad; maintenance man here and at La Fonderie; the Count's security man on many occasions; and lodgings for me and my wife, here present, whom I ferried back from Breslau in 1871. The children settled there and made families so we hardly ever see them.

'The Count and Countess, well. I wonder if the Count knew all Leonora's secrets. Did she tell him she was from humble origins somewhere in the east of Europe, that she had assumed the title Countess and the name Orlowski as she weathered the storm of life alongside the Prussian army as a canteen server, part-time cook and more recently full-time lover of one of the most notorious generals? The Count knows she married him in 1870 under a false name. She knows the Count's secrets, the same ones I know. They were perfectly compatible. Neither of them had any reason to betray each other, neither at the start when they were so desperately in love, nor later when they drifted apart.

'My goodness, I think back on the first years here and I think of the extraordinary beauty of Leonora. She sported a shock of red hair, strong wavy hair, which would not brush down straight, nor would she make the effort of putting her hair up. Maybe it wouldn't go, or wouldn't hold in a bun. She wore her hair with pride, sticking out and just as it was. She had strong eyebrows, a firm nose, red cheeks and a permanent smile on petite rosy lips. Her rounded chin had a little dimple, very sweet. Her body was superb; quite a big girl but not carrying too much weight. She loved her big breasts, firm ones not saggy, and so did the men. Her dress sense was risqué. When she was not in diaphanous evening gowns with a knee peeking through a slit, she wore skirts or dresses hardly below the knee, so her legs flashed in the light. She often took off her shoes and stockings; there was something natural and energising about her.

'She was always laughing and teasing even with the other senior military staff around and then later with clients of her husband. She pleased everyone around her. In fact when there had been some wine for dinner she could be overtly sexual with her body language. Even, frivolously, towards me. On occasions before Metz when, late in the evening, alone, washing, she saw me peeking through the tent door at her perfect breasts, she would wag her finger at me, reproaching me while smiling mischievously and doing little to hide herself. She certainly gave me much to exercise my imagination at night – forgive me my dear wife for I was always true to you all those years in the army – and neither she nor I would have dared any liaison.

'But her good looks, her young husband and the new life in Nancy were not enough to save her from herself, from her terrible tempers and what she has perceived as the frustrations in her life. It has been sad to see her fall apart, and now the death of Jean-Marc.

'Did she tell you about the miscarriage?'

'Yes.'

'It broke her apart. She must have loved the General and it was obviously his baby. It took a long time to recover and get back to work. Even then, although she was always ready with a smile, I could sense that it was wafer thin. Inside, she was not in good shape. You can imagine also that the Count immersed himself in his work, ten hours a day in the works, six days a week at least. She did not spend a huge amount of time with her young French husband. She was living in a place where they did not speak German and her French was pretty appalling, as it still is today.

'When you were born, Cécile, it did not lift her spirits as far as I could see. She drank. She sought the company of well-to-do friends, especially if they had a title or a good name. When Jean-Marc started growing up he turned out to have all sorts of issues. The Countess's frustrations and bitterness grew. Within four or five years of arriving here she was shouting and screaming at her husband, and, I regret, at her son. She could not accept that her son, her son and heir, was not a brilliant, healthy, future socialite and industrialist. It had all gone wrong.

'Later of course she started hating you Cécile, hating the fact that you were beautiful and talented – you could draw and paint, you did well in school, when the son couldn't. Difficult times. She had a wicked temper – still does. She attacked a gardener with a metal rake, because the roses were not in straight rows, and nearly killed him.

'But, killing her son ...' Binder's head dropped. His story was finished. There was silence.

'Your story Herr Binder... thank you. I understand everything you have said. Every detail. Every nuance. Extraordinary' said Natalie in German.

Les Oiseaux Familiers (1921)
Émile Friant (1863-1932)

She paused. 'I love you for this story Herr Binder. I think you are a remarkable man and I am proud to know you. The story also... strangely... increases my love for the Count. It's strange, but it's a good feeling. What you have all been through. Thank you.'

I added my thanks, in French, in a very small voice. The clock was ticking. I wiped a tear from my eye and looked at the clock; it was after ten. The fire and Frau Binder were quiet.

We sat in silence for five minutes. Binder spoke at last.

'I met your mother once, Natalie. In Pompey. In the Café des Boulistes. She came from Germany didn't she?' asked Binder.

'Angela. Well, Mama was a German-speaker but from Saarbrucken in France. It was French until the Germans invaded and took it over a few weeks before Metz. My Papa was a well-trained quantity surveyor, Alexander Büdenbaum who volunteered for the French army at the start of the war and was killed by rifle fire in a skirmish east of Metz in early August 1870, just before the battles you've described. Maybe you and the Countess were the other side of the lines. Mama, Angela Büdenbaum - she was born Paulitz, also in Saarbrucken - followed friends from home on the exodus to Nancy in late August with newly born me in her arms and settled here in Pompey. She has worked in Electrogène de Nancy, the electric generator factory, a few blocks from our house, all her life. She took the French name Duhamel and did everything to get a good education for me and to make sure I could speak French without a German accent.'

'She did well. What day were you born?'

'10th August.'

'10th August. Yes. 1870. Quite a year that was, wasn't it.'

The Count's cab arrived at speed up the gravel drive. Natalie jumped to her feet and ran out of the door. I lingered a moment to shake Ursula and Hermann Binder by the hand.

☙

Chapter 38 – The Countess's day in court

When I saw Mama in December there was already coverage about her case in the press, including apparent leakages from police and judiciary. My father was briefed every week by the avocat and I picked up snippets when I was with him and Natalie at weekends and over Christmas.

The court process against my mother became a complex one. There was an initial arraignment the day after Jean-Marc died at the end of October. Bail was refused and she was taken directly to the Charles III Prison where I met her. She had no idea she would be there for three and a half months before the case even came to court. Papa insisted on using the formal terms for everything. The Civil Court of Nancy ('tribunal d'instance') passed the case without hesitation up to the Cour d'Assises d'Alsace Lorraine composed of three judges and nine jurors. The judges consulted the Cour de Cassation in Paris, the highest court in the land and the only conduit for a possible appeal by the Countess. Given the status of the accused, they were keen to get their arguments and decisions checked by their superiors. In particular, as the Cour de Cassation established from time to time the long-lasting doctrine known as 'jurisprudence constante', they needed to check the direction of the prevailing wind in this case, even though there was no 'stare decisis' rule forcing lower courts to decide according to precedent.

From the start, within a week of the death of her son, Mama had no defence and pleaded guilty. Not even the Princess Ursula Poniatowski, who had broken the news to her after coffee on that fateful morning and who saw her initial calm reaction, was prepared to take the stand. The high-powered avocat, whom Papa had retained, informed him and Mama two days before the trial that the Procureur, the public prosecutor, with the agreement of the judges, had changed the count from manslaughter to murder. The prosecutor had established from the witness statements by Antoinette, the maid, Binder, Frau Binder, Franz, Marcel, Mimi, Bernard, Cécile and other eye witnesses, all of whom spoke in court, that the Countess had clearly intended to kill her husband's alleged mistress. French law did not distinguish in the case of murder between the intended victim and the actual victim. They contended that the death of Jean-Marc, at the hand of our mother the Countess, was murder.

The trial at last commenced in Nancy's law courts in the Place Stanislav on Wednesday, February 22nd, 1893. We were all there. The first minute of the trial provided a new cause for shock and gossip. The contremaître of the court room, introduced the accused as 'La Comtesse Leonora Orlowski, wife of Le Comte Geoffroi Orlowski, born 1842 in Metz, presently President-Director-General and 87.5% owner of the steel works at La Fonderie, living in Lay-Saint-Christophe, Nancy, married in Nancy on the 20th of August 1870...' A low pitched buzz went up around the courtroom as everyone could calculate that the date was only a few days after the start of the siege of Metz by the Prussians, a time when someone of foreign parentage might want to join themselves in marriage with a French national. He continued after a pause, and with difficulty pronouncing her real names, '...née Blanka Bohdanka Černý-Procházková, date and place of birth unknown'. The buzz was even bigger this time as the informed gentlemen of the press and the Countess's 'friends' took in the fact that she was Czech, from Bohemia, low-born, her birth un-recorded in church or town registers, and even had a surname of wandering gypsies. The Count winced; he knew the facts, but had not anticipated that the dirt would be dished in public. I knew from her own mouth that she had humble beginnings but she had not talked about her family name and Binder clearly had not known it.

The defence team was unable to find any witness or evidence to counter the prosecution's position. In the mid afternoon of the second day, the nine-man jury found her guilty after only 20 minutes deliberation. The court room was in total silence as the Countess awaited her fate, quite possibly the death sentence. I sat between Duchien and my father; I couldn't help sobbing quietly into my handkerchief.

The judge in summing up before passing sentence referred at length to an early Napoleonic statute, still in force, and two precedents in case law. He relayed the written advice of the Cour de

Cassation in Paris mostly word-for-word, such that even the legal experts present (lawyers and specialist press reporters) lost the thread of the argument. The court briefed the press afterwards and put out a written statement with the details, so the subsequent press reports were quite accurate. The first exceptional part of the case was that the victim of the murder was a family member. The fact that the intended victim was not a family member made no difference. There was also the consideration of the fact that prior to an hour before the murder, the Countess had no intention to kill anyone and that therefore there was an argument that the killing was not totally premeditated. The returning judge confirmed that, even though this would be a 'crime passionnel' if the victim had indeed been her husband's mistress, this could not in this case be used as a defence; the killing of the actual victim, her son, could not be deemed a crime of passion. In neither case would it commute the crime from murder to manslaughter (for which the sentence would be only a custodial sentence of two years). Everyone in the court held their breath for the sentence.

The judge declared their judgement and that of the country's highest court, giving in this case no room for appeal, that the court could defer capital punishment but was obliged to pass the alternative sentence of 'Life imprisonment without any possibility of early release'. The judge was about to stand up when the contremaître leant over and passed him a piece of paper.

'Yes, of course, thank you. I have also to announce, given that a further hearing is neither necessary not possible in law, that the marriage of the Comte Orlowski with the accused, in infraction of Penal Code Article 131-37-64, and I quote 'the accused having presented herself for marriage on 20th of August 1870 at the Mairie de Nancy under the false name of Comtesse Leonora Orlowski shown in forged documents, her real name having been Blanka Bohdanka Černý-Procházková, the marriage is deemed null and void.' All subsequent actions under the marriage regime including but not limited to agreements, cession of funds, legacies, properties and emoluments are deemed not to have taken place. The Countess does not, however, relinquish her own property ('restitution de biens') immediately.' The Count thanked his lucky stars that everything was in his own name. 'I can add that the Comte Geoffroi

Orlowski had adopted this name by deed poll in the same Mairie de Nancy some minutes prior to the wedding according to the registry of the Mairie and has not committed any infraction in this connection.' The Count, for the second time in a minute, thanked his lucky stars and consoled Natalie as she burst into tears of joy on his shoulder. The way was open for him to marry his young sweetheart.

The stunned silence in the courtroom as they took the Countess down was replaced in a few seconds by the sound of gathering of papers, snapping shut of attaché cases, a stampede of journalists to the PTT telegraph office and a crescendo of voices. Natalie hugged me as much in condolence for the long sentence for my mother as for a happy resolution for my father, and for her. I wiped my eyes. I hugged Natalie for the joy at the way open to her union with my father. We both, with a quick mutually complicit wink at the moment, and then with hours of chat over the next few months, acknowledged the role played by each one in the sexual liberation of the other. The Count shook Duchien's hand as if agreeing to the request, which he had not yet made, for his daughter's hand in marriage. Duchien shook the Count's hand to thank him for two commissions which reignited both his love of sculpture and his earnings, helping him on the road to banishing his demons, and to thank him for the gift of his lover, me. Binder, with his wife in the gallery, permitted himself a wry, omniscient, toothy smile.

L'Est Républicain carried the story across the four first pages of the newspaper with further articles every day for a couple of weeks. It was by far the biggest local story since the paper's creation in 1889 and the rise in circulation secured its long-term place as northeast France's premier paper. Their syndicated reports to the Paris national press also got huge coverage; The Times of London, die Zeit and daily papers in many countries of the world picked up the story. Certainly it would keep the gossip at Bernard's café and round the boules pitches of the Place Thiers for many years. The consensus was that this pantomime was such an amazing and unexpected story, you could not possibly have made it up.

২

Chapter 39 – A toast to a double wedding

'Welcome stranger' said Bernard. The welcome looked exceptional because he took his white serviette out of the glass he was drying and waved it merrily at Antoinette as she came in the door. 'Look who's here.' he said to Franz, Marcel and Mimi, temporarily idle and sitting at one of the tables. They all crowded around Antoinette as Bernard served her a regular little café serré and a pousse-café of Marc de Bourgogne.

'What have you been doing for two weeks? We haven't seen you since the wedding - the double wedding.'

'My God it's been so busy. I'm so glad to see you all and once again, many thanks for helping out on the Big Day. Without the friendly faces, and efficient and of course, it would have been a nightmare with all those contract staff doing the big meal and everything.'

'What's the news, what's the news' chimed Mimi. Antoinette drew a deep breath and proceeded for close to half an hour to relate everything that had happened at the Château. Everyone had seen the big piece in L'Est Républicain about the number of worshippers who had to cram into the village church, the 250 great and the good of Nancy invited to the reception and the traffic jam of carriages in the approach to the Count's house for the reception. Well of course, now, also the new Countess's house as Natalie, his new wife, was installed no longer as his mistress, but as mistress of the Château and Orlowski's wife. She had been in residence since a few days after the trial in February. Antoinette found it hilarious that Duchien, who I had said never revealed his first name, was obliged to provide it for the wedding service and the marriage register... Edmond! Edmond Duchien. The gentlemen listening thought it was perfectly acceptable as names go.

Natalie had not missed a day of work throughout the whole period of the trial and the build up to the wedding. She remained the Count's most faithful employee at La Fonderie and the most capable of future wives in organising the staff and preparations for the upcoming wedding. It surprised nobody that Natalie got a major promotion from 1st April and was now Commercial Director for the whole company. Her idea to stimulate demand for casting by making the half-size bronze statue in the office entrance (opposite the stone statute of the Count) and a series of social and media events had triggered a very big demand for the casting service. That ranged from casting objets d'art to steel couplings for railway wagons and detailed components for metal construction. The casting department had become profitable. Her straightforward approach and friendly manner made her popular in the company and with clients, despite, rather than because of, being the wife of the boss. In and around the Château she also made herself popular with the staff... a firm hand but a soft touch. She only made demands of the sort that she would buckle down and do herself if necessary. She also had a very respectful attitude towards the value of women in the workplace and even got the Count to understand the benefits of the new empowerment of women. He lapped up all this goodwill, efficiency and evolution of the species; the contrast with the regime of his ex-wife, now toiling in the Clairvaux prison for lifers 150 kilometres southwest; was noticed not only by him but everyone in the household.

Natalie's mother lived in an apartment in the stable block, recently refurbished in a simple way. It turned out that she had been a gardener when younger and she was very welcome to take charge of the vegetable garden, a task which she relished.

While the relationship between Natalie and the Count was one of maturity and authority, even though laced with true love, Cécile and Duchien were head-over-heels in love as if it were his first marriage. He absolutely doted on Cécile and spent every moment with her when he was not working. Antoinette realised that he was a passionate man not only by the way he spoke to her around the Château when they came to stay for a weekend but also by the speed with which they retired to bed after dinner, the occasional joyful noises heard fleetingly through their bedroom door and the gay abandon of under-clothing and bedding traipsed around the room when it came to cleaning the bedroom in the morning. They had kept the apartment, previously Natalie and the Count's love nest in the block next to Duchien's workshop. Its location was perfect and it was certainly big enough for the couple until they made further plans, children even, at which time they would look for somewhere bigger in Nancy. The Count offered to buy them a town house with a garden whenever they wanted.

Cécile had also made great strides in her own career. Since she had been employed by Daum full-time in August, she had continued to impress the Daum brothers. She had been promoted, before the death of Jean-Marc, to a new post of Chief of Resources, looking after the suppliers and contractors full time. She also had the mandate to give expression to her artistic skills; she had already created a complete range of chinaware for the home, slightly less complex than Daum's existing products, with a more homely and rustic touch. Daum promoted the range strongly and it was a best seller in many outlets especially *Art et Antiquités Montmorency-Laval* round the corner.

Presently Bernard offered Antoinette, Marcel and Franz to join Mimi and him for the 11 o'clock lunch service for staff before things got busy with customers. The chef as usual brought out food on the plate and sat with them to eat too. Antoinette marvelled at the strength and joy of the two young women in their lives. The gaggle of pals in the bar chatted enthusiastically about Paris-Nancy, art nouveau, the worldwide success of the style of the École de Nancy, the city's place in the development of psychiatry and the cures for mental illness, Bernheim's exploits like curing Duchien of his psychosis, of the new-fangled scientific theories of the evolution of man, of the empowerment of women. This latter hot potato, sub-titled the sexual liberation of women, triggered a frenzied discussion about Natalie and especially Cécile. Bernard, in his role of philosopher-in-chief, waded in 'I'm sure the Parisians rejoice in their role at the vanguard of sexual liberation, but here in Nancy there would be those who tut-tut at the thought of two of our pure young ladies being influenced by the decadence of the capital to unthinkable thoughts about the opposite sex.'

'What a prude, Bernard' said Marcel. 'They are both desperately in love with their men. The marriages remain pure and the weddings mark a great new beginning in the lives of four people we love.'

'As well that may be, my dear friend. But there remains the issues of youth. The age difference, for heaven's sake. Cécile is just

21 and Duchien must be approaching 40. Natalie is a year older than Cécile and the Count is, well, anyone's guess considering the uncertain details of the man's life story; late forties, nearly fifty? The mauvaises langues among us, and I have overheard such remarks here several times since the wedding, would say that two predatory male spiders have lured innocent virgins into their webs.'

'Ha, you're killing me.' Antoinette laughed out loud, and joyfully. 'Virgins? It would go way beyond my duty of care and discretion to the extended family which I serve to contradict your assertion, even if allegorical, but that does make me laugh. Women, in general I mean, have no fear of intimacy with men before marriage, nor even at quite a tender age. God made woman fertile and attractive to the opposite sex in the early teens, so let's not get carried away by indignant thoughts about young ladies over the age of 21. Besides, the men in question have nothing but the highest personal standards to maintain and are as genuine in their love as each of the girls.'

Mimi piped up, as she was fond of Cécile; 'I don't think for a moment you could include Cécile in any discussion of sexual promiscuity. She is the sweetest and most genuine person you could ever hope to meet; yes, very attractive, but she has some inner purity. That Duchien might not know how lucky he is.'

'Bravo. Long live youth' exclaimed Marcel; 'Vive la difference' proposed Franz, referring both to the difference in age between the man and the woman in each couple and on the difference in behaviour between Natalie and Cécile; Mimi cheered with a clap of the hands. Antoinette smiled broadly and consoled Bernard by briefly putting her hand on his arm. 'Certainly neither girl went in to any relationship other than of their own free will.'

Because they had known Duchien's depressions and other problems since his tragedy, they assumed that it was the charms of the young Cécile who had awakened Duchien from his dead mental state. They toasted this remarkable triumph of love over illness by emptying what remained in their glasses. Then Antoinette proposed they drink to Natalie and the Count. They had to get a quick refill to do this.

ৡ

Chapter 40 – Duchien writes to the hypnotist

46, rue Gambetta,
Nancy, Meurthe-et-Moselle

Nancy, 5th May 1893

Dear Professor Bernheim

Thank you so much for the letter and your good wishes. I'm glad you noticed the report on my wedding to Cécile Orlowski. I can tell you that I am even more glad than you.

You may have read about the death of Cécile's brother at the hands of their mother in October. She was present at the dreadful incident and held her dying brother in her arms; you can imagine that the traumas she suffered, including guilt at not being able to save him, were not dissimilar to mine. But what you did for me, just in two sessions, gave me the strength to assist her through the bad times. In perfect reciprocity, it has been Cécile's affection and encouragement that has driven the nail into the coffin of my demons.

I also thank you for the offer of a copy of the transcript of our sessions last year. Because I have moved on and embraced fully the therapy and advice you provided, I have entered a new and extremely positive phase of my life. It could therefore be a backward step to retrace the trauma, nightmares and depressions I experienced. I think that if you sent them I would read the first page and then burn the rest. It seems better to avoid any remaining memories.

I met your assistant Jacques about a month after the sessions when he was on his way to the station. He told me he was travelling to Paris and then on to Austria to set up a sanatorium. I thanked him then for what you and your team achieved in my case. I repeat these thanks to you now and I look forward to meeting you in a social context in Nancy in the future.

Please accept, Professor Bernheim, my sincere salutations

Duchien

La Petite Barque (1895)
Émile Friant (1863-1932)

Chapter 41 – The painter and the sculptor

Autumn 1893

The sculptor was working in his atelier as usual one morning when a call came from the front office. 'Duchien? Bonjour Duchien.'

'Come in. Who is it?' called Duchien.

He looked up from his drawing table to see a short young man with sparse ginger hair and a quizzical look on his face.

'My goodness. Émile Friant, the rising star of the Nancy cultural firmament. I am honoured by your visit.' Friant, at age 30 and coming to the peak of his powers as an oil painter, a naturalist and a romantic, was indeed quite famous. At age 15 his painting of a young couple dressed in white sailing up the river, *La Petite Barque*, had been displayed in the Musée des Beaux-Arts and acclaimed as a masterpiece. He had an eye for people in the natural surroundings of Nancy and also for the pomp required for society portraits, which paid the bills.

'Duchien, my dear sir, it is I who am honoured to be in your presence. Seriously, I have admired your work for some time, and... my goodness what is that beautiful sketch you're working on?'

Duchien was happy to show it off; a pencil sketch, in the way he would normally do in preparation for a sculpture, of two beautiful young females, straight-faced, naked as nature intended, standing together, touching at hip and shoulder. Several other studies for the same pose were on the desk.

'Yes. The two muses. I do not know whether I will ever do the sculpture. But I cannot help putting pencil to paper.'

'But they are so wonderful; you must complete the work.'

'Well it is delicate, Émile. One is my new wife Cécile and the other is Natalie, the new wife of my patron and father-in-law the Count Orlowski. Both the girls and the Count would really have to agree before it could be done and the piece displayed.'

'Yes, I see, I had not thought it quite through. Quel embarras de richesse. Your cup floweth over. All these beautiful people around you and you can't even commit them freely to stone.'

'Indeed, but what goes on in my imagination is my own business. Hopefully when Cécile sees these, and with the passage of time, she would encourage me to make it my ultimate nude sculpture.'

'I saw last week your new full-size stone nudes in the Musée des Beaux-Arts. Did they find a sponsor to acquire it for them? My goodness, one of the girls in these sketches looks rather like the new statue.'

Duchien had managed to keep a secret that the new Beaux-Arts statue was indeed of Natalie, started a year before, and the critics had not identified the sitter, or chose not to write it. Duchien was mildly peeved that the likeness was so poor that it was not obvious who the girl was. The museum had agreed not to publicise the fact that the Count Orlowski was the donor. Duchien was not going to divulge all to Friant, so he steered him away from his question.

'The two girls will look great together, don't you think?'

'Yes, ravishing.' Émile looked round the studio. 'I have never told you Duchien, but I have always found your work inspiring. I now find the desire to paint nudes, male and female, irresistible. So I am afraid it's your influence that has led me to have done three or four oils and several pencil sketches of which I'm quite proud. Nudes. I thank you for being my leader.'

'My goodness. I feel some guilt at being the older man who is perverting you to the evil ways of the flesh. Would you let me see them sometime?'

'Of course; I would be so pleased.'

There was a noise of somebody coming in the front door then Cécile's voice 'Dou Dou, chéri, are you there? I've done the shopping and got the stuff you needed. Oh, Émile, what a pleasure.'

Duchien had discreetly covered over the sketches of Natalie and Cécile and came to embrace her warmly. Émile shook her warmly by the hand and kissed her on each cheek.

'Cécile, good morning. How fortuitous that you arrive while I'm here. I'm tempted to call you Mademoiselle la Comtesse, or whatever the daughter of one is. But I guess those titles are reserved for Natalie.'

Two Muses (2020)
Robert Butcher (born 1961), as if by Duchien

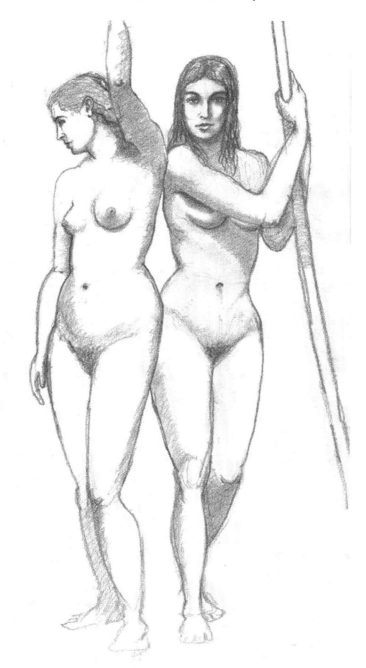

'You are funny Émile, stop. I am just the girl from Daum who is now Duchien's wife. Plain and simple. Have you got time for a quick drink with us?' She had put down her bag and reached for three glasses and a bottle of white.

'Well only for a moment, I'd be delighted. In fact I wanted to tell you both, the Count is commissioning some paintings from me. I'm absolutely delighted.'

'Tell us more.' said Duchien.

Chapter 42 – Two muses: two mothers

Nancy, a year later

Natalie and I were at Bernard's newly enlarged restaurant, the Excelsior, the boss fussing over us two young mothers and our toddlers. Jean-Marie and Élodie were just beginning to walk at ten months, so controlling them while having a Sunday lunch was quite a challenge. Natalie would have left Jean-Marie with the nanny or her Mama but she was keen to take every opportunity to get them together. Each was tethered on a home-made harness and held by her mother at arms-length; nonetheless they managed to approach each other, make eye contact, touch and embrace each other firmly. There was even a semblance of a kiss. We were delighted.

'Oh my God, look at them. Clearly they are going to marry and have beautiful children'.

I agreed.

'Yes. And their children will be fantastic with finance and very artistic. They will all live in a big château and have as much love and happiness as money.'

'In your dreams little sister.'

'Talking of which, I never told you that there were times last year when I wondered, facetiously, whether I should call you 'Mama', or 'yes, no, dearest step-mother'. You, my best friend, conquered and then married, my father for god's sake! It weighed heavily for a while. But our friendship won over and now you're back to being my big sister, uniquely.'

'Thank goodness, Madame Duchien. Before you knew about Geoffroi and me I did fear terribly that it would drive a wedge between us. That was part of the adventure which initially escaped my mind. Thank you for accepting us. Anyway I do adore your Papa, you know that. The adventure has developed into an extraordinary life. I could not have been more lucky. Your father is special. He is a strong man in many ways, but I like that. I am intolerant of weakness, in life, in bed, in business, anywhere. He leads, but at the same time he has his soft side, the side of him I grabbed with both hands, the chink in his armour where I was able to insert myself and get to his heart. You know how great a father he is going to be to our child because you have experienced it. You are his daughter.'

'I am indeed, and he was and is a great father.'

'I forgot to ask, Natalie, how do you feel about have a life-size nude of us two together in the Musée des Beaux-Arts? On permanent exhibition.'

'I never thought Duchien would go through with it. I remember the drawings. Has he done the sculpture now?'

'Yup, finished. Awaiting our approval. That's what he'd like.'

'It won't have our names in the title?'

'No, but it's pretty obvious. He's done our figures the same as each other, pre-maternity but not teenage. I am maybe a centimetre shorter. The facial features also show the differences between us; my nose not as pointy as yours; your eyes not as doe-like as mine; my lips not quite as pouty as yours. Duchien seems to have done our breasts in a size which is midway between us too, although, because I have not had the pleasure of seeing yours unclothed, I do not know the real difference in size. '

'There's only one person who knows.'

'Indeed. My husband. Duchien. He is the only one of the three of us that has seen us both naked. You at the sittings, a dozen times, and me in the bedroom (well mostly in the bedroom) every gorgeous night till the sixth month of my pregnancy. It's a good sculpture and the museum has found a patron to buy it in. Would you be willing to let him go ahead?'

'If you are agreeable with it then so am I. Especially if my bottom is less saggy than the one he did of me at the start, two years ago.'

Cécile continued. 'Duchien has also started on a quarter-size clay of the same statue, us two, for casting, a commercial piece. Fair warning given.'

'Dear Lord. We will have to get used to our relationship being cast in bronze for all time and sold to dirty old men - I mean, discerning collectors - all over the world.'

'When you sat for him, did he ever give you the impression he fancied you enough to make a move on you even though you were involved with Papa already?'

Natalie thought about that one for a moment, feeling the low winter sun through the window on her face. She reached out and put her hand over Cécile's to reduce the temptation to lie. 'Initially he did not know I was involved with your Papa. Or, could not be certain. So, if he did not want to make love to me I would be very disappointed. What man would not want to? And I had been totally brazen; even the first time, undressing without him even asking me to. But there must have been a time at which he guessed that I was in a relationship with your father and would have felt a professional duty to him, as his client. It would not be proper for him to seduce the client's mistress, if that is what he was thinking.'

'If his behaviour had been less reserved, dearest Natalie, our stories might not have developed to what we have now. When you first sat for him, brazenly, it was only a few days after he and I had first made... had first... got close.'

'You mean made love. You can say it to me.'

'Yes, made love. I can say it to my husband lover too. Anyway, if he had made a pass at you then it would have been totally unfaithful to me and would have shown that I was just another of his conquests. If you had fallen to his charms, you would have shown total lack of faithfulness to my father. Where would we have all ended up?'

'Yes, you're right. It must have been a curious feeling for him when I stripped off because of my similarity in appearance to you. The Twins. He would have been thinking 'who is this Doppelgänger. Why am I inexorably attracted?"

'Ha! That's ridiculous. Or is it? Anyway, I got Duchien in the end. He is such a lovely man to be with. I think he is going to be a super father for our child. Guess what, I call him DouDou, baby version of Duchien. Like the word we use for a little kid's comfort rag. He loves it.'

Both of them instinctively looked at Élodie, who was holding her piece of muslin to her mouth as usual. Her shock of red hair was like her grand-mother Leonora's. No doubting, despite the extraordinary stories, that Leonora, languishing in prison, was Élodie's grand-mother.

'Are you thinking of going to see your Mama?'

'I can't bring myself to see here again. It was not too bad that once, before the trial. But now, even just thinking about my mother makes me weep for Jean-Marc. That's the woman who killed my dear brother when she was about to kill me trying to kill you. What can I say to her that was not said then? How can I have any feelings other than hate and disdain? I have my own life despite her; I have a child, a husband her father, my best friend you, my elder sister you, my father your husband. I have never felt better. Why would I want to jeopardise that? Take a step backward? Also, on the practical side, my mother has been transferred to a prison 150 kilometres away near Chaumont. Travel there with Élodie? I don't think so.'

'You're right. Move on.'

৯

Author's note and acknowledgements

I wrote the first version of this book in eight straight weeks in March and April 2020 during the Covid-19 virus pandemic, a version complete enough for selected friends and two serious writers to read for errors and other comments.

I would like to thank above all my lockdown partner and wife Susie Bicknell who was both encouraging and constructively critical at three stages of the book's creation. She provided some ideas for the Count and Countess's back story including the Countess's miscarriage and the reasons for her attitude to her children. My cousin, writer, Alison Jean Lester gave enthusiastically of her time to introduce me to some of the disciplines of writing, as did Geoffrey Gudgion. I relished the opportunity to attempt to learn a new skill, but then came the 3 further months of re-writes, editing and improvements.

The geography of Nancy, the battles of the Franco-Prussian war and the history of the period are factual. The Count's escape from Metz as the Prussians invaded in 1870 is described over the factual background including the battles of Gravelotte, Metz, and Mars-la-Tour. General Constantin von Alvensleben was a real person but neither General von der Heyde nor his mistress.

Several characters used in the background to the plot are from real life. These include

• Émile Gallé (1846-1904), art nouveau designer who worked in glass, was born and died in Nancy;

• Auguste Daum (1853-1909) and Antonin Daum (1864-1931) art nouveau ceramicists, glassware manufacturers and designers;

• Émile Friant (1863 Dieuze - 1932 Paris) was a painter of classic-style landscapes, poetic scenes, society portraits and, after the period of my novel, male and female nudes; his pictures shown alongside my narrative are not to portray specific characters in my text but to provide imagery of people in Nancy in the period of the novel;

• Louis Majorelle (1859-1926) architect, designer and manufacturer of chinaware and furniture in Nancy. In 1885, Majorelle married Marie Léonie Jane Kretz (1864-1912), daughter of the director of the municipal theatres in Nancy. Their only child, Jacques Majorelle, who himself would become an artist, was born in 1886;

- Hippolyte Bernheim (1840 Mulhouse - 1919 Paris) physician, hypnotherapist in Nancy; Bernheim had a significant influence on Sigmund Freud, who had visited Bernheim in 1889, and witnessed some of his experiments. Freud had already translated Bernheim's *On Suggestion and its Applications to Therapy* in 1888; and later described how 'I was a spectator of Bernheim's astonishing experiments upon his hospital patients, and I received the profoundest impression of the possibility that there could be powerful mental processes which nevertheless remained hidden from the consciousness of man'. He would later term himself a pupil of Bernheim, and it was out of his practice of Bernheim's suggestion/hypnosis that psychoanalysis would evolve;
- Ambroise-Auguste Liébeault (1823-1904) physician, hypnotherapist in Nancy;
- Jules Henri Poincaré (1854 Nancy -1912 Paris), French mathematician, theoretical physicist, engineer, and philosopher of science;
- Auguste Dupont (possibly 1848-1913) of the Fould-Dupont ironworks. After Germany annexed the Moselle area in 1870, Dupont and Alphonse Fould transferred their Usine d'Ars-sur-Moselle to Pompey, near Nancy. They provided the iron for the Eiffel Tower for the Exposition Universelle of 1889. My fictional Count Orlowski moved his (originally smaller) business from Metz to Nancy in the same period; and
- Léon Goulette, the owner, editor and managing director of L'Est Républicain newspaper.

Bernard's café, which is fictional, was on the site which since 1910 has been the Hôtel Restaurant Excelsior in the Place Thiers (now the Place Simone Veil) opposite Nancy's SNCF railway station.

Jacques Rebière is a fictional character created by Sebastian Faulks in *Human Traces* (2005); Jacques and his English friend Thomas Midwinter set up a pioneering asylum in 19th-century Austria, in tandem with the evolution of psychiatry and the start of the First World War. In Faulks's novel, fictional Rebière spent some time in Nancy with Professor Bernheim, a real person. I read *Human Traces* when my book was half-written; I was inspired by Faulks to intensify my research into people in Nancy of that period and true historical backdrops. Faulks wrote a Bicknell into *Devil May Care* (2008) so I was delighted to reciprocate by including

Rebière in *Sculpted Love.*

Robert 'Bobzy' Butcher, a real-life artist, film-maker and international expo designer, was inspired in April 2020 to draw, specially for *Sculpted Love*, the 'sketches preparatory for sculptures' and the drawing of the fictional finished sculpture of *Mother and Child* which, like other images in the book, give the reader a visual impression of Duchien's life, art and times.

I am grateful to the literary or otherwise-coherent friends who read the proof, including Brigitte Berger, Alice Bicknell, Christopher Bicknell, Susie Bicknell, Will Bicknell, Anna Böhm, Diana Bunny Bunyan, Robert Butcher, Pauline Butcher, Alain d'Aboville, Geoff Gudgion, John Helliwell, Bruce Kennett, Alison Jean Lester, Paul Majendie, Sabine Noelle-Wying and Henrietta Usherwood.

Bruce Kennett designed the cover and advised on typography, art copyright and the rendering of the images into black and white. Thank you. The text is set in Matthew Carter's Miller 11pt. The cover title font is Delphin by Georg Trump (1896-1985).

I thank Muriel Mantopouluos of the Musée des Beaux-Arts de Nancy and Adriana Krohling Kunsch and Fernanda d'Agostino of the Pinacoteca de São Paulo for their speedy approval of reproduction rights and the warmth of their encouragement.

There are about 60 French words used in the book as a sprinkling of local colour. Because there are no hard rules about which words have fallen into usage in the English language, and for consistency, I have not italicised any foreign words.

July 2020

ঽ

Image credits

Map   Hand drawn by Marcus Bicknell ©2020.

Mother and Daughter (2020). Sketch by Robert Butcher (b. 1961) of the sculpture La Mère et Sa Fille (1888) by Duchien (Nancy 1855-1922), with the kind permission of Robert Butcher ©2020.

Four smaller initial sketches, as if for a sculpture, are also by Robert Butcher © 2020 Robert Butcher.

Place Thiers, Nancy (1890). Postcard. Bernard's café is behind the statue. Public domain.

Le Turban (1929). Émile Friant (Dieuze 1863 - Nancy 1932). Engraving, from pencil on paper. With kind permission of the Musée des Beaux-Arts, Nancy, inventory 2006.0.9. (703 à 738).

Venus after the Bath (c.1700). Commercial copy after Christophe-Gabriel Allegrain (Paris, 1710-1795). Photo, public domain, Wikimedia.

Dessin nu, Fiche 9717 (date unknown). Émile Friant (Dieuze 1863 - Nancy 1932). Engraving on laid paper with a watermark, Émile Friant's collection stamp 1199 verso. This engraving is the property of Susie and Marcus Bicknell. Photo Marcus Bicknell. Copies also in the Musée des Beaux-Arts, Nancy; inventory 2006.0.9. (463 à 480).

Dessin Nu (1918). Émile Friant (Dieuze 1863 - Nancy 1932). Impression on laid paper with a watermark, Émile Friant's collection stamp verso. Photo, public domain, Wikimedia.

Catalina Pietri de Boulton (1920). Oil on canvas. Émile Friant (Dieuze 1863 - Nancy 1932). With kind permission of El Panteon, Fundación John Boulton, Caracas, Venezuela. Photo, public domain, Wikimedia.

Saudade *(Longing)* (1899) oil on canvas by José Ferraz de Almeida Júnior (Brazil 1850-1899). Donated by Leonor Mendes de Barros, 1982. With kind permission of the Acervo da Pinacoteca do Estado de São Paulo, Brazil. Photo: Isabella Matheus

Jeune Nancéienne dans un paysage de neige (1887) (*Young girl from Nancy in a snowy landscape*). Oil on canvas by Émile Friant (Dieuze 1863 - Nancy 1932). With kind permission of the Musée des Beaux-Arts, Nancy, inventory 75.5.1. Photo, public domain, Wikimedia – Creative Commons

Q51756720

Professeur Bernheim, Faculté de Médecine de Nancy, 1895. Postcard, public domain.

Usine de Pompey (The steel works at Pompey), 1895. Postcard, public domain

Graphic designs as if by Cécile Orlowski, various sources, public domain, no rights reserved.

Les Amoureux (Soir d'automne, Idylle sur la passerelle) (1888) (*The Lovers (Autumn Evening on the Foot Bridge)*. Oil on canvas by Émile Friant (Dieuze 1863 - Nancy 1932). With kind permission of the Musée des Beaux-Arts, Nancy, inventory 771. Photo, public domain, Wikimedia Commons Q26924895. Used on the front cover and in the text.

The Mistress (2020). Initial sketch, as if for a sculpture, Robert Butcher (born 1961) in the style of an 'étude préparatoire' (1892), by Duchien (Nancy 1855-1922), with the kind permission of Robert Butcher © 2020.

Heinrich XVII, Prince Reuß, on the side of the 5th Squadron: Guards Dragoon Regiment at Mars-la-Tour, 16 August 1870. Emil Hünten, 1827-1902. Location unknown. Photo, public domain, Wikimedia.

Les Oiseaux Familiers (1921). Oil on canvas 163.8 × 119.4 cm by Émile Friant (Dieuze 1863 - Nancy 1932). Private collection. Photo, public domain, Wikimedia.

Prussian Soldiers Escorting French Prisoners of War, Metz 1870 [1888] by Gaston Claris (1843 - 1899) who served as an artillery lieutenant during the Franco-Prussian war of 1870-71. Oil on canvas. 140 x 200 cm. Location unknown. Photo, public domain, Wikimedia.

La Petite Barque (The Small Boat) (1895). Oil on panel by Émile Friant (Dieuze 1863 - Nancy 1932). With kind permission of the Musée des Beaux-Arts, Nancy, inventory 1462. A later version of the painting which launched Friant aged 15 on his career. Photo, public domain, Wikimedia Commons 2718.

Two Muses (2020). Initial sketch, as if for a sculpture, Robert Butcher (born 1961) in the style of an 'étude préparatoire' (1893) by Duchien (Nancy 1855-1922), with the kind permission of Robert Butcher © 2020.

Printed in Great Britain
by Amazon